SET OUT BEFORE ME LIKE SOME NIGHTMARE LANDSCAPE WAS DEATH'S SEA—

a sea of fire, miles and miles of glowing molten rock.

Suddenly three guards were upon me, their hands outstretched. I twisted to avoid their grasp, turned, leaned over the airship's rail. Still, I would never have given into the impulse for release had it not been for the child in my arms suggesting I throw myself over the side of the ship into a sea of lava hundreds of feet below. It was the *ridiculousness* of the situation that prompted me. The Universe had truly stunned me this time, and laughing, I leaned back so that I flipped over the rail. For a moment I felt a sense of liberation. The heat of the molten se[illegible] and the odd sensatio[illegible]ssness, brought me [illegible]other's arms, long [illegible]

Then the [illegible] fully aware of wha[illegible]

My speed i[illegible]ed. I plunged wildly toward destruction. . . .

POISONED MEMORIES

EARTH DAWN

Poisoned Memories

by

Christopher Kubasik

A ROC BOOK

ROC
Published by the Penguin Group
Penguin Books USA Inc., 375 Hudson Street,
New York, New York 10014, U.S.A.
Penguin Books Ltd. 27 Wrights Lane,
London W8 5TZ, England
Penguin Books Australia Ltd, Ringwood,
Victoria, Australia
Penguin Books Canada Ltd, 10 Alcorn Avenue,
Toronto, Ontario, Canada M4V 3B2
Penguin Books (N.Z.) Ltd, 182–190 Wairau Road,
Auckland 10, New Zealand

Penguin Books Ltd, Registered Offices:
Harmondsworth, Middlesex, England

First published by Roc, an imprint of Dutton Signet,
a division of Penguin Books USA Inc.

First Printing, March, 1994
10 9 8 7 6 5 4 3 2 1

Series Editor: Donna Ippolito
Cover: Boris Vallejo
Interior Illustrations: Robert Nelson

Printed in the United States of America

For Hannah and David,
who walked me through it.

And for Sam Lewis,
who let me write the
Earthdawn Trilogy
with ridiculous leeway.
Patrons are few and
far between these days,
but he was there for me.
Sam, thanks.

PART ONE

Prologue

1

Samael and Torran sat by the hearth of their home. The rainy season had come, and the nights had grown cool. More than the air, however, it was the last words of their mother's letter that chilled their flesh. The scrolls of the letter rested on a table between them. Samael, the better reader of the two, held the last sheet in his hands, its final words echoing inaudibly in the air between them. He held the scroll loosely, the way a curious, cautions boy might hold the bones of a monkey found by chance out in the jungle.

Glasses filled with rice wine, still half-full, caught the fire's light and gleamed. The fire crackled, and every so often emitted a sharp POP. The fire had grown low, the hour late. The firelight, deep red, caressed the faces of the men. Shifting blood.

They might have been twins but for the scars. Thick, smooth hatch-marks that cut this way and that across their flesh. The veins of broad jungle leaves. Both sat graven and thoughtful; Torran with a tinge of scowl, Samael with eyes bright. Each turned his mother's story over and over in his head.

Torran's sword rested across his lap. It had become a fixture since the reading of the long letter had begun a few days earlier. His right hand rested on the pommel now, one finger touching it gently. His feet in their thick boots rested on a stool.

Over the last six nights of reading the letter, Torran had slowly added one layer of protection after another, until now he was wearing a complete suit of leather armor bought from elves in the city of Bartertown outside the mountain kingdom of Throal.

Samael rested more comfortably in cotton pants and a shirt that had been dyed into a festive swirl of greens and reds. He was a storyteller, and the cheerful clothing served his trade well. But the dark, thick wood of the house, the low firelight, the somber revelation of the letter all dimmed the happy aura in which he usually wrapped himself—as much an armor as Torran's leather—and made his clothes seem ridiculous.

The walls of the house. Dark and red-stained and foreboding. Thick walls. Walls to keep things out. When the twins had built their home, paying for it with plunder from countless adventures, they had agreed, silently, tacitly, that thick walls were needed. Something solid. Something to keep things out. Neither one had ever understood what it was that haunted them, but they never ceased to feel it. All their lives they had shared the silence of being hunted. A slow exchange between the two of them as they camped under the stars. A shared nod as a plaintive wind rustled the leaves of a savanna. And it was so terrible that they never spoke of it aloud.

Yet the walls had never worked.

The two men had carried their ghost into their home every night, in their heads. Hidden memories of their father. There was no escape.

"We could have read the ending first," Torran said, his voice dry, strangely forced to be deep. "I told you."

"That's not how she wanted to tell it," replied Samael. He wrapped the scroll back up.

"Why did she go on so long?"

"She had things she wanted us to understand."

Without thinking, Torran brought his fingers to his face, touched his scars. He examined them carefully, as if they'd just appeared and he needed to acquaint himself with them. "Why didn't she tell us until now?"

Samael put the wrapped scroll on the table, picked up his glass of wine. "I don't know. I think . . . It would have been hard, of course. And perhaps she didn't want to hurt us."

Torran lurched forward, his hand suddenly gripping the pommel of his blade. "He's still out there! He wants us to come see him!" He stood, crossed the hearth, his muscular, armored body a solid shadow before the flames.

"He does."

"He's insane."

"Maybe."

Torran whirled suddenly, the sword up, a familiar rage on his face. Samael was not afraid. He knew it all too well. "MAYBE! What did you just read? Maybe! What is your problem this time? It's simple. He's insane."

"The dragon, Mountainshadow, who sent us the first letter, he spoke highly of Father."

"He's a dragon. They shred people for joy! I'm sure he and Father got along famously." Torran spread his arms wide, the firelight glinting up and down the blade. "It's been at the corner of my mind all these years."

"Yes."

"I can't believe . . . I can't believe . . . Maybe she lied. She could have, you know. To make us . . ."

"She didn't lie. You know that."

"MAYBE!"

"Feel it in yourself. Don't you see him now? Leaning over us." Samael began shaking. "I do. I see it. I see the knife . . ."

"Yes," Torran said harshly, cutting him off.

Silence.

"Are you going?" Samael asked.

Without pause Torran answered, "No." Then he looked carefully at his brother. "You're not. You can't . . ."

"I am."

"You can't."

"I am. I'm going."

"He's an old man. He betrayed us. He left us. He did . . ." Torran touched the scars.

Samael stood. "In the morning. I'm leaving in the morning. If you want to come, if you change your mind . . ."

Torran stepped up to his brother, put his hand on Samael's shoulder. They were identical twins, but Torran always imagined himself the older of the two. The older brother protecting the flighty, daydreaming younger one who could never keep his priorities straight and had never acquired the proper sense of the world's danger.

"Don't go," he said, very serious.

"Torran. He's our father. He wants to see us."

"I'm not afraid."

Samael lied for the sake of his brother. A man all of armor, all of weapons. "I know."

"Don't go."

"I want to."

"Why? He . . ."

"He has a story to tell. I listen to stories."

Torran lowered his head. "You're such an idiot."

"Yes."

"A story."

"He wants to tell us something."

"Why listen?"

"It will be a good one. I have a sense about these things. Now I know it as a gift from him, this talent for stories."

"And what did I get?"

Samael could not answer. Torran looked down at his armor, uncomfortable; he turned the sword in his hand. He asked, "And if he's still insane? If he still wants to hurt you?"

"I'll kill him."

2

The dragon, Mountainshadow, in the letter, told them where they could find their father—if they wanted to. Just southeast of the city of Kratas, deep in the jungle, he lived in a small, strange house.

Trees and flowers and vines formed its walls and roof, intertwined and cobbled together. Several of the branches and trunks had taken root again after being set in place, and sprouted green leaves.

The house was a shamble of rooms jutting off one another. A main section rested on the ground, but then small shacks, attached at odd angles, jutted out. Then larger rooms grew atop those, stretching out into neighboring trees. Samael had to step back a moment to take it all in. It was much bigger than he had originally guessed. The rooms tumbled up with larger and larger proportions, like an inverted hill constructed of living wood. The home twisted and turned and grew into the trees above, so that it was impossible to know where the semblance of order began and the sprawl of jungle life ended.

Finally he noticed a set of stairs, rising free and without railing, climbing up around a tree, spiraling up toward the jungle rooftop, and vanishing into the thick tangle of branches high above. At first he didn't know what that was about, then he remembered his father's obsession with searching the stars for meaning, mentioned in both Mountainshadow's story and his mother's. Getting to the top of the jungle would be the only way J'role could examine the glittering points of light in the sky.

The day was gray, and high above a drizzle fell. The thick canopy formed by the jungle growth kept Samael dry and turned the light around him an eerie gray-green. A dreamlike twilight where objects in the distance did not so much fade into darkness as simply lose their color and become insubstantial.

A door waited, made of rough wood and set into the center of the main section of the house. A curling brown moss grew on it, and for a moment Samael thought he saw the door undulate, as if breathing.

He smiled. The product of an overactive imagination.

He shivered. He didn't know anymore; how much is passed on from parent to child?

Singer, his magic sword found in the ruins of a shelter destroyed during the Scourge, tapped against his thigh as he walked toward the house.

He raised his hand and knocked on the door.

Silence. A noise. Something moving, scraping. Another noise—a pot falling, a clatter.

A pause.

Footsteps. The latch lifted from the inside. The door opened.

J'role, old and thin—gaunt—stood there, his skin chalky-gray. His eyes shone with the clarity of the stars against his murky flesh.

Samael looked for scars on the man's flesh, saw none.

His father stared down at him for a moment, curious, uncertain, intrigued. Beyond the man, Samael saw a maelstrom of clutter. Charts of the stars hung haphazardly on the walls, staked into the wood with knives. Treasure chests rested against chairs knocked over onto their sides. Silver and gold pieces lay scattered across the floor like dust. Cobwebs hung from the ceiling, and spiders scurried about as if excited by the arrival of a guest, finally, after all these years. Furniture, chairs and tables, were stacked up tightly in one corner. A stairway led up to one of the higher rooms. Stacks and stacks of star maps rested on the steps, making it look as if ascending the stairs would be as difficult as scaling a steep hill.

As what had been a shadow nightmare for thirty years now became flesh, the sight of his father brought too many memories into sharp focus. A panic gripped him. Samael wanted to turn and run, but it was not in fear for his life. It was purely and simply a need to escape the situation. What was he doing here? What could he say?

But he did not have to speak first. J'role, who as a boy had had no voice, smiled down, sudden recognition in his eyes, and greeted his son. He ushered Samael in.

The two of them stood awkwardly for a few moments, J'role gesturing to the treasures he'd gathered but now had no desire to own. He was a thief and he stole. He couldn't help himself.

J'role asked after Torran, and was disappointed to learn that his other son would not be joining them.

Samael mentioned that neither would Releana be coming. Upon hearing this, the old man turned away and asked if Samael would like some tea. He accepted, and soon father and son had settled down before the hearth, teacups in hand, the fire warming them.

Samael kept his sword with him, on his lap. His father noticed. Commented. The son only smiled, tight-lipped. J'role nodded, knowing. He swallowed. He understood, Samael knew, what their meeting was about. The sword rested between them, a barrier to be breached before any tenderness of touch.

Samael said, "You wanted to tell me something?"

J'role cleared his throat.

PART ONE

New Boy,
Old Magician

1

I stood on the platform I'd built at the top of the jungle. Just over a year ago. Stared at the stars, the lot of them, still and perfect above me. A tableau of order. They moved, but slowly. Not like our own frantic thoughts, but in a stately procession. Comprehensible. One can see the stars. Take them in. Map them.

I did that. Often. It kept me whole. Or busy. Calmed my thoughts. I sat at a desk on the platform, stylus in hand gripped so tight my fingers often numbed, marking out the stars. Their positions. Noting shooting stars, the loose thoughts of the universe. A fixed point of light pried from its proper place. Three of them that night. Terrified me. Things had come unstuck in my head years earlier, and I so desperately needed to know that at least the stars would stay in place. So I sat there, body tight, a child waiting for the unpredictable slap of an angry parent.

The sound of movement far below floated up to me, soft as a butterfly's passage. In the jungle, one listens; each sound a clue to survival. I heard leaves swishing, a branch snap.

A tiger, hunting? Too clumsy. People? I stood. Had I been found? The threat lay in my head, one snake among many, always coiling and writhing in my thoughts.

Voices now, calling. Shouts. "Over there!" The scream of a boy. "No! Please!"

Here and there, along my flesh, the prickly sensation of panic. I did not wonder who these people were. What mattered was that a child was in danger. What greater dilemma? I had to do something. But—BUT would *I* be a greater threat than the danger the child was running from? I'd not harmed any child since you and Torran during the Theran War. Still, the snakes writhed.

I stood, poised like a hunting dog, listening. Around me, the canopy of thick jungle leaves, a strange, frozen lake of black waves. The implacable stars above. Be still, I told myself. Be as the stars. To take action is to risk death. Not the death of the flesh, which I would have welcomed. The death of safety.

Far below, the shouts came closer, grew louder. He was fast, this boy. He deserved a chance.

I sprang for the steps, bounded down them toward a room some forty feet off the ground. No sound made. Thief magic cloaked me. A mantle of shadows. Comfort. To be invisible! There is nothing so wonderful as not to be known! To slip into the cracks of nature and become no more than a rock or a tree to the eyes of other people.

I made a dive for the door leading into the house, rolled inside, leaped up, and grabbed a sword that hung on the wall. A fight! Things began snapping in my body, a cacophony of muscles waking up, brilliant and shiny. Ready for battle.

Down the stairs of the house, as silent as ever. Laughing to myself. I was my own secret.

Through the front door. The air warmer under the canopy of leaves. Thicker. Stifled. A crack of branches ahead. "Spread out!" someone shouted. Old. A fish hook in my brain, that voice. Sharp, but too thin to be identified. Torches, blotches of glowing blood, bobbed in and out from behind trees. Patches of flesh revealed in the harsh light: an elf, a few men. They fanned out.

My house, built room by room amid the trees, covered now with vines, blended into the night forest. They moved on, about a hundred yards off, slowly, beating their way through the thick brush. Searching.

The boy was out there. Somewhere. Ahead of the hunters. The soft, wet ground only gave the slightest sigh as I ran on. My ancient legs took me from one swift leap to the next. The thief magic surrounded me, guided me. I turned and twisted and ducked, missing leaves and branches by a hair's breadth. Hide from the hunters, I thought. That's where the magic's safety could help.

I had to bury my desire to help the boy. Had to trick the magic. Not easy, but possible. Dangerous. Told myself over and over I didn't want to help him. He could prove useful. Valuable. If they were chasing him, he must have money. Or could lead to money. Or could create money. Somehow.

Tell the thief magic you don't care, only that you want. I've lived my whole life that way.

I could kill him if I believed it too much. I might get too selfish. Balance was the key. To think about the boy as a means to my own fortune, but not too much. I didn't want to hurt him, but then, I hadn't reached him yet. If I did and he wore a jeweled crown and I realized I wanted it, the magic coursing through my muscles making me desirous for wealth, I could do anything to him to get what I wanted.

Wealth I couldn't use. Wealth I didn't need.

The shouts rolled further and further away. My breathing increased. Raspy, old breathing thick in my ears. I stopped. Listened. The snap of a branch. Ahead, faint, the sound of hard breathing. The boy. He tried to stifle the noise. I thought, for a moment, that the boy was me, fifty years earlier, hiding from those who wanted the Longing Ring. It, his breathing, was a corpse raised by a nethermancer, desperate for true life.

I moved closer. Slower now. Tricks had been set for me before. Was this all a ruse? Absurd, perhaps, but solipsism speaks tender whispers to the man with no friends.

The hunters approached. Shouted instructions and agreement. Soft mumbling of insubordination. "Too late for this sort of thing." "We're in a jungle for the sake of the Passions." City dwellers, and they weren't particularly fond of each other. Good.

The boy had stopped moving. Had hidden himself, no doubt.

I heard something new. Moist. Ill. A sniffing, thick and full of decay. Beasts. But not from the jungle. Something new.

"Stay within a hundred feet!" someone shouted. The voice of the hook. My memories reeled. I was a man on a tightrope suddenly seeing the woman he'd killed sitting in the audience.

Mordom.

2

Dead fifty years earlier. Fallen onto spikes. Dead. Dead as flesh washed up from the sea. Ragged and torn. I'd seen the glitter of blood. No. I hadn't. I'd imagined that. There had been little light in the tunnels under Parlainth. But Mordom had fallen onto the spikes. That much I knew. The scream. The sudden silence. Dead.

But, then, Death is imprisoned beneath a sea of lava. His power fragile. Things happen. Resurrection. Birth. Hope.

Alive. Mordom was alive, here, now. Only a dozen yards away. I stifled a scream. Raised my worn, blotched hands to my mouth. Exhaled. Almost let the sound slip past my fingers. Memories crashed in all at once. The boy in danger. Me, the boy, now. Mother dead, father dying. Creature in my head. Garlthik, my mentor, traitor, torturer. Something had gone horribly wrong somewhere in my past. One ill-planted seed and you end up with the branches of your mind gnarled and twisted.

These questions plagued me, though. What had been my misstep? What had I done wrong?

I lowered myself to the ground, the weight of years

past pressing down on my shoulders, heavy and improbable. If I could simply sink low enough, he might miss me. They all might.

I was past sixty! What was he doing here? He was a memory, the source of painful nightmares! He belonged inside my head, a phantasm of despair and questions left unanswered. He had no business taking on flesh and muscle, walking with the uncanny precision of bones. His being alive was comprehensible, barely. But why did he have to be near *me*? Our lives had parted. I almost jumped up, shouted, "Look. I've lived my life in terror of everything that happened when I knew you. I have no quarrel with you. Let me go. Take the boy. You'll have no more trouble from me."

The boy.

Now, not me. A boy in danger. Mordom nearby.

His father dead? Mother insane? Stoned to death? Who knew? Horrible things happen. Wasn't there joy somewhere out there in the world? Hadn't I once seen a couple walk by, hand in hand, smiling? Wait. Hadn't *I* done that? Where do these things go? Just how does one go about being happy? And when one gets it, how does one keep it? Air is easier to catch and retain.

The strange, moist sniffing approached. "There's something nearby," one of the hunters said. Deep and gruff. A dwarf.

Through tiny tunnels formed by branches and leaves, I saw Mordom and the dwarf. Fifteen feet away, visible in the light from the torch the dwarf held. If he wasn't dead, Mordom was old at least. Thin, hairless. In the crawling torchlight the deep ravines of his flesh churned red and black. A blasted soil, cursed. His eyes were different. No longer open and white and blind, the eyelids were now closed, sewn shut with thick purple stitches through his flesh. My fingers dug gently at the damp earth, casually, checking for firm reality. His hand was raised, as it had been so many years before, searching. In the palm, a green eye, turning left, then right. A blink. Garlthik's eye.

Mordom's face wore an expression of malice. Too general a description, you might think. But no, it was malice, pure and simple. Imagine a sneer, then add to it such loathing as any name-giver might feel. Then add some more. That was his face. Full of passionless hatred.

The dwarf, standing to his left, leaned back. One hand held the torch. The other, with arm extended, held two leashes wrapped around the wrist. The strain from the animals at the other end turned his flesh red. The moist noise, a breathing, a hunger, came from behind the thick bushes where the leashes led.

"Should I let them go?" asked the dwarf.

"No, not just yet. They'll be difficult to retrieve. They have his fear. They'll find him."

They have his fear?

Horrors?

Horrors.

Mordom had handled Horrors well enough years ago. Now he kept them for pets. I hunched over, shamed by my lack of courage, trying to fold in on myself. The terror of the moment—the past smashing into the present—seemed worthy of such an extraordinary stunt.

Through the gaps in the leaves I caught glimpses of the Horrors. Two of them, different. Both black, the size of very large dogs. One with a huge humped back. The other nearly a skeleton covered with tight, wet fur.

I could be safe. I could remain quiet, let them pass. They didn't want me. The creatures were leading Mordom and the dwarf past me toward the boy. Too cowardly? Compare me to a hero, and the answer is yes. But I never claimed to be a hero.

The boy's breathing, again. A sniffle. Quiet. I turned just slightly. Beside me, a dazed, dead tree, its hollow innards cracked open, exposed. Inside the hole, a shadow shifted. A shaft of torchlight touched the boy's face momentarily, the flesh of his cheek smooth, uncorrupted by age and experience. A dwarf lad.

"Over there!" the dwarf with the creatures suddenly called out. The sniffs of the creatures, heavy footsteps through mud, growing louder. One growled. A tendril of thought curled through my brain, probing. For a moment I stopped breathing, stifling all emotions. The probing mind moved on.

"Listen," I whispered, leaning in toward the boy. "I can help you. We have to leave . . ." He'd thought I hadn't noticed him, thought he was too carefully hidden in the tree. He screamed.

I reached in, seized him under the arms with both hands. He kicked his legs against me as I dragged him out. "Leave me *alone*!"

I pressed my face against his, our noses touching, and snarled, "SHUT UP!" He did.

Behind us, the crashing of the Horrors through the bushes as they raced toward us, freed from their leashes.

3

I dropped the boy to the ground, then clutched his hand. It shook. He was crying. "Come on!" I said harshly. We ran.

So much happened, pierced my senses. The thief magic was no help now. Mordom's presence had confused me too much. No longer could I envision the dwarf lad as a possible treasure trove. I wanted to help him. He was no longer himself, he was more than himself. He was me, threatened by Mordom decades ago. He was you and Torran, threatened by Overgovernor Pavelis. My mind slipped beats in the rhythm of life, as all our minds do at times. Often things are not what they are, but more. He was a little boy, but with his pudgy hand in mine, he was all little boys, lost in a jungle, pursued by enemies.

The Horrors at our heels. The air become moist and hot, unnatural. A tongue of warm air descended, curled around me. The boy screamed again, and I knew why. The touch of the air lapped up against our flesh, began to melt into it. It disturbed my sensibilities. Something was in my skin.

We ran on. Branches grabbed at my flesh, scratched out blood. The boy gasped for air, drowning in thick leaves slapping against his face. My forehead slammed into a low tree branch. I reeled backward for a moment, but then pushed forward once more, ducking slightly.

Where were we going?

Shouts again. The hunters followed the Horrors, who followed us. "There's someone else!" one of them cried. A Horror reached us, snapped at the boy's calves, its breath exhaling sharply; a snarl. I scooped up the boy in my arms, stumbled forward. Awkward, unpracticed, an old man suddenly cradling a child.

The branches cracking against my body overwhelmed me. The exertions so draining I could not think of a plan. I could only focus on trying to keep my legs moving. If they failed me, all was lost. The strange, probing tongue of hot air moved into my body, sliding in and out of my organs. It took on a more solid texture, began to constrict, drawing my innards into a tight knot. I doubled over, nearly dropping the boy. In my arms his weight was extraordinary, stocky and solid. I gasped out loud. He, the boy, was crying again. I was false hope. A tease of the mind: Things might be all right. Then: No, not so, not after all.

I had been young once, strong. Now my muscles felt sore and weary. I longed for a rest, a long rest. Death. How had such a miserable creature as me managed to stay alive so long? I became light-headed. Could I just fall? It wouldn't be my fault. Old, running, trying to save a boy's life. Killed by a Horror for a good cause. It seemed a nice way to go, worthy of a few kind words in memoriam. Something that might erase the horrible child's rhyme as my only possible epitaph.

The rhyme wound its way through my head, and as I ran, its meter matched my footsteps:

"Who are you?"
"J'role, mad old clown;
I've always been so
Since my first sound.
Father and Mother
Crazy before me,
Juggle a razor!
Slice! Now you can't see!"

I had just finished the rhyme when the ground dropped out from under my feet. The boy and I fell forward in utter darkness.

4

Surprise gripped our throats, shaking cries out of us. The river greeted us, its water cool in the night. Our clothes, wet, snaked around our skin, clinging. I knew of the river, normally so much smaller. A brook. I had forgotten that it would be swollen from recent rains. The current moved us along with countless, formless hands. The thing that had been in my body, the probing tongue, was gone, but a lingering stickiness remained in my nerves. A strange mucus oozing through my flesh. The boy splashed in the water, called for his mother, water half-filling his mouth as he bobbed up and down. I grabbed him under my arm, turned him so he floated on his back. "Relax," I commanded, but he continued to slap the water, unable to stifle panic. The loss of all moorings had taken its toll; we think we know what life is, and then all that is familiar is gone, replaced by half-formed shadows, phantasms of people and places we do not recognize. What can one do but move about wildly, try to somehow transport oneself back to the world known before?

A splash from upriver. Above, the thick, leafy canopy blocked starlight; behind us only the low hum of rushing water. Something came toward us, swimming.

Breathing heavily. Moist. Hungry. I reached for my sword, which I had slipped into my belt in the house, but my hand found nothing. I must have lost it during the race through the woods or the jump into the river. Torches bobbed along the riverbank, following us, eclipsed and revealed between trees.

I kicked wildly, throat tightening, the Horror splashing its way toward us as I tried to get us to the opposite bank. The dark air, the dark water, the floating, all put me in mind of being somehow already dead. Closer came the Horror, and I pleaded with the boy to be quiet. I didn't think silence would help us against it, but it might keep the hunters from knowing where we landed on the bank. He settled down, aware he hadn't drowned yet, his mind suddenly careless of the danger all around. Relieved. He sniffled, loneliness and homesickness wearing on him more now than anything else.

The thing got closer, paddling. Even as I kicked the water wildly, I tensed, expecting the strange lapping, humid tongue to arrive again. When that didn't happen, I assumed that the Horror possessing that strange power was now leashed, following the hunters along the bank. The second Horror, the one in the water with us, remained a mystery to be revealed. They, Horrors, come in so many nightmarish forms and shapes, who could possibly catalogue them all?

Its breath was clearly audible now, heaving. Snorting up water as it paddled closer and closer. Only a few yards away. The boy heard it, started screaming. It lunged at us, propelling itself forward, inspired by the boy's terror. The lunge fell short, sending water into the air, splashing over us. The boy, his pitch high, tried to shatter his fear with another scream. He failed. He struggled to free himself from my hold, grabbing my arm and trying to pry free of my grip. I held tight, but then the thing was on us.

It came at me, a shadow darker than the darkness around us. A flash, teeth, a blur. The wound, an epicenter of cut glass. The boy slipped from my arm as I screamed, rolled over. My mouth, gasping with agony as I turned, filled with blood-stained river water. Paws, large, with nails like silver pins, pushed down on my back, driving me deeper into the water. The thing scrambled over me, paddling toward the boy. I became a non-object, and it kicked me without thought as it passed.

Around me, a void. No up, down. I floated without purpose. Lungs straining for air, eyes straining for sight. Then, a muffled scream. There, to the right. I broke the surface of the river. Coughing. The air I sucked in ripping heat through my lungs. The thing whirled before I had my bearings, a face—no. A mouth. The thing's head no more than a massive mouth, lips pulled so far back that only teeth and tongue showed. A peeled orange, and inside, nothing but a gaping void. The impossibility of the image froze my thoughts. The mouth lunged toward me. I fell away, rolling back into the water. The thing's nails drove down into my chest. A scream from me, and then a gurgling as water once again rushed down into my throat. I clutched at its shoulders, clawed for its neck, thinking without thought it could somehow save me from drowning. The two of us, the Horror and myself, submerged.

Twisting, rolling deeper down through the river's thick, coursing water. We struggled to get a solid grip on each other. My fingers slid up the neck, brushing against long, fine fur that felt oddly luxurious. The neck was long, strangely long for the enormous mouth it supported. I gripped it with both hands, tried to snap it. It writhed in my grip, a snake. A child squirming for freedom.

My mother's fingers on my chest. The ritual. The creature in my thoughts.

Teeth sank down into my arm. The pain forced my mouth open. The world inverted. Water became my air, stuffing my mouth, throat. The natural response of a gasp meant death. My hands fluttered in the water, searching for the mouth, desperate to pry it off my arm. My right hand did not respond. Limp. Searing. The left found the teeth, sharp and deadly. Pried back the mouth, cutting the fleshy palm of my hand. Free. Images of death floated before me, strange fish. My corpse floating down the river. My corpse flayed by Theran slave masters. My corpse, killed by my own hand at the suggestion of the Horror in my thoughts. How many times had I almost died? The lack of air made me dizzy. Time tightened, the work of a child, a ball made from a jungle vine, wound upon itself again and again. I drifted, uncertain of how old I was. Old, though. Old. Always old.

Always?

Always.

Some of us, it takes us our whole lifetime to catch up with our age.

Up, through the surface of the river. The torchlights distant on the other side. Alive! A moment of pleasure, the beauty of a still lake at dawn shattered by the ripples of the moment. The Horror. Mordom. The boy! Where was the boy?

I was confused. The pain in my shoulder so hot I thought it was on fire. The boy I sought—which one? For a moment I thought I could find myself. Drifting, tumbling end over end in the flood waters of life. Thoughts of my past brought me round and I somehow was a stranger to myself. An unknown, mysterious savior to myself. Did my childhood still exist? Did it live somewhere? Could I rescue the boy I once was and change my present? The thoughts crept up the base of my skull and I feared I was about to lose my mind. It happened on occasion, the fear, the threat of losing my mind. Out of my mind. Thoughts spinning so quick, like a child held by the hands, by the hands of his father, the father spinning and spinning and spinning, the child laughing and laughing until the fateful moment the father lets go. An accident. A slip. Momentum, and the child goes flying. Off. Out. Gone.

Lost my mind.

I feared I might truly come to believe that I wasn't myself as a child, that I was in fact two separate people. (From where came the idea? Where exactly do thoughts come from?) If I could believe that, if that belief came to pass, surely I would no longer know how to live in the world. I would wander the jungles of the land, living like a leopard, aware of the surroundings as things—a tree, an antelope, the sunlight—but my thoughts, the thoughts of a name-giver, would be gone. I would no longer know me as *me*.

Suddenly the boy again. The dwarf boy, that is. "Get off!" he shouted. A glint of metal, faint. A bright star on a cloud-covered night, piercing the veil. His small hand brought the blade down into the back of the thing's mouth. It roared in pain. I realized at that moment that I was dying. I floated away, an observer, delighted at the boy's blow and our common victory. Delighted, but certain I wouldn't be around for the celebration.

5

It whirled on him, the Horror, sending him a few feet off. A splash as the river swallowed him again. "What's happening?" someone from the bank shouted. We had made good time on them, the water sweeping us along past the tangle of trees and bushes that slowed them down. They stood twenty feet back from us. "I can't see!" chimed in another. "Where's the magician?" said a third. "Coming! He's on his way," said a fourth. A torch thrown by one of the hunters arced toward us. "There!"

The flame's reflection spilled over the river's surface, a scarlet oil, a hot point of white at the center. For a moment I saw the boy, young, chubby cheeks smooth and beardless. Eyes a mix of fear and the resilience of mountains. Something had snapped inside him. The strange strength of children, underestimated by sentimental adults, had been tapped. The alarm sounded. He flailed to stay afloat, but did not sink. In one hand, the dagger, stained with green globules.

The long neck of the creature extended from the water, its massive, wide, obscenely impossible mouth peeled back in a parody of a scream. No sound emerged. It just could not close its mouth. It turned. I had no idea how it saw; eyes could not fit anywhere with the mouth taking up so much room. It moved toward the boy.

The torch struck the water, hissed. Steam rose, lit by the last flare of the torch's light. Darkness, a mother's suffocating embrace, returned.

The threat of annihilation, the fear of it, rocked me. In me woke the passion of conflict. Was not life a series of jabs and feints? Were we not only alive in struggle? A punch. A stab. Perhaps the rough tumble of sex. If I had found any purpose in living, it was this: Draw blood.

I clamped down on the pain, swam toward the thing, its presence marked by the shout of the boy. "Let me go! Let me go!" The waters ahead slapped and rippled from the struggle of the boy and the creature. It didn't seem to be hurting him, only carrying the lad off toward the bank where the hunters waited. As I approached I heard the sticky penetration of the boy's dagger into the thing's flesh. Again and again he raised it, plunged, and withdrew. He exhaled heavily with each blow. The creature grunted, a high-pitched sigh of pain in time with the boy's exhalations, but it seemed to sustain itself against the damage.

My hand touched the thing, caught it on the back. It started, turned awkwardly in the water. The boy shouted in surprise. I realized that the creature had the boy in its mouth. Cradled him. The creature kicked at me with its hind legs as it tried to keep moving for the bank. "Give me the dagger," I demanded, but the boy did not respond. I reached up with my left arm, the good one, found his face by accident, gripped it tight in my fingers. I'm sure he thought I was about to crush his cheeks. "Give it now!"

His hand fell down toward me, a soft blur of sound in the darkness. I let go of his face, ran my hand down his arm, found the dagger. "Let go." He did. I flung my right arm, useless and pained, over the creature's back, desperate for a grip of some sort. My shoulder felt as if it might crack, my arm falling off, drifting down to the river's bottom. I managed, despite numbness, to grab the thing's fur with my fingers. The grip tentative, but good enough for the moment. Like most of my life.

A fierce thrust with the dagger into the thing's belly, a jagged turn, a raking back and forth. The creature cried out. The boy splashed into the water. Shouts from the bank. A new wetness, a different texture from the water, thicker, poured out from the wound, drifted over my skin. The mouth came for me. I drove the dagger up, my arm erect. The mouth engulfed my arm, teeth boring into my flesh. A wave of blackness through my eyes. I pushed the agony away, twisted the dagger, cutting into the roof of the mouth, the tongue. The thing opened its mouth and screamed. I splashed into the water.

Without pause I swam back to it. Droplets of its strange blood rained down on me. A void, the mouth, rushed at me. I rolled in the water and the mouth splashed up a wave. Pulling my arm up, I cut blindly for the neck. I found it, flung my right arm over the neck, pulled myself closer. I sawed at the neck with the blade. The neck, the body, splashed. I clung desperately, dragging the edge of the blade deeper and deeper into the thing's neck. It thrashed in the river; a terrible racket of cries and churning water. Then suddenly, with an almost suspicious abruptness, it went limp. Water flowed over it, soothing, as it sank. I held on, even stabbed it a few more times, certain it had somehow conceived a trick for me. Some of them thought like name-givers. The one in my head when I was a boy certainly did. The thing I rested on, semi-submerged, had behaved like a well-trained animal. But it could be more. One, I knew, could never be too careful. Enemies on all sides. The Universe had created a playpen of despair. All we had to do was let down our guard for a moment to be rendered crippled—physically, emotionally—once more.

But the Horror sank. Still. Quite dead. I floated away, oddly afraid that being near it would somehow suck me down to the bottom of the river. A perverse magic.

The torches of the hunters still followed, but were now forty to fifty feet upriver. With the creature dead, we would be able to move silently. I floated, the river carrying me, doing all the work. "Boy?" A shivered reply. "Yes?" Something clicked in me now. The danger past, I could feel my natural tendencies returning. I had saved him. He might be of value. There might be money in it after all. "Stay calm. Here, come here." He drifted toward me, his small arms extended. I caught one of them, gently. Pulled him close. "We'll be all right now. We'll be all right. We just need to get to the other side. Here. See. Here we are."

I encouraged him to be quiet as we caught some roots that trailed into the water and then made our way up the bank. He obliged. In fact, he became peculiarly quiet. A fear stirred in me: Had the creature done something to him? Entered his thoughts? Turned him mute? "Speak to me," I whispered.

"What?"

"Never mind."

Behind us the hunters had entered the river, swimming carefully, like strange fish with luminous organs, their torches, protruding from their flesh. They had lost sight of us, however, and our silence held. They did not know if we were nearby or already further downstream. We made our way into the jungle, me doubled over with pain, the boy shivering, the night engulfing us.

6

We doubled back to my house. Mordom and the others obviously did not know I lived nearby, and would probably think we had continued downstream. A person seldom looks for something right in front of him. The mind thinks that if something is not handy, it is well hidden, though this is not always the case. My home would serve us well for food and shelter until I found the means of gaining money from his presence.

I fixed him up. Rice and vegetables. Several blankets. A fire.

For myself, I sought a healing potion or two. I ran up and down the stairs, wandering the labyrinthine arrangement of rooms that was my home, tossing back the lids of trunks and yanking open the doors of cabinets gone stuck with years of disuse. I sorted through crystal pendants, magical daggers, silks with patterns of trees that rustled in the wind when moved. I found vials of clear blue glass, stoppered flasks carved from ivory, and tins sealed with layers of wax. I had to pause and consider each one, re-weaving, in my mind, the narrative of how I had come to possess the item. Only then could I remember exactly what the fluid in each container actually did. Even then I could not be certain.

I see them now, these glittering goods, as organs, like stomachs or lungs, found lying about the world. I'd picked them up, thinking that they could do me some good. A spare stomach. A spare lung. Who couldn't use an extra organ when the world constantly chipped away at one's flesh? Anything to stay alive despite all the troubles. Once they were mine, I tried to stuff them into myself, make them part of me. Lonely? Uncertain? But think! I have a surplus of goods resting inside me. How many lungs? How many hearts? Too many. I'm the envy of any other person. Who wouldn't be jealous of what I've got? I'm really quite fine.

But despite the surfeit of artificial body parts, I never really felt any better. They never fit very well, these baubles. I'd think I was finished each time, and then realize I still felt empty. Time for another intestine. More hearts. Out for more and more and more. The accumulation kept me busy, and at least numbed me to the stirring of disquiet in my soul. But never was I done. I see now that the fake bits of life cost me too much blood as I shoved them through my flesh and cut myself open again and again.

One after another, holding them up to the light, all beautiful, feeling for a tremor the excitement that had been mine when I first possessed the thing, and then wondering where that feeling had gone.

I tracked blood everywhere around the house, and each time I passed the boy he seemed drowsier and drowsier. Firelight lapped gently at his round cheeks. His flesh, seamless. Finally I found two vials of the healing potion, one taken from an abandoned kaer, the other from a trade caravan I'd helped raid just a few months earlier. They made me dizzy, and I sat down opposite the boy, letting the fire reheat my flesh. Soon I was asleep.

I woke, the night still as a corpse. Coals, red, blinking to shades of black, still burned in the hearth. Without stirring a muscle, I stared at the boy. Very peaceful, he. By dwarf years, not yet an adolescent. Not much older than you and Torran when I'd seen you last. He rolled over, sighed, his breathing relaxed. Innocent. I want you to know, I felt no desire to hurt him. The same way I felt no desire to hurt either of you. But sometimes it seems that we must hurt people.

Enough equivocating. I'll come to it all soon enough.

I remained awake. Wound and tight like an archer's string. Though my wounds had already become soft and pink, Mordom's return from the dead had called up too many memories for me to feel healthy. Through the final hours before dawn I imagined my life. The narrative felt terse. My memories came colorless, which, in fact, is how I often perceived the world. A lack of vibrancy. Only in shadows did I truly feel alive.

Haphazard pinpricks of pink cast themselves against the walls as the morning sunlight cut in low through the jungle, and passed through my windows. The boy stirred. Rolled over. Opened his eyes. Stretched. Realized his surroundings were unfamiliar, panicked, sat up, looked around, stared at me in fear.

"Good morning."

He held his breath, then breathed quickly. "Where am I?"

"My home. Do you remember last night?"

He looked away. Bit his lower lip. A thoughtful boy. He reminded me of someone, but I could not place it. Meeting my gaze, he said, "Yes. You saved me."

I bowed slightly, spread my hands apart. In such circumstances, always appear humble. This compels the person from whom you want something to make up for your humility with a bigger reward.

He smiled. "Who are you?"

"My name is J'role . . ."

Immediately his face betrayed terror.

"Not," I said with a laugh and an overdone wave of my hand, "the infamous clown who mutilates children. An awkward situation, for my name is my name. But more people know of the character from that rhyme than know of me."

The boy swallowed. Relaxed. "I don't think he really exists, anyway."

"You're a bright lad. Most children can't distinguish stories from life."

"My father taught me you have to know the difference. Both are valuable, he says, but for different purposes. For different reasons."

"What's your name?"

"Neden. Son of Varulus."

The world tilted me backward in time. I closed my eyes. Gripped the arms of my chair. I looked at him once more. "Neden. Son of Varulus. Your father is King Varulus the Third? King of Throal?"

He smiled. Leaned toward me. Pride radiated from him like sunlight. "Yes."

"Your father is King of Throal?"

"Do you know him?"

"We met many, many years ago."

"It's said that my father gave the order to hunt down that clown."

"Is it?"

"I don't believe he did, though."

"You never asked?"

"No." He looked down.

"Why not?"

"I don't think I want to know."

"If he says yes, the clown exists," I said, finishing his thought for him.

"He's probably dead by now."

I thought of Mordom. Of myself. "Probably. Most monsters die eventually."

"He wasn't a monster. The clown. He was a bad man."

"Really?" Revealing nothing, I felt a giddiness course through me. I imagined myself the villain of a turgid melodrama as I let the little tyke tell me about me, my infamous deeds. I could move up closer, feign interest, interest, interest, then pull out the blade, fulfilling the rhyme's prophesy. No desire within moved me forward. Yet suddenly the idea was born in my head for the first time. What if I attempted to fill the shoes of the legend I'd inadvertently created for myself?

7

His legs, stubby, swung freely as he sat up on the bench where he'd slept. Relaxed now. The chatter of a child who knows his subject. "The clown was a man who went crazy. Maybe from a Horror. Maybe from the Theran War. My papa says war can drive people crazy."

"Yes."

"But at the end of the war, he killed his children. He killed them and ran away. His wife told my father what happened, and my father tried to find him. And he ran and ran, and tricked children. He made himself seem nice. But he killed them too. That's what I heard."

"I don't think he killed his sons," I said. "He cut their faces." The boy looked at me, curious. "That's what I heard."

"Why would he do that?"

"Some people . . . some people confuse . . ."

He waited, a child not indifferent to etiquette and the respect for adults.

"I don't know, exactly."

"He was crazy."

"Yes." What did I think I was doing bringing a child here? Into my life?

"Are you all right?"

I'd obviously revealed too much. My face was not the mask I always wished it was but never turned out to be. Time for cheap tactics. "What happened last night?"

"You mean those men?"

I nodded.

"They attacked my guards. They wanted to capture me. One of them, the man with his eyes . . . his eyes sewn shut . . . he kept saying, 'Take the boy alive.' My guards all died. Even Bombim." He looked down.

"Do you know why? Why they wanted you?"

He remained silent a long time, and I thought he hadn't heard me, his memories, stirred up, clouding his senses from the moment at hand. But he finally said, "No. Or maybe. I don't know for sure. My papa, he sent me from Throal. He said I was in danger. Said there was a plot to hurt him and me. Sent us out . . . I didn't know where we were going. Bombim knew. He was my teacher. Anyway. I didn't know. I don't know."

"The people your father was worried about, they probably caught up to you."

"I want to go home."

"I'm sure you do. But that's what you *want.* You have to decide what you think you *should* do. If you want me to get you back to Throal, then we'll do that. If you think we should hide you—like your father wanted—then that's what we'll do. You decide."

"You would get me home?"

"Oh, yes."

"It's very far away."

"I know."

"There'd be a reward."

"It wouldn't be for the money."

"Still . . ."

"I wouldn't refuse a reward. That would be rude."

"Yes." He laughed.

"What's so funny?"

"You, trying to be clever."

I smiled. "Is it that obvious?"

"You mean, does it show?"

"Yes."

"Yes."

"I'm getting old. The games are harder to play."

Laughter again. Not the malicious laughter that children are so capable of. A delight in life. I liked him. He reminded me of someone I'd once wanted to be.

"Why don't you think about what we should do." I stood, preparing to go upstairs and get some more sleep.

Fear crouched around the edges of his eyes, ready to spring.

"What is it?"

"I don't . . . I don't know what to do. I'm . . ."

"Yes?"

All his confidence and good nature shattered. "I'm just a little boy. I don't know what I'm supposed to do."

A memory, but not quite a memory, stirred within me. A sensation, a truth from years past. I couldn't see it quite clearly. It passed. "Well, you have to make a decision now. You can't hide behind being a child."

He blinked, stared at me. "I didn't mean . . ."

Something tightened inside of me, my flesh. "It doesn't matter if you meant to or not, Neden. The world is full of danger. You have to accept that, deal with it. You've got to learn how to make decisions on your own."

He stifled something, his face a mask. He nodded. Toughened. A pleasure tickled me; I felt myself a father. Passing on something about pain and life and how it all comes together.

"I . . . My father wanted me away from home. Until the danger passed. So I think I should stay away. That's what he wanted."

"So we'll hide you."

His stubby fingers folded themselves into fists, then relaxed, then repeated the motion several times over. "But I won't know when I can go home."

"Don't worry about that. We'll go on to Kratas. We can stay there, hiding, and I can send word to your father from there."

This eased his concern and he sat back down. Sleepiness overcame him and he began to blink. I got up and eased him down onto the bench. Already his eyes were closed, and his breathing deep. By the time I stood straight he was fast asleep. Inspired by Neden, my body so wanted a heavy sleep. But I stood rooted to the spot, staring down at him. I felt the desire to become his father, to *possess* him as a father. I wish I could say there was love behind this desire, but what was there to love? I'd known him for the half-hour of our conversation. No. What had roused in me was the same desire to own the trinkets and jewels and treasures scattered about my house. Something for me to revel in owning, but not to enjoy.

I should mention as well, though I am loath to do it, the other sensation. It was present, strange and formless in the muscles of my arms and hands. The desire to hurt him. I wish I could say otherwise, but it was there. And as always, when these feelings coursed through my thoughts, I sensed the shadow lurking nearby.

Unlike the white shadow that had been the Horror's spirit in my home in the kaer years and years ago, this one was rich in darkness. I never saw it clearly. Never took a sharp look at it, never tried too hard to see it. Did not want to. But I knew it was there. I'd felt it growing since the time I'd gotten my voice back. It had grown stronger and stronger over the years. Now it was in the room with me. With us, Neden and I.

At once I felt shamed by the desire to hurt Neden, but I also believed it to be a true impulse, good and strong. The same way I knew what I had done to you and your brother thirty years ago to be good and strong. I had meant what I said then: Our scars make us what we are. I felt that I must hurt Neden for him to grow up and understand what the world was about.

How to hurt him? How much? I didn't know. It didn't seem the right time. I turned from him, leaving him be for now. The shadow retreated. Never fully gone, but out of sight. The impulse slipping from my mind, I went off to sleep. I climbed the stairs to the bedchamber, the highest room in the house, and shrugged off the exhaustion that had gathered on me for so many hours.

8

Later in the afternoon I awoke to a sound filtered through a dream—the claws of rats sorting through a pile of refuse. When I opened my eyes, patches of dead yellow sunlight crawled on the walls. A moment of hesitation, listening to the sound, wondering, then a quick, alert sitting up. Where was Neden? Had Mordom somehow found us?

I slipped out of bed, floor cold against bare feet, crept to the door. Down the dark stairway I heard nothing but objects shifted carefully. Someone trying to be quiet. No words spoken.

A dagger waited on the wall by the door, tucked behind a tapestry. They're everywhere. I don't even know if I could find them all for you, I've planted so many in this house. Just in case. I withdrew the dagger from its hiding place. Started down the stairs, silent. Not a creak from the floorboards. Dagger in hand, held for a stab. One flight, then two. Only the sounds of the treasure-sifter from the room ahead caught my attention. The stairway and the lower rooms were dark, lit only by lanterns hanging from walls. It seemed likely it would be Neden. Mordom's henchmen seemed more the sort to clumsily scatter everything this way and that, and then claim they could find nothing of value. Still, one can never be too careful, I thought. I have always thought that. I lived like an archer's string. You know, of course, a bowstring should not remain permanently on the bow. It bends the bow. Strains the string. It's astounding how we can so clearly recognize the mistreatment of objects, but be so unaware of what we are doing to ourselves.

I turned the corner into the doorway. The light of a lamp hanging on a hook in the hall threw my shadow forward. Neden turned, gasped, as the shadow appeared large and wavering on the wall before him. "J'role," he said, and smiled. He was kneeling before a trunk. Scattered around him were silver coins and glinting necklaces and jewel-encrusted goblets. Part of the haul from Parlainth the day the creature in my thoughts died.

The day my life changed.

The day everything stayed pretty much the same.

The day things got worse.

For a moment, looking at him, I thought he was me, kneeling down before the treasure, back in the treasure room in Parlainth. The elements of my dreams had finally come true: The monster killed, treasure chests opened. An adventure! My confusion cut deep, shaking my bones. Who was I, if he was me? I became a bodiless spirit without a time or place. It was a common problem of mine. I spent a great deal of time in my head. I often forgot about my flesh. Or rather, it seemed a distraction. If only I could be aware without having to be alive. The sight of Neden kneeling before the treasure I had knelt before decades earlier only exaggerated the problem. My voice left me. What can a ghost say?

Neden stood, concern on his face, distancing himself from the treasure. "I'm sorry. I didn't . . . didn't . . . I just wanted to . . ." He stepped away, starting to shake. He wanted to get away from the treasure, but I blocked the door, and apparently I was not something a child would want to be near. What was the expression I wore on my face? How did I hold my body? I cannot say. Something had slipped. The center gone. My perceptions of self fraying, a sail in the storm. Tense, I would imagine, the muscles firm and locked. My face taut. I don't think it was anger. Anger is comprehensible to a child. I imagine the confusion on my face ran so deep, a great ravine extending down into darkness, that Neden had never seen anything like it. An adult with the lost expression of an infant. Now that would be disturbing.

"Neden," I said, not looking at him. I had no body, so I had no eyes. How could I look at him?

"Yes?"

"Come here."

Nothing happened. No scrape of footsteps against the wooden floor.

"Please come here."

A hesitant step. Then another. His voice creaked, filled with spiders, I thought. "Yes?"

"Take my hand."

"I . . ."

A pause. Then the touch of his stubby fingers against mine. They slid up to my palm, and then he gripped my hand. Reality, swift and solid, flowed up through my flesh. His touch anchored me back in place. A place. A time. I was warm once more. I stood, swaying, uncertain. Glad. I held his hand a bit tighter. "Are you all right?" he asked. I nodded. I was. I felt myself coming to me again. I looked down at him. Smiled. He returned the smile, but hesitantly. "I'm all right."

"What happened?"

"I get confused sometimes. Confused—does that ever happen to you?"

"Sometimes. I guess."

"Never mind. I'm all right now." I sensed that he wanted to take his hand away. But I held onto it, selfish. Needed to know he would be uncomfortable for my sake.

9

I had planned to spend a few weeks hiding here, in my home. There seemed little need to risk a journey immediately. Varulus had obviously meant for Neden to be out of sight for some time, and as my home had escaped the attention of soldiers and bounty hunters for a decade, it seemed the perfect place for us to wait out the time before our trip to Kratas.

For three days I showed him my trinkets, hauling them out of lonely storage. He showed little interest in the treasures themselves. Why should he? As the heir to the kingdom of Throal he had wealth aplenty. His scale of wealth and power involved the movement of armies, trade negotiations, the construction of whole cities. I realize now I must have made a ridiculous sight, hauling out my treasures, tossing them before his gaze.

But the stories that accompanied the treasures—Ah! These caught his attention. "Now these rubies," I'd say, knowing I had him hooked, "I acquired from the lair of a corrupted elf who led a band of thieves against caravans."

His eyes widened like a beggar's hands, fingers

spread wide, waiting for more. "You've seen a corrupted elf?"

I knew that the Elf Queen and others from Blood Wood sometimes visited Throal. "Haven't you?"

"My father never lets me see them." He pouted, a boy knowing he'd been robbed of the birthright of seeing the strange and horrible of this world. "He says they're a bad influence."

I thought of the Elf Queen's thorns raking through my flesh as she embraced me so many years before. "Yes. And no."

He cocked his head, catching on that there was more in my cryptic reply than merely ambiguity. "Have you ever been to Blood Wood?" he asked slyly. I nodded. "Is it terrible? I've heard it's absolutely terrible." He leaned in, little-boy energy crackling around him like a magician's spell, eager to hear of things disgusting and repulsive.

"It's pretty bad," I answered. The setting sun cast a rosy light, and my gaze followed the shadows of leaves on the wall. I didn't know if I could begin talking about the matter without breaking into tears.

Softly, a truth dawning on him, he said, "You can tell me about Blood Wood." Then, abruptly, loudly, "You must tell me all about it. Please. My father doesn't tell me anything about the Corrupted Court." As an afterthought he said, to bolster his argument, "And I'm to be *king* some day!"

"Your father has his reasons for not speaking to you about it, I'm sure."

"My father wants me to be *nice*." He spat out the last word as if it reminded him of carrots forced on him at dinner.

I thought of the Elf Queen, of blood. Of you and Torran, faces ruined. Of all the pain I'd caused your mother by my irresponsibility. "Nice has its place in the world."

"Please, please, please, tell me about Blood Wood. I hear they take their skin off at night."

"No. No, they don't do that. Their skin is always on them, and the thorns always prick through their flesh. They can't ever stop the pain. It's always with them." A chill began to crawl along my arms and into my shoulders.

"They did that to save themselves. From the Horrors."

"Yes. They made themselves hurt so much there was no pain left over for the Horrors to feed on. The Horrors went elsewhere."

Neden looked down, putting it all together. "But now they still hurt. How come they can't stop?"

"Their magic cost them a great deal." I laughed, thinking how much the metaphor of money had crept into my thinking over the years. "And some things, once you purchase them, are yours for life."

"Like a dog?"

"Somewhat."

We sat in silence, our thoughts drifting in different directions, but orbiting the same ideas, like stars floating around the earth. He said, "So you don't want to talk about Blood Wood?"

"No."

"Pretty bad, huh?"

"Oh, yes."

"I guess that's why my father doesn't want me to know about it."

"He also hates them." Neden raised an eyebrow. "They represent everything he is fighting against. They sold themselves to corruption to save their own lives. Your father thinks people should rather die than become monsters." My voice betrayed a bitterness.

"You don't think Father's wrong, do you?"

I smiled, laughed, a ridiculous attempt to throw the boy off track. "No. No, not at all. Of course not."

With the cautious eyes of a pup who had yet to learn what was good behavior and what bad, he stared at me. "You think people should become monsters to survive."

"I'm saying it happens. We do what we must."

Fear turned his face into a mask. Then, cleverly, he relaxed. "Can I go outside to play?"

"I don't think that's a good idea."

"Hmmm."

The splintering of the front door rushed up the stairs, making us jump. We looked at each other, startled, waiting for an explanation.

"Hurry," someone shouted.

"Are we in trouble?" Neden asked.

"Oh, yes." I answered.

10

With the thrill of possible death tickling me forward, I rushed toward the door. Neden slipped further into the room, willing to let me protect him once again. I grabbed a sword from a wall. With thoughts of the Elf Queen in my mind, I realized that all of my weapons served me as thorns of the mind, walls of sharp metal, pricking me constantly with thoughts of the world's pain, never permitting me to let down my guard.

But who was it attacking? Mordom and his henchmen? Bounty hunters finally come for me? Or perhaps even soldiers from Throal, come to rescue Neden after somehow tracking him to my home. The sounds of swords being drawn greeted me as I made my way down the last flight of curved stairs to the main floor. A faint shadow on the wall, a creak of the stairs. They wanted to be quiet, but silence was my friend, and he spoke to me of all the noises that intruded on him. I dove for the wall opposite the mercenary, sailing for a moment through the air with ridiculous ease—a dream made flesh—and smacked my back into it. My abrupt arrival caught the mercenary off guard. A young man, dressed in black armor, he wore a determined scowl, which he must have hoped would accentuate the nihil-

istic armor. The look changed to horrified surprise as I swung my sword into his stomach. He cried out, fell back down the stairs. His companions, a motley lot of young mercenaries like himself, as well as the dwarf I'd seen with Mordom, caught his body.

I rushed back up the stairs as they tried to push their way past the corpse. "Neden!" I cried, "Time to move on!" When I reached the room I discovered him—gone. A cursory search behind treasure trunks and a few large sacks of gold and silver coins revealed nothing. I called his name again, then ran from room to room, the panic of the moment sending a thrilling heat through my flesh. It occurred to me I might have lost my mind. Had the boy really been in my home? Where, exactly, had the shift in my sanity taken place? Had I fantasized my mother placing the creature in my head, her fingertips touching my chest as the creature's ritual required? Or perhaps it was the arrival of Garlthik in my village? Or even my father's death? Did he still live somewhere? Then all the thoughts tumbled and collapsed at once, hundreds of pearls cascading down a flight of stairs—clickity-clack, clickity-clack. Was I really me? Where did the knowledge of who I was, how I was supposed to behave, how I was fated to live, come from? Had I only dreamed all of my misery? Maybe it was all a mistake. Perhaps I'd been living the habits of someone else after all. Could I be happy?

I found him shaking within the confines of a closet. "I . . . ," he began, apologizing, stuttering with fear. I grabbed his wrist, dragged him out, letting his muscles sort out the problems of abrupt motion as we moved. No time for pleasantries. When we reached the door two mercenaries stood in the corridor. One raised his sword, the other stepped back. Faster than the first thought I could move, I thrust my blade into his chest. I jerked it hard, pulling it out, and shook it at the second swordsman. "Have you no shame!" I said sharply. "Harassing an old man and a little boy!" Cowed, he stepped further back, and I raced up the stairs with Neden in tow. Only a moment later I heard a surprised shout from the young mercenary. "Hey," he called, "wait a minute."

But we were up the stairs, rushing along, birds with wings spread wide, the wind lifting us up, the thrill of motion, the chase, the threat of death exciting us both. I responded with manic inspiration, having lived long enough for my perceptions of myself to fray; I felt my life a story, and death would simply be a convenient but abrupt close. Maybe I would even merit a few tears shed by those who heard my tale. The boy, though, still held the belief that his life mattered. He gripped my hand tightly, using my presence to stave off fear. His faith in me, need of me, pleased me to no end. I knew I could never truly be a father, but these odd, desperate flirtations with the role gave me strange comfort. Perhaps, his warm hand suggested, I could succeed where my father had failed, after all.

The footsteps behind us came louder. I whirled, slashed my blade at the young man I'd dressed down earlier. He ducked out of the way, thrust his sword point toward me. I parried, my ears filling with the sound of metal sliding against metal, raspy as a dry throat. My grip on my pommel strained as his youthful strength drove me back. My arrogance now earned its reward as I lost my footing and began to trip on the stairs behind me.

Neden saved the day then, roaring out a dwarf oath and lurching forward. With his small but stocky arms he grabbed the wrists of the swordsman, lifting the man's arms up and knocking him off balance. Our blades parted and the swordsman teetered for a moment, his left arm making a wide, frantic circle as he struggled to stay upright. I lifted my left leg and gently touched him with my toes—just enough to send him rolling down the stairs with a surprised cry. From below, more cries of surprise as he bowled into the mercenaries running up the stairs.

But there was no time to savor the moment. At least not outwardly. I wanted Neden to think me of grim purpose, so I hid my joviality. Is that not what boys want from their fathers?—a solid man, one with serious thoughts in his mind, who knows the proportions of danger when in the thick of it, but can laugh about it later? Inside, though, where I created my narrative of myself, I laughed. The invasion of my home filled me with glee. I'd remained still, you see, for so long. After finally cutting myself off from all people, there had been no more reason to run off. So I had sat around. But—and I want to make this clear—I didn't run off only because I couldn't make a commitment. There's always been a strong bit of the Passion of Floranuus in me. Motion, even more than your mother, has been my companion, and I love it for its own sake.

You know it, too? Don't you? As a troubadour, the love of the tale, the gestures of the hand to toss off the word, the tilting of the head to portray one character or another. Subtle motion, to be sure, but motion nonetheless. The motion of a small gesture that conjures up great passions, deep sorrows, and glorious victories.

Out of the house we ran, and up the stairs toward the platform. Neden gasped as he looked down at the gulf between us and the ground. I felt his hand tug away as he swooned, and I pulled him along. "Don't look down if you can't," I shouted.

"I can!" he declared, suddenly, stubbornly a boy. He began leaning over the edge to prove it, and I shouted, "I believe you. Come on!"

We rushed up to the platform. The vibrations of a half-a-dozen mercenaries behind us shook their way up the stairs. Standing now on my observation platform as the stars began to twinkle to life, surrounded by the broad-leafed canopy of the jungle, a young boy in danger beside me, villains with swords clamoring up the stairs like noisy vipers, I felt one thought nudging every other out of my head, and it was this:

How strange life is, and in particular, my own peculiar permutation of its possibilities.

"WHAT ARE WE GOING TO DO?" Neden cried out, clinging to my hand so tightly I'm surprised it didn't drop off from lack of blood. It was a fair question, worthy of a well-constructed solution. Unfortunately, I had nothing to offer.

Yet, luckily, I was under no obligation to immediately admit this to the lad. The ruffians at our back charged and screamed up after us, and I used their impending arrival to distract him from the trap I'd led us to. I grabbed the table where I'd spent years mapping out the stars, and rolled it toward the steps. Again, screams of surprise from the mercenaries, this time mixed with horror. The table knocked some of the swordsmen off the stairs, sending them plummeting dozens and dozens of yards to the jungle floor. Most survived the table's assault, however, and were re-grouping and preparing to charge up once more.

Nonetheless, Neden shouted "Hoorah!" (or something in that vein) and I felt a momentary surge of joy in my heart. After living the second half of my life as the bogeyman of Barsaive, the fact that I could still please a child meant a great deal to me.

The excitement turned to terror within a heartbeat. A shadow passed over us, and I turned slightly to see a Theran airship floating toward us, its stone hull skimming over the leafy roof of the jungle.

11

Directly opposite us from the ship floated the scarlet setting sun, and it created a brilliant aura of blood around the magical vessel. Therans—humans, elves, and trolls—all dressed in red and black armor, hung from either side of the ship on rope ladders. All held swords in their hands and wore smiles of anticipation on their faces. At the ship's bow stood Mordom, his eyes with lids sewn shut, dark pockets against the shadows of the day's end. His hand with Garlthik's eye stared down at me. Here we were, confronting each other once more after so many years. This time, however, I was an adult, in full command of my capacities and myself. It seemed we were beginning a battle that would bring us both to the edge of our abilities—and then drive us beyond them.

"So," I called to him (more than a little melodramatically, I'm afraid), "we meet again."

The ship floated closer. Mordom's face crinkled in confusion. "Do I know you?" he shouted down at me.

I nearly laughed, thinking the magician was trying to trick me. "I am J'role, the boy who stole the Ring of Longing from you more than half a lifetime ago."

"No," he shouted back. "I can't say I remember you."

"The city of Parlainth," I declared, hands on hips, still standing as if posing for a statue, but increasingly alarmed at my resolve for an epic confrontation. It appeared that my significance in the Universe was even smaller than I had originally imagined.

For a moment Mordom's face seemed about to relax in recognition. Then it wrinkled in deep concentration again. And then finally he said, "AH! The boy with Garlthik One-Eye!"

"You know Garlthik One-Eye?" asked Neden with awed curiosity.

"Yes," I said softly, attempting to diminish his interest in my mentor. It seemed ridiculous that the boy should have heard about the ork and be impressed with him. I had half a mind to tell Neden that I was in fact *that* J'role from the rhyme of his childhood, the one responsible for mutilating children. *That* would put things back in perspective. But I put my focus on Mordom. It was with him that I truly wanted to settle matters. I had killed him, and his dismissal of me made my accomplishment more than moot; it was as if I'd never been born. I shouted, "The one who landed you in a pit full of spikes. I should think you'd remember that!"

Neden tugged on my hand. "They're really close, J'role."

"I only remember things of significance. You killed me. But I live now!" He laughed, put his eyeless hand on the railing and leaned forward. "What use is it to dwell on it? I had a whole new life to lead. Did you expect that I'd been brooding over it since my resurrection?"

I almost shouted, "Yes! Of course I expected you to brood about it!" His point of view was far too removed and mature to suit my tastes. Little-boy energy crawled through my flesh, demanding attention, daring a reprimand. Me, an old man, body thin and skin wrinkled. And yet, as you know, I've retained a bit of myself from youth through all these years. "I just wanted you to know who it was standing in the way of your plans again." I laughed a hollow laugh that I carried off with great aplomb.

The ship was only yards away now. The air had chilled on my flesh, the evening's remaining heat buried under the shadow of the vessel. Neden tugged my arm several more times, speaking my name with soft urgency. The surviving mercenaries had reached the platform, carefully ascending this time, their swords thrust forward like the beaks of cautious, hungry birds. The Theran soldiers clung to the airship's rope ladders, like drops of blood on the thorns of a corrupted elf, waiting for the impending moment when they could slide off and let loose a wash of red on the platform.

I crouched. "On my back, boy." Neden hesitated only a moment, then did as I said, wrapping his thick arms around my neck. He was heavy, I tell you. But the touch of his flesh against mine sent a shock of magic through me—the magic of memories and emotion. Once more I focused, aware of a boy in danger. I would have to do better than was done for me so many years earlier when I was in his position. I didn't want him simply to survive. I needed to pull him out of the adventure as quickly as possible. I needed him to go on with his life *untainted.*

The airship swept over the platform. A Theran troll dropped down, landing only two yards away. Then another Theran soldier and then a third—a human and an elf, respectively. As with all the Therans, each seemed a perfect example of his race—stones smoothed by centuries of wind and water so that all that remained was the perfect core. Beautiful. Essential.

Out the corner of my eye I took stock of the mercenaries. In awe of the airship and the Theran soldiers, they seemed content to block my exit down the stairs and watch as the Therans slaughtered me.

The Therans, each armed with long swords gleaming with the last rays of scarlet sunlight, lunged forward. Neden screamed, his arms tightening reflexively, his grip choking me. But we had a chance. I moved forward, as if about to try to break past them somehow. They adjusted themselves accordingly, spacing themselves so I could not charge past them.

As all of this happened, the airship continued to fly on over Neden and I. A rope ladder swung toward me, and instead of rushing forward, I jumped up, catching a rung with the tips of my fingers. Neden screamed again. My fingers slipped off the rope and we dropped quickly—a burp of suspense—until I caught another rung, this time with a better grip. "Neden," I gasped as loudly as I could manage, "you're choking me."

He loosened his grip for just a moment, then tightened it again, this time with a shriek, as the ladder swung wildly. "J'role!" he shouted. "Look."

I looked up and saw a human woman armed with a short sword making her way down the ladder to us.

"All I want is the boy," Mordom shouted down at me from the airship's railing. His voice scratched like the scuttle of centipedes on stone walls. "There's no need for this to continue. If we've had a grudge in the past, it is of no concern to me now. Just give me the boy."

We'd traveled beyond the platform by this time, and only yards beneath my feet the broad leaves of the jungle rooftop rushed by like the deep-green waves of an ocean. Back on the platform the mercenaries and Theran soldiers stood staring at us, somewhat dimwitted it seemed to me, like childhood bullies surprised to learn that their soft-spoken victim would rather run than get the snot kicked out of him.

"What are we going to do?" Neden whispered softly. He'd gained control of his nerves, and though still frightened, there was a touch of slyness in his voice. He was ready to follow whatever plan I produced.

Again, however, no plan existed within my skull. It was at that moment I realized the boy was more than just a burden on my back. He was a burden in my thoughts as well, limiting the strategies available. Chances I might take that might lead to my death were not available to me.

As these thoughts filled my head, a terrible urge overwhelmed me. I wanted to shrug Neden off, be free of him, live my life as foolishly as I pleased without concern for others. The thief magic coursed through my muscles, begging this choice of action.

My muscles tensed.

He would die from the fall, I knew that. His stocky body would crack through branches and leaves until it smashed into the ground far below. But *I* would be better off. I could move more freely. I could take actions without concern for anyone but myself. I might well be able to leap to a branch below, cling tenaciously, and then make my way down the tree. Without the boy, it was possible.

Rationalizations piled up thick in my skull. I had not asked him to enter my life. And if he died, it would be as if I had never involved myself with him.

In fact, he would be better off dead. It was clear the magician wanted the heir to Throal alive. Memories of Mordom torturing Garlthik with the strange, black Horror came to the fore of my thoughts. And the torture he'd inflicted on my father's mind, finishing the work begun by my father's alcohol, turning him into a babbling, broken rag doll of a man. Could I risk Neden falling into Mordom's hands?

Of course not.

"Sorry, boy," I said, though I was not. I reached one hand up and undid his clasped arms from around my neck.

12

"J'role?" he said, his voice just a sigh, the silent death of a beautiful flower drowned by too much rain.

I turned my body, twisted him off my back. He cried out, and fumbled for a grip on my shoulders. Anger filled me now. How dare he resist me, after all I'd done for him! I struggled to shove him off me. He slipped further down my back, grabbing my waist at the last moment. The sudden tug on my body almost sent the two of us sprawling through the air. Above me, Mordom shouted for me to come to my senses.

Confusion of past and present caught me up again. A lost memory of emotion entered my thoughts—water rushing around me, choking the corridors of the *Breeton*. My father on my back. Enfeebled and incompetent, he'd clung to me, dragging the two of us back into the water flooding the deep corridors of the riverboat. He was so weak. I'd hated him for that! Now I had the boy dragging me into the confrontation with Mordom. But then, after I had—after I had—after I had killed him—

Killed my father.

Killed my father.

Had to free myself, you see. Had to get him off my

back. To get clear of the sinking ship. On with my life. To move on. You carried a sword here, you see. You know. You know.

But after the death. So much—

A torrent of regret, both for my father's murder and for my actions with Neden, washed over me. I gasped at the terror of it. The thief magic began to drown, gurgling for me to listen to reason. To live alone. Apart.

The Theran soldier, having made her way down the rope ladder, was upon us. At the moment I felt my muscles tighten. A spell from Mordom, I realized immediately. The grip of my hands; frozen on the rope rungs, did not allow any action on my part.

"Here," said the woman. "Come here, boy." I was forgotten. She stretched her arm past my head, down along my back, extending it so Neden could take it.

"J'role," the boy said, still desperate for an ally in a world of enemies.

I could not answer him. I could not move my jaw.

"Ignore him, boy," the soldier said. "We've got to get you back home. The men who were after you—those mercenaries—they wanted to hurt you. We're here to help you—"

"No. You—"

"Listen. We're here to help you."

Neden swung himself around on the rope ladder. The moment his weight lifted, loneliness consumed me. I wanted him again on my back. Somewhere a balance existed between love and suffocation. Where was it?

Now that I no longer supported the boy, the soldier was free to do with me what she wished. Though my muscles had frozen, my eyes could move, and I glanced up to see her smiling a wicked smile. She raised her sword. Moments like this had occurred throughout my life, but this time it seemed I was surely dead. I hadn't counted on the boy. His morale was made of stronger stuff than I'd imagined, and neither Mordom's overwhelming forces, nor my inconsistent loyalty was enough to break him. He reached up and grabbed the soldier's right foot with both hands, then fell back, dragging her leg through the gap in the rope ladder, dangling from her leg, his face a fury of concentration and fear. She lost her balance and toppled down on top of me, her sword dropping from her hands and tumbling down.

She clutched at me as she twisted around. Luckily my hands were frozen around the ladder, or the sudden jolt would have loosened my grip and sent us after the sword. Neden's face was now even with mine, and he stared at me with panicked eyes, silently asking, "What should I do now?"

With nothing but the exhalation of breath at my command, I wheezed, "Let go!"—though it sounded more like "Hett ko!" through my paralyzed lips. But he caught my meaning and released the soldier's foot and took hold of the ladder rungs once more.

Suddenly relieved of her ballast, the soldier's balance gave out. Her grip on me loosened and she fell from my back, clawing for a moment at my shoulders. Her scream was silenced by the crash of her body through the upper branches of the jungle canopy. At almost the same instant Mordom's spell dissipated and I was free. Without waiting another moment I began scrambling up the ladder.

The memories of my father's death—murder—left me with no choice but to try to help Neden. The question before me was this: By the time I died, what kind of life did I want to have led? Things had already gone wrong so often in the past, but that didn't mean I couldn't try to recover a sliver of my spirit. Redemption is one of my favorite themes in stories, though not particularly fashionable these days—we live in a time when no one wants to feel bad or be responsible for his actions—but I'm somewhat old-fashioned.

Actually, I think I'm lying. It's hard, you know, looking back, trying to remember how one framed one's life in the past. The perspective one has, the story we make up for ourselves to give meager order to our existence, changes with time, as new details accumulate and we need to reshape our narrative to accommodate them. Only upon our death can our true tale be told. By picking and choosing we form the arc of our narrative. It's all arbitrary in the end, I suppose. But I think that believing one's life to be a story helps one get through the day. At least around four in the afternoon, when things seem a bit sluggish.

So the thought of redemption had not been in my head through most of my life, nor even as I scrambled up the rope ladder in the Theran airship. In no way did I think myself redeemable. As I scrambled up the ladder I thought of myself only as a miserable man, seeded with misery in his early years, and doomed to bear the fruit of misery.

But I could not wake up the next day with another murder on my hands. I tried to save Neden simply because I was tired of feeling bad.

I suppose turns of the soul have to begin somewhere.

Up the ladder. "Wait there!" I cried to Neden.

Mordom waved his hands in order to cast a spell, and I felt my muscles tighten for a moment. But the spell did not take hold, and I continued. Another soldier came down toward me, waving his sword. I dodged the cuts, back and forth, then made a feint that sent me lunging off to the right. With one hand firmly gripping the rope of the ladder, the other reached out and grabbed the crossguard of the soldier's sword. I tugged the sword forward, pulling the soldier off the ladder. A moment of surprise on his face (he was the hero of his story, and not supposed to die so awkwardly) as he fell forward, shifting wildly and uselessly to keep his balance, and then plunged off the ladder. His grip on the sword loosened as his life loosened from the world, and I plucked it from his hand.

Without a moment's hesitation, I cut at the left, vertical rope of the ladder, slicing it through. The ladder collapsed, so that for the last thirty feet of it—from my cut to the bottom—the two vertical ropes hung together and the rope rungs hung doubled up between them.

"J'role!" Neden cried out, clinging desperately to the ropes, twirling slightly now. I shouted back for him to just hang on.

As I was distant from Neden now, soldiers armed with crossbows appeared at the airship's rail and began firing. The bolts rushed by me, one or two clipping my arm or thigh. Meanwhile, I began working my way down the ladder, slicing each rung as I passed it. Soon the left side of the ladder was drooping past me, reaching down to Neden.

A bolt caught me full in the thigh, and I cried out in agony. Blood rushed up from the wound, soaking through the cloth of my trousers, spreading out with frightening speed. For fear of causing further damage, I let the bolt remain, hoping to take it out when I was safe. I continued down the ladder, cutting the rungs, until I reached Neden. I dropped the sword. "On my back," I gasped. "Your leg!" he cried out. "ON!" I shouted.

He crawled up, his weight worse now for the crossbow bolt, which made all my flesh feel as if it had been scraped off with dry bones, leaving my nerves directly exposed to every touch. But there was little time to contemplate pain. Mordom finally grasped my plan and shouted, "Raise the ship! Raise the ship!"

But too late. The ladder, now split in half, reached down an extra thirty feet, dangling as a single rope rather than as a ladder. I gripped the rope with my hands, and began moving quickly down it. After twenty feet we reached the treetops. The airship, though, was already beginning to rise. I moved down faster, and we plunged beneath the tops of the trees, dragged through their leaves by the forward movement of the airship. Only a few feet of rope remained.

I turned to face the onrushing leaves and branches that slapped against us, looking for a branch sturdy enough to support us. That's when I felt my muscles freeze up once more. We were rising. "Jump!" I wheezed through my paralyzed lips. I said it over and over again.

"But . . . !"

"JUMP!"

I saw his small hand reach out for the branches in front of us. Twice he tried to grab a large, sturdy branch, and twice he failed. On the third try I saw his hand make contact, and suddenly his weight was off my back.

The airship continued to rise. Above, sailors dragged the rope ladder up, hand over hand, until I was brought over the airship's rail and onto the deck.

13

You'll recall that Mordom, since I'd last seen him, had not only risen from the dead, but had sewn his eyelids shut with thick purple thread. These terrible stitches held my attention as the magician grabbed my throat with his eyeless hand and slammed my head against the rail of the airship. "I do remember you now," he said with great spite. "You're the Meddler-Boy. Had a Horror in your head, if I'm not mistaken." His one eye, green and set into the palm of his left hand, stared down at me, blinking with rage. "The Horror's gone now, it seems. But I think I can take care of that. You must miss having something slithering around in you."

I did not. His words brought me close to tears. Paralyzed and in the hands of my old nemesis, who was threatening to manipulate my mind with his strange affinity with Horrors, it seemed that no time had passed since last we met. I thought of my near-murder of Neden only minutes before. Perhaps no time had passed.

A soldier beside Mordom, a troll with milk-white canines that protruded from behind his lips, said, "Sir, should we . . ."

Without turning the magician snapped, "Yes! Bring the ship down. Find him!"

It was my hope that Neden would soon reach the bottom of the tree and make his way into hiding, as he had already managed to do when first we met. Then I realized I did not know if he actually had gotten hold of the branch. And even if he had, whether he could climb down. A thief adept could manage it with ease. But a young dwarf? Was he now trapped in the tree? Had he already fallen?

Had my wish for his death come true after all?

"Take him downstairs," Mordom intoned, a trickle of glee slipping into his raspy voice.

The ship spent some time hovering over the spot where Neden had vanished, but he could not be found. We then sailed to a clearing where the ship could land without the risk of its riggings getting tangled in the thick branches. From there, a search party was sent out for the boy. Also, another magician created a pair of wings for one of the soldiers so he could fly back to my house and lead the mercenaries and soldiers back to the ship to join in the hunt.

I learned none of this directly, but from shouts that spilled over the upper deck or from orders that echoed down the corridors. It was my fate to be tied to a table in a dark room buried in the heart of the ship. Mordom huddled over me, a hungry man set before a feast, unable to decide what to eat first. His hand with the green eye, held two feet from me, examined me carefully. On his face, a smile. It was the first time I'd ever seen him smile—really smile, the way other people do when happy. The only illumination came from a few glowing crystals set into the wall, which produced something like light, but something different from it as well. It seemed to skim over the surface of objects in the room, rather than fill the room, so that we all—Mordom, myself, two soldiers—seemed to radiate a kind of bluish glow. Mordom noticed my examination of the light and said, in a tone more generous than I would have thought him capable, "For my pets. It's closer to the environment they came from."

My mind actually puzzled over that for a moment, despite all my previous encounters with the man. Then I thought simply: the Horrors. They came from another plane of existence to our world hundreds of years ago. They had to have come from someplace, and undoubtedly it wasn't like our own world.

"We can do this the easy way or the hard way," he said. "What do you know of the conspiracy?"

Knowing nothing of the conspiracy—*the* conspiracy or *any* conspiracy—I paused, open my mouth, unsure of how to answer.

"The hard way, then," he said, and turned from me, humming. I looked to the guards for some indication of what was about to happen. Both had already fixed their gazes on the ceiling.

"I don't know anything about any conspiracy. Listen, we're both old men now. Why don't you just let me go? The boy's gone. He stumbled into my life, and now he's stumbled out. We'll just go our separate ways."

He was out of sight now, standing several feet from the head of the table. He continued to hum, and I heard the sound of glass clinking, as if he were moving jars around. He said, "Ah," and began walking back.

Stalling, I said, "How is it you live? You did die in Parlainth, did you not?"

"Oh, yes," he said casually, more intrigued with what he held in the jar. I could not make out what his hand stared at. It seemed to be a shadow moving within the confines of the jar.

"Who raised you?" I asked. I wanted to say, "Who in their right mind would allow you to draw breath again?" But I was a prisoner of a magician with an affinity for Horrors, and the better tactic seemed to be to remove the verbal bile if possible.

He set the jar on a small table beside the one to which I was strapped, and rummaged about in a small box of metal tools. "A group of Therans who investigated the city. They found me about twenty-five years ago."

"Therans have been to Parlainth?" I said with complete surprise.

"It was our city, Meddler-Boy. I don't suppose you have any objections to our returning home?"

I did, for the city was claimed by the people of Barsaive now, an urban wilderness rich in magical treasures and ancient secrets. But I said, "No. I just didn't know."

"We're not much welcome in Barsaive." He plucked a dangerous-looking item from the box, a stick about six inches long and with a glittering hook on one end. "We often have to travel secretly. Of course, I'm certain you know of many of the places we've wanted to visit. And now I'm going to find out which of those you do." He stretched both his eye-hand and eyeless hand down toward my head, near my right ear.

"I really don't know anything, Mordom. I really

don't. I've been hunted myself for the last thirty years by King Varulus. I haven't been much involved in politics."

He stood up, pulling his hands away from me, and I breathed with relief. "J'role?" he asked, intensely curious. "*The* J'role. From the children's game? I've heard of the insane clown, of course. Everyone has. But that clown is you? How does it go . . .?" Then he recited the infamous children's rhyme I'd inspired:

"Who are you?"
"J'role, mad old clown;
I've always been so
Since my first sound.
Father and Mother.
Crazy before me,
Juggle a razor!
Slice! Now you can't see!"

He said, "Quite delightful, I think. Are you really the source of that?" He waited for a reply, truly intrigued, and to stall, I nodded. He smiled that genuine smile of his again. "I wouldn't have thought the rhyme to be based on a real person. More a gathering of vague fears, formed and shaped by a need to pluck fear from the soul and shove it out of oneself, into an imaginary being. Certainly I never could have imagined the Meddler-Boy would have grown up to be Barsaive's personal Horror of childhood." His eye stared at me a while, and he remained silent.

Now I was curious. "Why couldn't you imagine it?" *I* had always imagined myself miserable, and since the murder of my father, more than a little dangerous. It seemed almost fated that I grow up to be an inspirer of fear for children. I thought of all the years I'd traveled as a clown. How much of it had been to try so desperately to win the love of children, a love I thought I could never have?

He laughed. "You're a bit of a do-gooder, you know. I would have expected the mutilator of children to be more obviously a monster." The eye-hand hovered close to my face now, hungry for any flicker of uncomfortableness across my flesh. "So tell me. How many children have you killed?"

In my thoughts: the murder of my father, the mutilation of the faces of my sons. On my face: nothing. A mask. I said, "None."

The hand remained close, prying for any flicker of discomfort. "None?" he asked coyly.

"None," I said firmly. The bond on my ankles and wrists strained me for the first time and I wanted to rush from the room. I realized that I'd always wanted someone to worm the truth of my horrible deeds out of me, but I wanted it to be someone worthy of moral prostration. Mordom certainly didn't meet the requirements; he would lap up my actions like a happy dog at its gruel. For some reason the thought of him torturing me hadn't been horrible—almost expected, really. But I suddenly realized he would use his monsters to draw from me secrets I'd kept tight to my thoughts for decades. That I did not want to happen.

The thought of having to repeat it all pained me. Wearied me. I would rather have died than be held at the command of Mordom, tortured by some foul creature, spitting out all the crimes of my life. But it was not an immediate concern. Shouts came down the corridor.

Neden had been found.

14

He was not well, as Mordom took pains to explain to me on several occasions, as if it were my fault. All I learned of Neden was that he had fallen from the tree when he tried to climb down from it. For the next several days, as the airship sailed south toward the Badlands, no one paid me any attention. The wound from the crossbow bolt remained untended, and a hot pain grew in my flesh as it festered. No one fed me, and hunger, fitful with misdirected revenge, ate at me as I lay strapped to the table. I slipped more and more into delirium, unable on occasion to remember where I was or why I was there. I tried, in the few lucid moments, to undo the straps that bound my wrists and ankles. But each was enchanted, and they changed as I tried to study their nature, so that any progress I made was lost before I could apply it. My thief abilities were useless, and I realized that for the first time in my life I might truly be trapped.

On occasion images of your mother, or you or Torran, came to me, and I apologized profusely. I spoke to phantoms of my imagination, knowing full well my words were not directed to any of you. I do not think I would truly have been capable of apologizing to you at all.

It was with surprise that I regained consciousness one day to discover that Mordom had slipped a Horror into my skull. I do not know to what end he did this—experiment, torture for information, maliciousness (I think all three)—but the effect was clear enough.

It was not in the same way the Horror had lived in my thoughts years earlier, with its body in one place and its mind invading mine. No, Mordom had cracked my skull open and slipped something terrible inside. Blood trickled down my neck from the wound, and a disturbing tickling cut along my flesh at the point of the entry. Although aware of all this, and of being in a dark room with shadowy figures standing around me, I also slipped into the past. Memories as clear as reality smashed into my senses. I could feel the bed of my youth at my back. Smell the trapped air of the kaer where I had grown up. Saw my mother, alive and young, standing next to me. The touch of her fingertips performing the ritual to place the Horror in my thoughts. I'd remembered the moments so many times over my lifetime, but never with such clarity and reality.

Yet something new was added to the experience. Saying exactly what it was is difficult. My thoughts—they doubled up upon themselves. Mordom, I think, drew my *thinking* to the forefront of my brain, so he could pick through it, using the small creature he'd placed in my head to stir up my thoughts. It wasn't just memories he was after—the tactile sensations of years past—he wanted the thoughts, *the logic,* of despair.

For the first time in my life I understood the thinking that had taken place when I was just a boy. My mother's touch, her betrayal, flowed from her fingertips across my skin, transforming me, as if my soft flesh became the chitinous shell that bugs wear on their backs. Because, you see, I knew she was doing something terrible to me, but I couldn't imagine that she, my mother, would do something bad without a very good reason. All kinds of thoughts slipped through my head to help account for the inexplicable actions taking place. Key among these was the fact that I must have done something horribly wrong, that I deserved to have a monster placed in me. That, in fact, I was monstrous myself. Capable of committing terrible evil. I was horrible; a Horror.

As I lay strapped down under Mordom's examination, I felt a part of myself floating away from my body, examining myself from a distance, fascinated. My mother's touch, I saw clearly, was like the first star in the sky at twilight. One single point of burning light. But with time, as my life passed, the sky filled with stars. They dotted the sky, forming constellations of pain. Looking to the sky, I could remember how the Universe worked. A set of rules found by studying the stars; the rule of pain. Everything, it seemed, flowed from that moment. A moment that no little boy should have lived through. A moment that was, far from being a rational point from which to begin a life, an aberration. An aberration! How much work I had applied to the task of trying to give sense to my mother's actions. A lifetime spent defending a monstrous construction of constellations. More than the constellation—a fortress of stars—burning hot and brilliant. Endless corridors of white light and massive ramparts and high towers. A chill coursed through my flesh. I imagined myself walking through the corridors of such a castle, trapped there all of my life, a prisoner within my own thoughts.

J'role, the legendary clown-thief, trapped in the only prison that could contain him—

His own mind.

"Fascinating," Mordom sighed, and it was little comfort that in that moment he sounded just like the Horror that had inhabited my thoughts in my youth, lapping up my misery with relish.

The images of the star castle, the memories of my mother, left me. I snapped back into the moment. Without warning a pain such as I had never felt crashed into my head, just behind my right ear. I screamed, my throat becoming instantly hoarse. I could not stop screaming. I thrashed madly against the bonds that held me tight. The wound in my skull demanded to be tended, staunched, scratched. I became frantic with the desire to be free. From the bonds, of course. But also, at the age of sixty, I saw my entire life as imprisonment. As I rocked wildly back and forth on the table, I rocked to be free of all my bonds. "Ignore him," Mordom shouted to the guards as they stepped toward me. The magician laughed, stared down at me, pleased.

A baby appeared on my chest. An infant. Eight months old, no more. I stopped screaming just long enough to acknowledge this new element in the bizarre tableau. A sharp intake of air on my part. It stared down at me, serious. The pain caught me up again, and I began screaming once more, but glanced at Mordom to see if he was aware of the baby sitting placidly on top of me. The magician acknowledged nothing. I could not be certain, however, if this might be merely a ruse. Had he somehow created the image of a baby to confuse me, and now was going to mock my sanity by pretending it was not there? It seemed a tactic too subtle for him, yet there might still be wells of malicious strategy waiting to be tapped.

I noticed that the child did not rock back and forth as it sat on my chest, though I thrashed back and forth in my pain. The baby seemed above my agony. He reached out his small hand and touched my face. He smiled. With the light lilt of a child, but the vocabulary of an adult, he asked, "J'role? Do you wish to be free?"

"Yes," I gasped. "Yes. But the straps . . ."

The baby frowned in confusion, then laughed with understanding. "J'role, J'role. The bonds that hold you are not these straps. The freedom you seek is not from this magician . . ."

"YES, IT IS!" I screamed at the infant.

Out the corner of my eye I saw the guards looking at Mordom for some explanation of my words. Mordom had no answer, though he smiled with curiosity, his eye-hand staring. "I think he needs a rest for now," he said. With silver prongs he withdrew something shiny and white from my skull; placed it in a thick jar. Then he returned to me and applied a magical salve to my cracked cranium. These actions were at the edges of my perception, for the baby held my attention.

"Do you truly wish to be free?" the infant asked.

."Yes," I sighed. Death—any kind of release—would satisfy me now. "Please. Help me."

"Promise me something."

"Yes, yes, yes."

"You will throw yourself over the side of the ship."

This gave me pause only for a moment. I couldn't imagine why I would want to fall to my death from an airship. But, for such a possibility to exist, I would have to first be free of Mordom. I decided to humor the infant. "Yes. All right." He smiled at me, as if he understood the nature of my deceit.

Mordom walked toward the door, saying, "Keep an eye on him." He left, and the guards relaxed a bit.

The baby said, "You are on your way to freedom."

The straps, with no effort on the part of anyone in the room, undid themselves, sliding through the buckles and flying wide. The soldiers gasped. I sat up.

I was free.

15

The soldiers lunged forward to grab me. My head ached; my wounded thigh burned with furious pain as I moved. Yet I was inspired now, and even if I could do little but fall off the table, I did it with the grace that had been mine all my life. I slipped past the grasping hands of the soldiers and up onto my feet. Balance came with difficulty, and for a moment my vision turned dark as though I must certainly pass out. Even as this happened, I wasted no time. I whirled around, raising my hand and balling it into a fist, and smacked one of the soldiers across the face. He cried out and tumbled to the floor. The attack raised my spirits. The other guard drew his sword and swung. I ducked under the blade, caught his arm, and swung the weapon into the other soldier who was just getting up. The edge caught him in the face, splitting flesh and bone. He dropped to the floor, dead.

The guard whose arm I held gave out a cry of alarm. I twisted his arm back. A crack. He cried out now in pain. I drove him forward, slammed him onto the slab I'd just rested on, smashed his head repeatedly into the slab. I did it for much longer than was necessary.

But they had just stood by while Mordom had done those things to me.

Out the door. I had to find Neden. With drunken steps I made my way through the corridors. Yet I had only just enough energy to keep myself moving. What could I possibly do to help him if he was in trouble? But I knew I could not surrender him. From down the corridor, shouts of alarm. I had only moments.

As I passed a door, I heard voices. Mordom's was among them. "There are fewer ships over Death's Sea," he said. "It's worth the extra time."

"But," said someone else, most likely the airship's captain, "we can catch an airstream that will take us directly to the Badlands."

"The process is going to take a long, long while. Mountainshadow has assured me of that. I'm in no rush. And if we go over the sea, we help guarantee that we won't be disturbed. All that matters is that we finish the process. If it works I'll be able to control the boy with my will. With Varulus dead, the conflict with Throal will end with a peaceful surrender."

"Very well," the captain sighed. "But I've got to get the vessel back to Thera as soon as possible."

"I understand. You and your crew will be freed from your father's debt as soon as you deposit us at my cave."

Another voice said, "We've made contacts with people who know where King Varulus is hiding."

"Good," said Mordom. "Any trouble hiring the assassins?"

"None."

"Just make sure Garlthik One-Eye doesn't get any news of this. His contacts are scattered far and wide."

"I've worked with Garlthik in the past. He's always . . ."

"I said don't use him! He and I go a long way back. No love lost."

"He doesn't even leave Kratas anymore. From what I've heard, he's an old, broken ork."

"From what I've heard his information network is big enough he doesn't *have* to leave. Just keep all of this tight."

The baby appeared, floating in the air beside me. I moved on. "You promised," it said. "You have to jump off the ship. Soon. Very soon."

"I know. I know," I muttered. "But he . . . he's just a boy." We came up to a door and I paused, listening. I heard the shouts of sailors as they played a game. Neden was most likely not in there.

"Like your sons were just boys . . ." The infant's voice trailed off, suggesting all the events of thirty years earlier.

I looked down at him, scowling. Who was this annoying baby?

"If you won't leave him be on my advice, what if I show him to you?"

"You know where he is?"

He rolled his eyes, uncomfortable. "Yes."

Down a corridor, up the stairs. The baby gave me instructions as I cradled him in my arms. Third down on the right.

It was unlocked. Dim. Only the wash of orange moss-light from the corridor let me see the sight within.

The boy, eyes closed, still breathing, was dissected and tacked to the wall.

"Spirits," I whispered.

"Yes," said the baby, and he hid his face in the crook of my arm and trembled.

Neden's flesh, flayed and set out in flat strips, could not possibly be alive. Yet the chest, located a few feet from his beating heart, still rose and fell as if a part of a living person. "How is it possible . . .?"

His muffled voice said, "Mordom is exceptionally talented."

"I have to help him . . ." I took a step inside.

"J'role, you can't help him. Only someone he could depend on can help him. You're not that person. Not now."

"What I've done for him . . ."

"You're there when it's convenient. What you must do to help him, if you're the one to do it, will require a commitment of the sort you're not able to make."

"But . . ."

"Jump, J'role. It's over. It's time for you to give it all up. You think you know how to live. You don't. Jump."

The sight before me caused me to stagger back to the wall behind me and lean against it. "I can't leave him . . ."

"You can try to help him, J'role. But who you are now—your efforts will only kill him. You didn't quite kill your boys. But that doesn't mean you won't succeed this time."

That made me angry. "It wasn't my goal to kill them," I snapped.

He smiled up at me, knowing and coy. "So you tell

yourself. But you have certain beliefs about the lives of little boys. And death is a major part of those beliefs."

"I didn't want to kill them."

"That's another matter. I don't think you *want* to kill anybody. But as we both know, you sometimes do kill people."

I had an impulse to take him by the shoulders and smash his head against the wall till it broke and bled.

"Ahhhh," he said and shook his small finger at me.

From down the corridor echoed shouted commands. I took one more look at Neden, his face like a mask on the cabin wall, his innards stretched out like trophies from a hunt. "All right," I said, realizing I wouldn't know how to help him, no matter what my intentions. "Overboard."

With the baby still in my arms I rushed along the corridors, further up the stairs. A few times soldiers came upon me. I was too weak to fight, but I managed to elude their grasp and the swing of their swords. Even as I moved on I sensed something extraordinary was happening—each move I used to dodge my opponents was faster, more efficient than I was normally capable of, let alone when half-dead. The baby was obviously the source. Yet this fact remained at the back of my thoughts, for he was also a baby cradled in my arms, and I did not truly make the connection between him and my freedom.

As I pushed open a door to the main deck, a wash of hot air enveloped me, nearly knocking me down the stairs. The night air was thick with mist, a mist illuminated from below by red light. "I know where we are," I gasped.

"Over the side!" the baby cried. It sounded like a baby now, wailing and begging. "Over the side! Over the side!"

Several sailors spotted me and rushed forward. I had a choice. To return to the lower decks or throw myself over the ship's side. It really wasn't a choice.

I raced across the deck until I reached the ship's rail. There, set out before me like some nightmare landscape was Death's Sea—a sea of fire, miles and miles of glowing molten rock.

"I'll die."

The baby suddenly sobered. "Now you're beginning to get it."

"I don't want to do it."

The child became impatient. The guards rushed toward us. "I know you don't want to do it. If you did, I wouldn't ask you to. In any case, I don't see what choice you have."

Three guards were upon me, their hands outstretched. I twisted to avoid their grasp, turned, leaned over the rail.

"Choose to do it!" the baby screamed. "It must be a choice!"

I did not choose to do it only because the guards were suddenly upon me. Or even because I had no idea how to save Neden. Or even because if I did save him, I might prove to be dangerous.

No, at the core of the choice was a weariness with it all. A life born in pain, lived in pain, and desperate for the release of death. Yet, I would never have given in to the impulse for release had it not been for the small infant in my arms suggesting I throw myself over the side of the ship into a sea of lava hundreds of feet below. It was the *ridiculousness* of the situation that prompted me. For all my misery, I could still appreciate a good joke. The Universe had truly stunned me this time, and laughing, I leaned back so that I flipped over the rail. For a moment I felt a sense of liberation. The heat of the molten sea caressed me, and the odd sensation of falling, the weightlessness, brought me memories of being in my mother's arms, long before everything went wrong.

Then the baby vanished, and I became fully aware of what was happening.

My speed increased. I plunged wildly toward destruction.

PART TWO

Flames and Flesh

1

Tumble. Tumble. Tumble.

The fall, though brief, carried me with the deliciously interminable sensation of a nightmare; each moment stretched out endlessly, with the promise of another terrifying moment to follow. Red lava below and dark night sky above flashed before my eyes quickly, repeatedly, blurring, and before long I had no idea when I was looking up and when down. This disorientation mixed with thoughts of death. Confusion and terror gave way to acceptance. Of course I would die by plunging into molten lava in the middle of Death's Sea, with not a single soul to ever know of my fate. What else could I expect from my miserable life?

Crack.

My body slammed into hard rock.

Crack.

I bounced.

Crack.

Tumbled forward.

Already the agony of the impact scrambled through my flesh and bones. But I was not yet done. I tumbled and smashed forward, bouncing against one rock after another.

I was supposed to have struck molten rock. Not solid rock. *I should have been dead instantly!* I screamed out, not only from pain, but bitter frustration. I was tumbling down a low pile of rocks, then came skittering to an awkward stop.

Silence. Stillness. Breathing in air, calmly. For a moment the lack of motion soothed me. I lay on my back, spine ajangle, right arm raised strangely, hand twisted off to the right. This did not bother me. The fall had ended. The smashing into rocks had ended. Things were simply better.

I waited, resting. Didn't want to rush. Above me the stars were obscured by the sea's heat. A thin vapor flowed across the sky, catching the light of the molten lava. A massive sheet of thin, dyed cotton cutting me off from my fixed, icy points of light.

Off in the distance I spotted the airship. The sea lit its gray hull a dim red. In my pain it looked very much like a comet, slow and stately, burning across the sky. A portent sent from the Universe. Dictating something of significance in my life. But I was without my charts and maps, and its meaning was beyond my comprehension.

The ship turned about, sailing back toward the island. It then orbited the island, as if looking for me. Oddly, it drifted over the sea as much as over the island I had landed on. Equally strange was that apparently no one on the airship spotted me. This was a signal to the strangeness of the island, a strangeness I would not understand for many, many days. The airship circled several times and then sailed off into the red haze, growing smaller and smaller.

It was upon this sight that I fixed my gaze as I

waited for enough energy to move. As the ship drifted further and further away I wondered why they did not come back for me. They were low enough to know that I had not struck the sea, but had fallen, impossibly, upon an island. If they wanted me, they could come back and get me. But on they went, and though Neden was still on the vessel, I felt relief. It would be some time before I would be ready for another confrontation with Mordom.

The airship drifted into the deeper red haze and out of sight. I waited a few moments more, then tried to rise.

I could not move.

My right arm, held upright, frozen, beside me, refused to lower itself. My body did not roll at my command. Panic rose within me, and I realized I could not feel my body. With the panic came an awareness that I should have died. That I had not was miraculous. For some reason this thought had taken its time winding its way through my mind. Having survived so many dangerous situations so many times, I must have gotten into the habit of it. Become inured to the threat of death.

Of course I was paralyzed! I'd just fallen hundreds of feet from an airship onto a rocky island.

More thoughts came: Even if I could move, how would I ever get off the island? Why had I interfered in Neden's problems? Why had the child made me leap off the ship? Was this the freedom he had promised? And where *was* that damned baby!?

Turning my head as best I could, rolling my eyes as far as they would go, I searched the landscape around me. Nothing. Just black rock—sometimes towering up into small hills—pocked with countless holes. The only light came reflected from the red haze above. No sound. No wind. Nothing. I remained frozen, lifeless, in a desolate, lifeless land. The freedom I had earned by trusting the child had been the freedom of utter stillness.

Still, I puzzled over chances of escape, considered what I knew of the sea. Ancient stories related that long, long ago some of the Passions, in their love of life, tried to prevent anyone from ever dying. Though Death could not be killed, they banded together and created Death's Sea, transforming a massive body of water hundreds of miles across into a thick sea of molten rock. Within this fiery sea they imprisoned Death, sealing him as one might lock up a prisoner.

Their plan did not work as expected, for it's obvious that people still die. But they say that before Death's imprisonment people could not be raised from the dead, as they can today. He can claim the living, but sometimes, like Mordom, they escape. It is also said that when enough blood is spilled across the land of Barsaive, Death shall be freed and wreak havoc throughout the world.

It seemed strange that I should have survived such a tremendous fall, only to land on Death's prison. Yet it made sense in its own strange way. Death was perhaps trapped thousands of feet below me. What could he do about it? There were only so many lives he could claim from his fiery cell.

I'd spent some time as a mercenary on the sea, escorting Barsaivian airships as they mined the sea for elemental fire. Sifting through these memories, I began to realize how strange were my circumstances. Sailors who spent a great deal of time over Death's Sea had told me that "islands" did form on occasion, but they were only slightly more stable than the hard crust that floats over the molten sea. All in all, the crust constantly melts and cools, so that—even ignoring the terrible heat the crust radiates—only a fool would try to camp on such an island.

But what had I landed on? The crust never had the kind of hills on which I now rested.

Where was I?

It seemed that the rocks I lay on must certainly melt down and sink below the surface of the sea. But if these other conditions were not typical of Death's Sea, could I also be on a permanent island? Something that would retain its shape despite the heat around it?

It seemed possible, if not likely, that I had dropped onto a strange island in the middle of Death's Sea, with nothing to do but wait patiently for Death to come and take me in his own time. Perhaps this was why I had not died immediately. Death knew I was ripe for the taking at his leisure.

2

The night passed slowly at first. I'd never developed the habit of stillness. Motion, motion, motion had been my companion through life. For hours—or at least that's how long it felt—time wriggled through my flesh. Irritable children waiting for a nap to overtake them, but too full of energy to sleep.

Given my nature, there was nothing to do but try to move—despite the impossibility of it. I tried to lift my head, wiggle my fingers, lower my upright arm. Useless. The lack of success was frustrating, but only motivated me to try harder. Soon my breathing was fast, despite my absolute immobility. It was as if I had itches all over my body. All I could think of doing was moving! I had to move!

But nothing came of it. Soon, through exertion of will if not muscle, I was exhausted. I closed my eyes. I thought I might sleep. But images of waking up, finding myself in the same place, the same position, filled my mind. It seemed I would go to sleep, only to guarantee waking up to a nightmare. My fidgetiness returned in full force. Though I no longer tried to move, I became intensely agitated.

Memories began parading themselves through my

head. All lost opportunities. Lost love. How much I wanted to find someone who could soak in my excess energy! Someone who could handle me. Perhaps even calm me. My wife. My children. All gone from me. To be missed. That is what I wanted as I lay on the island, waiting for interminable death. All I could think was that everyone would be relieved that I had vanished. Who sets off in their life with such an ambition? Who had succeeded so well in it as I?

Finally sleep did come. Fitfully and in small chunks of discomfort.

From the changing position of the stars, just barely visible through the red haze, I knew that an hour had passed between each of my dozings. Each time I was more miserable than the last waking. My flesh felt scratchy, my throat dry. A dizziness passed over me, coming in rhythmic waves. Soon I longed for the respite sleep gave me from the pain. I wondered, more and more often, if there was any way to hasten my death. The thought that my condition would grow worse, the pain increase, the scratchy despair become more intense, made me long for movement again—if only so I could smash my skull to death against my stony grave.

The sun rose, and when I opened my eyes, I was at first startled. The heat of the air above made the sky shimmer, but the bright blue of the cloudless morning was a sharp, pleasant contrast to the distressing red of hours earlier. Though still lifeless, the black rocks surrounding me could be seen clearly now. I was not trapped in a world of round, obscure shadows. My imagination let me believe for a moment that the worst had passed. That if the memories of the previous night had not been a nightmare, then at least things would now be better.

I tried to move.

Failed. Only my left arm, at my side, broken from the fall, moved a bit. Not enough to propel me anywhere.

I waited. Took in a breath. I did not want to scream or cry, but the terror of the situation made it hard not to. I was still alive, and might live out my days trapped as I was. I looked about, frantic, pathetic, mindlessly searching for a clue, a means of help.

It was then my gaze fell upon the tower at the island's center.

Red stones, each lined with black swirls like smoke and flame, rose up from the rocky ground, forming a round tower two hundred feet tall. Windows showed intermittently along the wall. At the base was a huge doorway formed of solid black stone. The doorway was without a door, and seemed at once inviting and challenging.

I had not seen the tower the previous night because of the darkness and because it was slightly behind me. Now I craned my neck as far as I could for a view of it. Was anyone inside the building? Anyone walking around it?

Not that I could see. More than that. The tower was steeped in loneliness. Against the bright blue sky, its dark red stones seemed incapable of containing any life. Yet what choice did I have but to hope for rescue from some inhabitant within?

I tried to shout, but my voice, like the rest of my body, was weak. It cracked, making nothing more than the dry rasp of pain. I tried again, this time managing to get out the word "Help!" It seemed loud enough to carry to the tower, and I waited for a response. I waited and waited, fearful that if I cried out too soon I would not be able to hear the response.

Finally I called out again.

Not a sound came back.

I stared at the tower. Watched the door. My gaze flickered from one window to the next. I saw only the darkness of the tower's interior framed by each window.

Staring up at the sky I continued to shout, calling and calling until my voice was sore and I was forced to believe that even though someone had once taken the time to build a tower on the strange island, it was now deserted.

For a long time after I had given up my shouting, I closed my eyes. Hope once again denied me, a bitterness crept into my thoughts. Not odd for me, I know. I've created a bitter outlook for myself, and have viewed most of my life from a bleak point of view. So I thought once more of how terrible everything is, how miserable is the end result of every action. Life is nothing but a series of longings, leading to one disappointment after another.

What is strange is how I quickly left this thinking behind.

The heat of Death's Sea overwhelmed my mental construction—my castle of stars. Misery in the face of living my life was one thing. Moping and complaining was fine as long as I was free to do other things with my life. Now, however, I was trapped with myself. *All* I could do was complain about the misery of life. That was sheer terror. If I was going to starve to death on a barren rock, I didn't want to spend my last hours listening to myself whining. For the first time in my life I couldn't afford my self-loathing or my self-pity.

But what else *could* I do? The tower, deserted. The island, barren rock. The sea, hundreds of miles of molten lava. My body, frozen into inaction except for one broken arm. All was hopeless.

It occurred to me, though, that even if the tower were deserted, it might contain food. Even healing potions. It might even possess a means of getting off the island. A moment of hope.

Yet, given my life, what hope could I afford? What could I possibly do to reach the tower? Even if I somehow made it that far, could there be any doubt that some terror awaited me within? Something like the decayed, reanimated corpse of my mother, perhaps? My life was full of thinking I had finally reached safety, only to realize things were still abysmal after all. What point was there to hope?

I rested on the ground, spent. The strain of arguing myself from one extreme of despair and hope to another had exhausted me. The fingertips of my left hand scraped against the rough stone, but I barely felt it. Nothing really mattered.

Memories of the fall came back to me. A realization. I really could have died. I should have died. If I had died, what then? Nothing. Eventually, someday, someone who knew me—my wife, my children—would notice that they had not seen me in a long, long time. Or Mordom might meet someone and say, "There was a boy once who killed me. Now he's dead." He might smile as he said it. That would be that. My life, all the terror and hopes and fear and stabs at love I'd made, would amount to nothing. Vanished. A star dropped into Death's Sea, swallowed up.

My fantasy drifted on. I imagined myself dead and gone. All my life I'd been clutching at something—a longing for love. In death the panic for that love was gone. There was no more need. I had no more expectations. Whatever I had expected from life was now beyond me.

I began to relax, let the lack of need sift through my muscles. My breathing lightened. I had feared death not because I feared dying, but because I was afraid I would die before I got what I wanted—love. Now I was, for all practical purposes, dead, and that fear left me.

What if I pretended I really was dead?

What would I lose? Nothing. Life had already robbed me of all joy. I spent each day bracing myself against hope so I would not be tricked again.

What would I gain? Nothing. Except . . .

A lack of need. Since I was dead, there was nothing more to think about. If I was dead, I could finally relax. There was no more need to get anything, to prove myself. To steal useless trinkets I didn't care about. To seek out love and attention from people I didn't know and would never know. And there was no fear of hope anymore, because I had no reason to expect anything.

There and then, bones shattered and nearly dead from exposure, I smiled.

I wasn't dead.

And as I wasn't dead, I might as well live. Live not because I felt I had to do something, get something, accomplish something. But live because I chose to. I began to laugh. My life, already spent, was mine now to live as I chose. Why not have hope? If I was already dead, what would another disappointment cost me? I could no longer lose.

My hand, touching the harsh, coarse black surface of the island, felt for the first time since the fall, *alive.* The heat of the rock soaked up through my flesh. The coarse stone pricked delightfully at my fingertips. It was much like the sensation I felt when using my thief magic to scale a wall to steal a precious bauble. But I hadn't noticed the texture of walls in a long time. Not with the fascination I felt for the rock on which I now rested. Not for years and years. I thought back to the tavern where Garlthik had initiated me into the ways of a thief adept. Then all the particles of the world had been connected. I was part of it. Everything mattered, fascinated.

What had happened? I had simply stopped noticing. The goal of the bauble had supplanted the fascination of the *action.* Motion, motion, motion. Rush, rush, rush. Always had to get somewhere. Steal something. Make a name for myself. Become a legend. Could I gain love then? No one, I knew, could ever love *me*. It would only be a collection of activities and accomplishments, the tag of notoriety, that would make me valuable to someone else.

And in my insane rush I had, of course, attained that notoriety.

"Who are you?"
"J'role, mad old clown;
I've always been so
Since my first sound."

My fingers scraped against the rock. Where had my

life gone? Could I really have been happy? Why did I let all the years slip by?

Tears, tears from years ago from the present, welled in my eyes. I began to sob. I could not wipe the tears away, and they rolled down my cheeks, sticky and stinging. I thought of Releana, and of you and Torran. And I wished so desperately that you could be there, so I could tell you how sorry I was. Not just for hurting you, though there is shame and sorrow enough in that. But for not sharing myself with you. For in that moment, in the mourning for a lost life, I knew that there was actually something good within myself I might have given my family. I had just been too frightened to do it. I radiated pain instead. I had wanted to show you all how harsh the Universe was, so I made sure to be harsh for the Universe.

3

I cried for a long, long time. When I was done, I did indeed feel better. I had never believed much in the power of tears. They suggested a weakness I thought others would exploit. I remembered Releana's constant suggestions that I release my pain openly to her. How I thought it would be too much for her to bear. That my pain, openly expressed, would drive her away. Yet what did it amount to? Tears on my cheeks.

I looked back at the tower. It stood lonely and somewhat threatening. I had one arm that moved slightly. I tried a simple wriggle and found my hips could also move a bit. It was possible; I might be able to crawl and wriggle to the tower. On my back. Slowly. Over a hundred yards of rough rock. But what other choice did I have? And why not? Thoughts of my false death came back to me, and it seemed I might as well try, if only to give myself some purpose with my second, unexpected life.

The thought actually caused me excitement. The ridiculous impossibility of it teased my mind, tasted like sugar on my tongue. I was doomed to fail, trapped halfway to the tower, starving to death before I reached my goal. Thus, there was no pressure. The safety and perfection I'd always sought was well beyond my grasp. The attempt was all that was left to me.

I shifted my weight, moving my shoulder blades off to the right, pointing my head toward the tower. My left palm pressed hard against the rough ground, and I slid myself forward a little. I then shifted my shoulders a bit, moving slightly to the left as I scrunched up my spine, dragging myself forward. In this way, like a man using one paddle in a small boat, I moved forward, slipping left then right as I alternated using my shoulders and left arm.

Although my progress was difficult, the awareness that I *was* making progress sent another wave of ridiculous enjoyment through me. I could barely feel my body, but what I could feel was struggling, alert, and alive. I was living to stay alive, rather than to prove a point about misery. The lightness of this made me giddy, and despite my exertions, I smiled as I moved on.

Then I paused to rest and rolled my eyes to look at the tower. No more smiling now. In my thoughts I'd traveled yards. In fact, I'd moved only several inches. It was only then that I took in the full difficulty of the task. Yet I set myself to do it, and with a long intake of breath to launch me, started again.

I stopped later that day, falling asleep. When I woke, the sun had passed into late afternoon. I began again. Although tempted often to check my progress by looking toward the tower, I made it a rule to do so as little as possible. Only when I needed to confirm the direction I was traveling. The slowness of my progress was all too depressing.

Rises in the rocks caused terrible difficulties. I had to push myself uphill, the pressure scraping hard against my back, ripping into my already ragged shirt. I suspected I was bleeding along my shoulder blades, but could not be certain. Because I could not maneuver myself with any dexterity, the trip downhill did not go any easier. I was still obliged to push myself along, and with my head tilted back as I moved, I could see the tower clearly and how much farther I had to go.

Night came. I slept again. Woke in the middle of the night. Feverish. Dying, I think. I weighed out the choices. I could rest and try to get better, and then die later. Or struggle on, hoping against ridiculous hope that some sort of comfort waited for me at the tower.

I chose hope.

On the fourth day from the fall, hunger began gnawing at me like a rat inside my flesh. My body, in its efforts to keep me alive, had burned up whatever food had been in my stomach, food I had eaten days earlier in my home in the jungle. Waves of dizziness started to pass over me, and I often woke up with no memory of stopping my journey. Sensations came to my tongue. Pears and apples, sticky and juicy in my mouth. Roasted boar, cooked crisp on a spit. The taste of rice wine, sweet and dry. These thoughts supplanted concern over my interminable progress, though the exchange gave me no comfort.

I continued on.

Late in the morning of the sixth day I was still at it, though I had no idea if I really was moving forward. It seemed I might simply have been rocking back and forth, and no more. Thus, I risked a glance at the tower, needing to know I was closer, but afraid to learn how much farther I had to go.

It turned out that I had, even in my stupor, made tremendous progress. I remembered how far away the tower had been when I'd started out, and now, at late morning, its shadow fell over me. It seemed possible I would in fact reach it.

Then, in one of the windows of the tower's third story, I saw a shift of gray. I blinked, uncertain. Hunger, exhaustion had already taken their toll. You and Torran had come to visit me the night before as little boys, wondering where I was. Begging me to come home.

I looked back toward the tower. No. There was something. Someone. A woman. A shout formed in my throat. Shattered on the way out, my voice unused for so long. I tried again, calling over and over for help.

The woman, thin and delicate, old, as old as me, with thick gray hair, walked slowly past the window. Her hand touched the window frame as if leaning against it for support. She paid me no attention.

Shouts poured from my raw throat. I filled the air with as much noise as I could. Still, she did not acknowledge me. She moved on, and the last I saw of her was the back of her simple white gown as she vanished out of sight.

I paused, confused and frustrated. If only she had heard me, everything would be so much easier. An anger built up in me. How I wanted to hurt her! How I wanted to do something to cause pain. Things are never as easy as they should be! And I wanted someone to pay for that!

But, unable to take action, I was stuck with my own thoughts again. In the midst of inaction, there seemed little choice but to calm down. I do not know how long my rage lasted, but by the time it was spent, I thought this:

"Well, she didn't hear me, so there's no more to be done about it."

It seems obvious, perhaps, to you sitting listening to this tale. Of course, I should have simply driven on. But I think sometimes in the middle of our adventure, our life, we become confused and think things should be a certain way. Which is the way we want them. Which, of course, they are not. Things are the way of the Universe. And we know that the Universe created all of us and the Passions so that things would be difficult and interesting. So there it is.

She might be deaf, I thought. Or the tower might have magical protection that, among other things, prevented sound from entering it. *But* there was someone there. Rather than viewing her not hearing me as a problem, I realized that her presence was a good thing, and I decided to focus on that.

I wriggled on.

It was not until evening of the next day that I reached the tower door. The sky above glared red as thick clouds passed over the sea and caught the lava's glow. The clouds were thick and bilious and churned slowly. It seemed for a moment that I had drifted below the surface of the sea, so that molten rock floated above me as well as below.

At the base of the door I shouted again, several times. From the dark doorway came only silence. With a long breath, I braced myself and began to writhe into the tower.

The room, an entrance hall, was round, and I imagined that the other floors above would be so as well. A broad stone staircase wound its way up the tower wall, vanishing into the second story. Brass handrails, shiny even in the tower's darkness, flowed up along either side of the stairs. It took me a moment to notice that both rails floated in the air without support.

At the entrance hall's center rested a large fountain, much like the fountain of my kaer. Its round wall was two feet high. At the fountain's center stood the statue of a man, who bore, it seemed to me, a striking and disturbing resemblance to Mordom. However, unlike the magician's robes Mordom wore, the man wore armor and an elaborate cloak—the cloak of a Theran official. From the statue's surface flowed water, pouring down as if his very being were the source of life. His face was uplifted, as if taking in the rays of the sun, in typical overblown Theran fashion.

The room held no other ornamentation. There were no lights, nor empty sconces on the walls. The hazy red light of the lava sea crept in through the doorway and three windows, but beyond floated only a deep darkness.

I called again for help, but no reply came. The silence that followed my shouts seemed especially harsh, and I waited a long time, trying to discern any sound. I heard only the sound of my heart beating and my deep, moist breathing.

I shouted some more, and listened some more. But nothing came of either the noise or the quiet. Eventually, having reached my goal, exhaustion claimed my attention fully. Although I wanted to know where the woman had gone, there was nothing to be done to find out. At least not as weary as I was. I slipped into a deep sleep, a sleep more relaxing and enjoyable than any I'd had on the island, and did not open my eyes again until I heard the sound of footsteps.

4

They came hesitantly, softly, and not without fear. In my dreams it was the sound of a monster approaching, something snakelike, with small claws that lined the body, working its way toward me as I lay staked to the hot sands of the shore of Death's Sea. I woke with a start as I realized that the sounds existed outside of my dreams. At once I tried to move, only to discover that I was still paralyzed.

Memories of what had befallen me flooded my thoughts. I remembered being in the tower. I remembered the woman I'd seen earlier. But everything looked different now. Bright sunlight blazed through the windows, striking the well's red stones, creating the sensation of being in a furnace. I tried to shield my eyes from the afternoon light, but it was impossible to move my left hand far enough.

When I looked toward the sound of the approaching footsteps, I expected an enemy. Someone with a sly, but undisciplined walk, probably carrying a dagger, or a magical amulet capable of melting my flesh or possibly some other terrible, arcane effect.

Instead I saw the woman, and in that moment my heart reached out with unselfish pity.

She was as old as I. But where I had kept my health despite my misery, the woman on the stairs had been ravished by her six decades. Her limbs were thin, and her skin showed countless bruises and scabs. Her gray hair—possibly beautiful, for it was thick and long—was so matted and dirty that I immediately imagined vermin living in it. She clutched the inner railing that floated inches from the wall, her hand pressed tight around it as if she feared floating away. Her footsteps were taken with inordinate care. Desperate care. Not just the care of the blind, but of the terrified, as if trying to prevent any more dangerous missteps.

It took me a few moments of study to realize that she was indeed blind. I had seen the movement of blind people before, including those moving about in a place familiar to them. Usually they moved with a certain, careful, grace. They knew their homes very well, and maneuvered as you or I might when waking in the dark from our beds. But the woman did not move with this ease. Her footsteps were harsh, dangerous. Not risky, but powerfully deliberate. She would slide her foot out along the edge of each step until it slipped over the edge and she nearly plunged forward. Then, with a firm and hard step, she would place her foot on the step below as if try to smash the stone of it underfoot.

"Help," I whispered. My voice was nearly gone, and I felt needles prickling the inside of my throat.

She continued on her way, picking her way down the steps without a glance toward me, nor any apparent awareness that I was only four yards from her.

Behind her, along the wall, I noticed that an inscription of sorts had been carved into the stone. Beginning at the base of the stairs, the inscription wound its way up the wall, following the rail. The words seemed to be in the language of the Therans, though from my distance I could not be certain. Strangely, they had not been created with the same precision and beauty as the rest of tower. Even from the floor I could see that they had been forged roughly, with chips and awkward cracks splitting open the red stone's smooth polish.

Finishing her progress down the stairs, the woman was moving along the floor toward the fountain. Her steps were more confident than on the stairs, but still careful. She kept herself bent low, hands held out before her to keep from bumping into the fountain. As she walked, she counted out her steps. Silently. Just moving her lips.

She was blind, deaf, and perhaps mute as well. The scrapes and scabs on her flesh suggested that she might also be deficient in the sense of touch, for her flesh seemed often to misjudge pressure and pain. If there was any way to make contact with her, it would be by forcing myself into her closed world in whatever limited way I could. I had to be next to her, to grab her.

Immediately I started for the fountain, hoping to arrive before she finished whatever it was she was going to do there and was on her way back up the stairs. Although I was weak, frenzied energy drove me on at a quick pace. Using my slightly mobile left arm and my somewhat flexible waist, I wriggled closer and closer, twisting my body from one side to the other as I moved forward. Luckily I'd had days of practice, and against the smooth stone floor my motion carried me successfully forward.

I glanced at her and saw that she had lifted a silver cup from a small shelf built inside the fountain. She dipped the cup into the pool of the fountain, raised the cup high, and then drank the liquid down.

Not so fast, I thought. Not so fast!

She placed the cup on the shelf, and turned back toward the stairs.

"No!" I shouted. I was only a few steps away from her—so, so close. "Please wait!" I pleaded. But, of course, she heard nothing. Extending her right foot, she started toward the stairs. Desperate, I rocked back and forth from side to side. The rocking grew fiercer and fiercer until I had enough energy to roll over onto my stomach.

My left arm was now several feet closer, and I stretched it out toward her departing left ankle. The strain was tremendous, as if metal hooks had been placed into my shoulder to limit my motion. Her ankle lifted up, just an inch or two off the ground, and I was certain I had missed my opportunity. But she moved slowly, and the end of my finger managed to snag her ankle. My grip wasn't solid enough, and my finger slid off. Still, in that moment she knew something or someone was in the room with her.

She gave out a scream. An awkward sound, high-pitched and terrified. But more. The noise sounded slack, as if her jaw and tongue weren't used to working in coordination. I knew that people who are deaf lose, over time, the ability to speak properly. They can no longer hear themselves, and so can no longer test how they speak against how they sound.

Her hands waved in front of her as she tumbled to the floor in her panic. I winced at her impact, for she cried out again, this time with even more fear. For a flash I imagined being in her place; a soul trapped in a void. On occasion something would happen to her, and she would not know what or why it had occurred.

Uselessly I tried to explain who I was. She scrambled up onto her hands and knees, trying to look toward me, but staring off three feet to my right. She backed up quickly, then got onto her knees, raised her arms, and waved her hands as if to fend someone off. From her mouth came the distorted noise of twisted and elongated vowels. It took me a while to realize she was saying, "Who's there? Who's there?" I tried to answer her, but to no avail.

She stopped her questions, and her hands slowed their frenetic motion. I could see her trying to piece together what had happened. There, in that moment, in the small changes of expression on her face, I saw the intelligence the woman still possessed. As she tried to pull herself together she reverted to old habit, undoubtedly from a time before the loss of her senses and her life on the strange island. She seemed to have a kind of regal bearing. There was something of the Theran arrogance, but with the addition of something else. Most Therans, it had always seemed to me, puff themselves up with their preening, but possess little substance. But this woman had a true strength to her. Noble. Not in the nature of bloodlines, but in character.

When no further attacks came, she began to relax. She shifted her shoulders, assuming a posture of composure. Calmly, or perhaps with an exaggeration of calmness, she began to stand, as if saying, "See, nothing is wrong after all."

I realized then that she thought she'd merely tripped. A panic rippled through *me,* and I began making my way as quickly as I could toward her.

She turned and began to walk, arms extended, searching for the stairs, the matter already settled in her mind. My heart sank, for though I assumed she would eventually return, I didn't know if I would still be alive.

But then her pace slowed, revealing a hesitancy. It wasn't a matter of her hearing me. It must have been second thoughts. The kind that plague us even after we've done everything to convince ourselves all is normal. And more than that, perhaps. Just the sense of awareness people have of each other; knowing that someone is staring at you from behind, knowing someone is in the room though the lights are dark.

She turned slowly, and on her face I saw the lines of fear and doubt. She had reviewed the scene once again in her head, and now *knew* her world had changed. Lowering herself to the ground, crouching, she extended her hands. Not, this time, to fend, but to discover. She lowered herself to her knees, and with one hand on the ground and the other stretched out before her, she began searching for what had snagged her.

From the start she headed off in the wrong direction. I tried to cut her off, but though she moved slowly, she was too fast for me. For far too long she searched for me, and I did my best to let her find me. Soon the pain in my back was so intense from exertion and tension that I simply gave up and sighed. With my eyes closed I tried to come up with a new plan. I decided to head for the stairs. She would have to leave at some point, and thus find me there.

Just as I made the decision, I felt her fingers brush against my face.

5

She cried out, as did I. Paralyzed, I felt horribly vulnerable at her touch. I realized I was ultimately within her power. Why had I assumed she would help me? What made me think there was safety within the tower?

She spoke again, though I could not understand her. My Theran was limited, and the distortion of her speech made the task more difficult. Once again she was on her knees, fending off my nonexistent assaults.

When she realized that no attack was forthcoming, she lowered her arms and asked slowly, "Who are you?" Then she raised her hands to her face, pressed them hard against her cheeks in frustration. "I can't . . . I can't . . ." She seemed to be searching for a word, and finally said, "Listen."

I wanted to move toward her, to touch her and get her to understand that I could do no harm. She was *my* only hope. I laughed loudly at this thought, for it seemed ridiculous that my salvation should rest with the actions of a woman completely cut off from the world. What could she possibly do for me? How could someone so damaged bring the clown-monster of Barsaive any comfort?

She was close now, and had a sense of where I was. She moved toward me, the fingers of her right hand extended. Trembling. I waited, silent, expectant. There was nothing for me to do. Nothing I could do. The situation was so strange, for all of my life I had tried to keep moving fast enough to at least create the impression I was in control. Now I was so obviously out of control. Powerless. And yet, in that moment, I wondered how much I'd ever been in control before. I had stolen countless treasures. I prided myself on my skill at eluding capture. Through the amassing of wealth, always at the expense of others, I had believed myself clever. Yet, as the trembling hand approached, it came to me that all I had ever wanted was a touch of comfort. And certainly nothing I'd done with my life had encouraged that.

Closer and closer came the fingers, until she pressed them into my right cheek. The touch was not the comforting caress I'd just been thinking about. Awkward and heavy, the fingers dug deep into me before the woman was sure she'd found me. She then pulled back, suddenly startled by the discovery. She did not retreat this time. Instead she put her hand forward, her fingers now spread wide. They bumped into my forehead, then she pressed harder and ran them over my face.

I felt horribly young. Thoughts of my mother came to me, thoughts of that day, of her fingertips on my chest, performing the ritual to place the creature inside me. I wasn't paralyzed then, but just as helpless. The helplessness of a child under the power of a trusted adult.

The woman brought her other hand forward, using

them both to explore the shape of my face. The care she took with the examination made me think she had perhaps never seen anyone before. Babies, when they first see another baby, are immediately intrigued. Perhaps I was the first person this woman had ever encountered. If so, she would need time to confirm that yes, she had finally met someone like herself. Then my gaze fell upon the statue at the center of the room. It occurred to me that she might be trying to determine if I was someone she knew.

When she found my mouth she awkwardly jammed her fingers into it, cutting one of them against my teeth. I knew this, for I tasted a drop of blood on my tongue. But the woman did not respond. She continued on without a cry of pain, without even inspecting the damage. I knew now she lacked the sense of touch. That would explain the cuts and bruises I'd seen earlier, for she would not be aware of when she hurt herself. It would also explain the clumsiness of all her actions. She could not feel when she touched my face. She could only interact with the world through resistance.

What had happened to this woman?

She drew back, worried. Then placed her hand on my neck, checking, I suppose, for a pulse. She found it. Touched my forehead. With elaborate effort, she said, "I can't hear you. But I need to know if you are all right." Her words, despite the care she took in enunciating each of them, sounded high-pitched and clumsy. I could tell she knew her words were awkward. She turned her face up and away from me as if to hide the clumsiness of her mouth. But there was also the beauty of character I'd noticed earlier. "If you need help, nod your head."

I tried to nod, and believed I did succeed in nodding. But it was not enough motion for her to notice. "Please!" she said, and the sound came from her like a wail. I realized she did want to help me, but not only for my benefit. I began to suspect she hadn't retreated to the island for safety, but might well have been left there, exiled and alone. How many years? She said, more frantically now, "Can you understand me? I'm sor . . . sorry . . . It's been so long . . . Do you understand Theran?"

Her hand was near my mouth and I said, "Yes."

She stopped. Smiled. She maneuvered around, placed her fingers on my lips. "Can you understand me? Open your mouth twice if you can." I did so. She laughed. An awkward, heartfelt, lovely laugh. A laugh full of memories. "Do you need help?" I opened my mouth again. "I don't know what you need. Do you understand? I can't see you. I can't hear you. I can't even touch . . ." Her face became wracked with grief. She looked away, thinking I could still not see her clearly. She stifled her pain, then looked down in the general direction of my face. "Are you wounded?"

I did not know how to answer that—paralyzed? wounded? How would we ever communicate? Instead I laughed a bitter laugh. Years earlier Releana had asked me similar questions, and we had played similar games in our attempts to communicate. I had been mute then. Now I had my voice, but the only person who could help me was deaf and blind and lacked all sense of touch. My life was full of ruined people.

Where did they all come from? Wasn't there supposed to be some happiness floating around in the Universe?

She asked me if I could get up. She told me to open my mouth three times for no, twice for yes. I told her no. She asked if bones were broken. I said yes, if only because it was closer to the condition I was in. She stood. "I think I have something that might help," she said. She started leave, then realized she had completely lost her orientation. She started off again, determined, reached the wall, followed it until she found the stairs. Then was on her way up. Slowly. Painfully slowly.

I did not want her to go, and said as much, knowing full well it was futile. But the thought of lying helpless on the floor was too much. How long would it take her to make her way up the stairs? How long to find whatever it was she thought might help me?

I watched her ascend the stairs. Just seeing the effort of her steps made me tired. I wondered briefly why she had come all the way down the stairs to get a drink of water. I knew the water might be magical in nature. But if that was the case, why didn't she just remain in the entrance hall?

During our strange chase, when she had been trying to find me, I had moved closer to the stairs. I could just now make out the Theran words carved into the wall. As I had suspected, they were not part of the tower's original design. It seemed possible that the woman herself had placed them in the wall, carving them with incredible care and concentration.

I was not fluent in Theran pictographs, but could, with work, translate them. So, with nothing else to do as I waited, I began to read the words. The first two sentences said:

MY NAME IS KYRETHE. I DO NOT KNOW WHERE I AM.

As I read the words, I once again felt the "shadow" present in the room—the same one that had haunted me all my life. The same one that had been with me when I had held Neden's hand. I turned my head as much as I could, but could see nothing. Sunlight still flooded the room shiny yellow. The sight was incongruous. The day seemed so light and airy, yet the mood of the tower so brooding and solitary.

Looking back up at the two sentences I'd translated, a tension began working its way through my chest. The tower held a terror I had not—could not—have anticipated. Even with the limits on my knowledge of her situation, I could surmise that the woman, Kyrethe, led a more miserable life than anyone I had ever met. I wanted to leave. I was already soaked in my pain, and did not think I could take in any more. I thought I would drown in despair if she and I became connected in any way. I resolved to take what help she could offer, and help her in return, but to keep myself safe from her. To keep a wall—a wall to prevent our souls from meeting—between us.

When I turned back to the wall to read further, I found my vision had blurred. Exhaustion had returned—the encounter with Kyrethe had drained me. Sleep slowly overcame me. Dying, I thought, would not be bad if I could do it in my sleep. An easy escape from it all. I drifted off.

* * *

I did not die.

Kyrethe woke me when she shoved her hand into my shoulder. Before I could even take in what was happening, her hands were upon me, clumsily searching for my face. She found it, found my jaw, then squeezed my cheeks together to make me open my mouth. "This is a healing potion," she said. She had brought me a crystal vial filled with sparkling blue liquid. I wanted to ask her how she could possibly know that she'd selected the right vial, but the potion was already pouring into my throat. It did indeed taste like other elixirs I had used to heal myself over the years. More potent than most. The aftertaste brought to mind cool days in the jungle, along a wide river, with fruit and cheese sitting on my lap.

"Does that make you feel better?"

She put her hand over my mouth and I opened my lips wide twice.

"Good. I was hoping it was the right potion."

I opened my mouth wide again, this time in horror.

She laughed. "Just joking. Just joking." Unlike her words, her laugh was unaffected by her inability to hear. Her joy came out clear as a stream tumbling over a cliff, sparkling down to become a lovely pool of water. Her smile transformed her ruined and scraped flesh, bringing forth a person full of life and passion.

She forced her mirth down, and touched my chest. "I hope it helps. I have more if we need it. I hope you feel better. Everything will be all right." Then she said, "There is something I must know before I retire." Only then did I realize that the sun had begun to set. Hours had passed while she had been laboriously ascending and descending the stairs. "I don't know if this will make sense to you. I don't even know if my brother still lives. But did a man named Mordom bring you here?"

6

"Who are you?" I asked abruptly, my voice creaking with fear.

She had her hand at my mouth, expecting me to use her simple code to answer yes or no. "I can't understand you," she said awkwardly. "Please." I could see she was very disappointed with herself for not understanding me. Despite her condition, she still expected so much from herself. My initial fear, that she would drag me down into an emotional quagmire, seemed unfounded. I became envious of her. She had a strength I had never known.

"Do you know Mordom?" she asked, and this time I replied yes, using the code.

"He sent you here?"

I didn't know how to answer that question. He did bring me here, but he didn't send me here. I decided to answer yes. Her smile returned, slowly this time. "Did he send you to free me?" I said no. Her smile left her, and for the first time she looked very sad. Finally, after a heavy sigh, she asked, "Then, you are here by accident?"

I thought of the child, encouraging me to leave Neden behind and jump off the ship. (Where was that damned baby?) I did not mean to arrive on a solitary island in the middle of Death's Sea. But I did choose to jump. Accident? It was impossible to answer. When one really tries to speak the truth of one's life, answers of yes or no seldom do. I think that's why we all spend so much time talking. In creating so many sentences and words we're trying to stumble across an explanation for ourselves.

I finally settled on the answer yes. I did not want her thinking I had come to find her.

"How is my brother?" Her tone reminded me of my castle of stars. Precise. Sparse. Just the outline of pain, allowing for rooms of heat. Then, realizing I could not answer, she smiled ruefully. "I'm sorry. Here. Let me get you something to drink." She made her way to the fountain, pulled the silver cup from the small shelf, and scooped up some water. When she returned she knelt beside me, and after finding my mouth with her free hand, carefully poured the liquid onto my tongue and down my throat.

If the potion she had given me was astounding, the water was more so. Never had I tasted anything so wonderfully full of life. A warmth spread out through my flesh. I felt sleepy, as if I'd just eaten a full meal.

She stood. "I will let you rest now. You are very hurt, I think, and it will take time for the potion to help you." Without another word she turned and left. Her departure was again painfully slow, and I was asleep before she had gotten even halfway up the stairs.

Dim red light flowed into the entrance hall, weak against the overwhelming darkness of the tower. My body felt ragged and stiff, and memories of days spent as a slave of the Therans came to me. It took me a moment to realize I *could feel* again. I raised my right arm, held it up before me. *I could move!* With growing excitement I propped myself up—and immediately fell back down. Although I could move, my body was exhausted. Gently I rolled over onto my side, just to feel motion again. I smiled. A child comfortable in bed. Somehow things would be all right. I fell asleep again.

When I next opened my eyes, it was still night. Again I tried to get up, slower this time. Although a buzz still cut through my thoughts, I could sit up. That task done, I rested.

The red glare of the sea shone brilliantly on the water that flowed from the statue's surface. Was that a statue of Mordom in his youth? I did not think so. The man portrayed seemed stronger. More of a soldier.

I stood now, testing my sense of balance. Wobbly, but I believed the worst was over. A terrible thirst raked at my throat, and I started at once for the fountain with the wonderful water. After the first two steps, my knees buckled. This happened again and again. But with successive steps I improved—remembering, in a way—how to walk.

When I reached the fountain I sat on the edge of its round well. The red illumination that drifted in through the windows made the well water look more than a little like blood. For a moment I wasn't certain if I truly wanted to drink the stuff. But memories of its taste and my own intense thirst prompted me to dip the cup in and scoop out some water. When I drank it down, I once again felt refreshed.

Stronger now, I decided to see if I could find Kyrethe, or at least explore a bit more of the tower.

With stealthy steps—old work habits become part of our nature—I made my way up the stairs. There was no need for any lights in the tower, for Kyrethe was blind. Thus, no glowing moss grew from the walls and no sconces with candles waited to be lit. The shadows grew deep as I made my way up the stairs. But even in the growing gloom I could see that the words carved into the wall continued.

The second floor was as sparse as the first. Windows let in the lava's light, mixing the room with shadow and blood. At the other side of the room, opposite the stairs where I stood, were more stairs leading up to the third floor. The inscription continued around the wall and then kept moving up the stairs to the next floor.

At the center of the room was a large bed, with white sheets. Four posts stood at each corner, and white gauze floated around them, forming a delicate, airy canopy. The sea's warm air lifted the gauze, making it float and quiver. The lava's light illumined the sheets and the gauze making the bed look like a device of pain.

On it slept Kyrethe. The red light through the windows was gentle on her flesh, blurring the wrinkles and bruises of her body. Her long white gown flowed down along her limbs, and melted into the sheets. She seemed quite peaceful, as if the gown and sheets had grown up around her, cradling her.

I do not know what, if anything, your mother told you of the time she and I spent together. I do not know now how much I want to tell you. But it is important for you to know that—because of who I am—because of so many things—when I saw Kyrethe in that bed of blood, I was very drawn to her. The mix of pain and flesh had an arousing effect on me. I moved toward the bed, without a specific plan in my head. Just going, because I simply wanted to. Because I wanted to touch someone, and I wanted to feel pain, and because . . . I really didn't know why.

I walked up to the bed. Stood beside it. Looked down at her. She was so thin, frail. Her thick gray hair fell about her shoulders, curled up over her neck. I placed my hand, carefully, just the fingertips, against her cheek. Her skin . . . How I wanted to . . . I ran my fingertips over her lips. She did not stir. It took me a moment to remember she could not feel.

This revelation sent confusing feelings through my flesh. On the one hand, I was drawn more to her. The thought that I could—do things to her without her knowing . . . Caress her. Kiss her. Excited me. Gave a sensation of power. A power found not in strength, but in safety. No threat of rejection. I could simply have my ways. As long as I did not jostle her too much, as long as my desire remained the shadowy actions of a thief, I could touch, and she would never know.

But the realization also disturbed me. I felt repulsed by my desires. She could feel neither pleasure nor pain. I could give her nothing. Only receive. And then, if I did it secretly, I could only receive what I was willing to take. Your mother, the things that . . . When she made me bleed with bites and nails, I knew that a part of her liked it. She later said . . . But at one time . . . Kyrethe would offer none of this. I cannot explain. But to know there was no interaction, no exchange of sensation, drove me away from her. I stepped away, my hands trembling.

Wanting intensely to occupy my mind with other

thoughts, I made my way up the stairs to the third floor. This was the top floor of the tower. Wooden shelves lined it, all packed with vials containing potions. On each shelf were labels, all carved into the wood. Written in Theran, the labels identified potions of healing, regeneration, sleep, and a few to induce pleasant emotional states. Few of the vials had been touched. Aside from the water, Kyrethe seemed to need little.

How had she ended up on the island? Why did she bring so much she never used?

The answers, I knew, might be waiting for me in the inscription. Although the words covered the walls around me, I decided to go downstairs, to start from the beginning.

7

I read:

My name is Kyrethe. I do not know where I am. I write this for you; whoever is reading this. I want my story known. Only if stories are known can things change.

I am the daughter of Veras Churran and Quorian Churran. Veras, my father, was a Theran governor in the province of Herrash. Proud. We all lived in the mansion, but it was HIS mansion. We all ate the food, but it was HIS food. We each longed for our dreams, but we were HIS family.

My father advanced in the Theran ranks. Promotions. He conquered people. Did it well. At dinner he would laugh about his power. Joked that he was a new Passion, a Passion of conquest. My mother and I did not laugh. My brother Mordom did.

After the Holy Day Massacre, my mother and father began to argue. She wanted him to change his policies. He would not listen. He ruled other people, but it was HIS land. My mother was also Theran, but it was HIS decision how to represent all Therans. Other people died, but it was all a part of HIS life.

My mother did not relent. Asked him to relinquish

the post, to permit us all to return to Thera. She wanted him to rest. He refused. She asked again. Again. Again. Again.

He struck her.

She asked, he struck. Again, again, again. On some nights I heard him rape her. Her cries filled the mansion. I rushed to stop him, but his guards prevented me. I screamed, "You know this is wrong." But they were HIS guards.

He killed her.

I did not see the body, but she was gone. My father said she met her fate. He smiled; a joke. He thought HE was fate.

I cried, as did Mordom, for we missed her. My father asked us what was wrong. I told him I saw my mother, and Mordom did the same. My father said, "Stop seeing her." We could not. We missed her. I did not want to forget her. I wanted to hold her memory as proof of my father's crimes.

My father knew this. He locked me up in a small room. He starved me. He beat me. But he would not kill me. In his strange way, he loved me.

I did not relent. He called us into the council chamber and told us to swear to forget our mother. We said we could not, that we saw her in our thoughts. He then called down a curse upon our eyes. A shadow loomed behind him. He did not know this. He said, "You will not see your mother; you will not see anything. I imprison your sight."

He blinded us.

A week later he called us into the chamber. He asked, "Have you forgotten your mother?"

Mordom said yes. I said, "I hear her voice when I lie

down at night. I hear her say, 'You are my love. You matter to me because you are you. Everything about you is what I love, the good and the bad, because without both, you would not be what I love.' "

My father said, "You will not hear your mother; you will not hear anything. I imprison your hearing."

A week later he called me into the chamber. He wrote in the palm of my hand, "Have you forgotten your mother?"

I said, "When I lie down at night, I feel her arms around me, giving me comfort. She asks nothing from me, but gives."

My father said, "You will not feel your mother; you will not feel anything. I imprison your touch."

From that moment on all my contact with the world was removed. People moved me around, fed me. After a long time, many years, I think, I was put on an airship and the air eventually became very hot. Then they took me off the airship. Put me in a round room. There is water here, which I can taste, and it is good. There are stairs, which lead to my bed. And more stairs which lead to magical potions.

I spent a few nights sleeping on the floor of the first floor. There is a statue in the middle of the pool, and water pours from it. When I touched the face of the statue, I realized it was my father's face. I will not sleep in the same room with such an image. I will sleep upstairs from now on.

I walked around outside the tower today. I fell many times. The air is very hot, and I believe I am in a dangerous place. The tower is my only place of safety. I will stay here.

I do not know how long I have been here. No sight.

No sound. No touch. The world is beyond my comprehension.

Much time has passed. I wish I could die.

I do not want to die. If I die, my mother is forgotten. She must be remembered. What my father did must be remembered. What my father did must someday be seen, spoken of, felt.

I did not know what loneliness could do to a person. I cannot find the words. Pain, true pain, does not come from the flesh. There is a thing in my soul. It grows larger. Has claws. Eats my life from the inside out.

I had to re-read this to remember. It is good that I wrote it down.

I had forgotten I had written this. The events came to my mind as I read, but I had forgotten.

I cannot believe this is my story. Yet I know it is.

How long have I been here?

When did I write that question?

How much longer till I die?

My name is Kyrethe?

Are there other people in the world? Does anyone yet live? Are they lonely like I am, cut off from life like I am? I lose faith that I am really a human. I remember other people. They are happy, smile, hold hands. I am not like that. I am outside of people. I am not a person. I am a thing. Disconnected. A collection of thoughts floating through life, without flesh, without passion.

Should I kill myself?

I was twenty when I came here. How old am I now?

Why do I still live?

How many years?

8

The words stopped. I stood on the third floor, in the storage room. Through a window I saw Death's Sea roll on and on, endlessly, drifting off into hazy scarlet and black. The sun had just topped the horizon, and the sea's molten lava seemed to float into the red-tinged morning air. Despite the warmth, a chill crawled along my flesh.

As I walked down the stairs I kept my hand on the rail that floated alongside the inner edge of the stairs. I moved slowly, and I needed the rail to keep my sense of place. Without the touch of the cool metal, I thought I might wander into thoughts of pain and terror and never return.

The things parents can do to their children.

The things I have done.

Thoughts and memories tumbled through my head. I stopped on the stairs occasionally, frozen in place, transfixed by some horror from my past. I forgot I had a body. Forgot I was in a place. Forgot that around me life moved on. As if my senses had become connected to the past, the immediate world blocked by distant experiences.

When I reached Kyrethe's bedroom I stood for a

long time and watched her. The gentle rise and fall of her chest under her gown. The occasional turning from one side to the other. A bit of breath moving some strands of gray hair. In sleep, so much like a child. In sleep, we are all children. The masks we wear to prove ourselves safe, successful, and strong are unsustainable. Helpless and unaware in sleep, we are just children, needing a place to rest, shelter from a world with so much pain. We depend on the people around us not to harm us. A tacit, unspoken agreement between parent and child. Between siblings. Between lovers. All sleeping near each other; all needing to know that at least here, next to these people, I am safe.

For a moment she became so many people to me. My sons. My wife. My father. Each had trusted me, and I had betrayed them one by one.

I wanted to give her something. Not because she was she, but because by giving her something—easing her wounds somehow—I wanted to redeem myself from previous, horrible deeds.

When I approached her bed, I approached silently, craftily. The old habits. This should have been my warning. As I had done hours earlier, I extended my hand. Touched her cheek. Brushed away her hair. She felt none of it.

The bed shifted slightly as I sat on its edge. She did respond to this, for her weight shifted. She turned toward me. Her eyes fluttered open for just a moment, then closed and she fell deeply asleep once more.

With all the grace my thief magic allowed me, I slipped up onto the bed with her, propping my back against the headboard. Not once did I consider my behavior ghastly. I had cloaked it under the guise of a gift of comfort I was giving her. Trust, you see, was something I did not understand. Neither was it something I could expect, or know as something another might need before becoming intimate. The concept was outside my skull, outside my understanding of the universe. A child might think that the sun revolves around the Earth. Until someone explains the true nature of things to him, he cannot truly know the relationship between sun and Earth. So it was with me and trust. No one had ever explained its nature to me, and so I did not understand the relationship between fathers and children. Husbands and wives. Between lovers.

I took her hand in mine. Raised it carefully, as if wary of setting off any traps or alarms set around a beautiful jewel in a king's palace. Did I know I was trying to steal something from her? I would like to think not. But could I really have been that unaware? What we do without knowing, we really do without listening to our souls. But the truth was around me. The shadow was in the room. It hid behind me, near the wall, not daring to come too close lest it force me to acknowledge its presence. But it was there. And I knew it.

I took her arm, draped it over my lap. Remember, gentleness and comfort were still my intended goals. Affection, it seemed, would be a good thing for both of us. I told myself I did not want to wake her. I did not want to startle her. Disturb her.

Interestingly, though she could not feel the warmth of my body nor the texture of my clothes, she wrapped her arm around my waist, pulling herself closer, tightening her grip on me. A deep instinct must have taken over, the memories of hugs and mothers. She nestled her head first against the side of my abdomen, then let it come to rest on my thigh.

Now, still staying true to my intent, I brushed her hair. She was so much like a child; helpless. I was so much someone in power. I had not thought that sexual desire was any part of why I had approached her. But now with her so close . . .

And, indeed, now I can say, sexual desire had so little to do with it. Once, my father nearly dragged me down into a sinking ship, and I killed him. I would not let him destroy me; I destroyed him first. Once, my wife did not know what to make of my pain and darkness. I led her down my path, making her do things to my flesh she never would have conceived of without my insistence. I forced my perversions on her. Once, my boys did not know what to make of me, and turned always to their mother for guidance and love. I ruined them, justifying it at the time, but all the while seeking power. And now, a woman, asleep, lay beside me. I wanted power once more. I could do things to her, and she would not even know what was happening. What was more, her father had already beaten her down. I felt so, so safe in what I was doing.

I slid my hand along her neck. The skin, worn and warm. She was so beautiful. Peaceful. She began to tremble. Aware of motion. Of something happening. I leaned down, kissed her on the neck. Picked up her hand. Her nails were long. Slid them lightly along my face.

Did it again, pushed them harder into my skin. Nails into the flesh now, leaving white lines. She moaned.

I leaned over her, running my hand along her side.

She woke. Eyes wide. Terror on her face as she frantically tried to comprehend a situation she could not see or hear. Straddling her, I pushed her back. But I did not pin her arms down. Left them free. Her arms raised, slapping at me. Clawing. She scratched me, and the sharp pain of it pleased me. She gasped, gulping in air, drowning in fear.

Around my pleasure, in the darkness of the room, I felt the strange presence. It encouraged me. Her struggle against me grew fiercer. For her, it was a matter of survival; terror forcing her to uninformed desperation. For me, an act of pleasure.

The shadow, as wide as the room now, moved closer, creeping up behind me. Part of me was torn, for I wanted to turn and see. Never had it been so close. And never so obvious. I knew now that if I did turn, if I did look, I would finally see it. Curiosity, like an itch, demanded attention.

Yet, part of me did not want to know. I suspected just enough of the truth. Ignorance has its virtues when such ugliness is involved. I was afraid that if I looked I would see something so terrible that I would stop what I was doing. And that I did not want to do.

I shoved my forearm into her mouth. In quick reaction she clamped down. Her teeth squeezed blood from my flesh. She considered it a victory. Wrong, wrong, wrong. She served my purposes. She, to me, was a tool of muscle, blood, and flesh. Not a person, but something that existed only in response to my desires. No. Not desires. Anger. Rage. Revenge.

I cried out in pain and pleasure. Thoughts of the Elf Queen rushed through my blackening vision. Confirmation that pleasure in life could only come from pain. The darkness closed around the edge of my vision. Lurked. I longed to see. What had haunted me all these years? Not the Horror in my head, but the terror it left behind. No. Not the Horror. Everything. Life. I confused life sometimes with *the* Horror. But how many horrors had there been? Each piling up upon each other, influencing each other, until there was no separating what I had wanted with what was. Dreams no longer mattered. I lived in a void of shattered expectations. I shattered them now, unable to distinguish what I did from what others had done to me.

She was tight-lipped now, my blood on her lips. Down her throat. No emotion from her. Just closed eyes—closed from pain. How much of what I was feeling wracked her with agony I cannot say. But I suggest that what the Horror did to me in my youth was no worse.

The thing at the edge of my vision breathed on my neck now. It cloaked me. Offered protection. From what? From any decency I had left. From the shame or remorse that might rise up in response to what I was about to do. I wanted to look now. Knew I could. Could stare into its face and would see myself and I would accept that. The final release. The culmination of pain and the acceptance of pain. Pain as life.

I grabbed the collar of her gown. The cloth tore evenly down the center. The sound of a jagged torrent of raindrops against jungle leaves. I closed my eyes. Turned my head. Prepared myself to see my shadow. To embrace it with this horrific offering to brutality. Control. Power.

My hands plunged toward her body, grabbed her abdomen.

And before I could enjoy either her scream, or the sight of the shadow, my fingertips encountered something most strange.

9

I jerked my head around. For Kyrethe, time had frozen. Her face remained grimaced in terror and pain. But the flesh of her face did not waver. Not a sound escaped from her mouth.

The skin of her abdomen was now translucent. There, rising from her flesh, was a child, glowing with golden light.

The infant from the airship, different somehow.

The child pushed up through her flesh, passing through her skin. My fingers rested on the child's chest. Confusion rushed through me. For a moment I was my mother, years earlier, her fingers on my chest. Thoughts tumbled quickly and I forgot all about the thing at my back. I could not move, though I wanted to turn and run from the room.

I had always thought my mother had acted from fear. Fear of the Horror. I had thought she wanted to protect herself. That consumed by her own fear, she had betrayed me. But now, lost to my identity, feeling the emotions she felt—possible emotions she felt—I thought differently. What if she enjoyed it? What if she saw herself as deserving to do to me what she wished?

The baby rose up from Kyrethe's stomach, free of

her flesh now. I saw in its face my own features, young and innocent. Uncorrupted. My thoughts reeled at the passage of time since my youth. Sixty years old! And in that time, how many horrors had I perpetuated on the world? When I was a baby, had I considered such actions? Would I have wanted to do them if I could even have imagined them? No. No. No. How, then, had I come to commit these acts of terror?

Kyrethe's immobilized form should have provided me some comfort. At least my actions were now safe from her awareness. No glare of her blind eyes to accuse me. But it only increased my terror toward myself. How helpless she was—devoid of all senses! Yet what I would do to her! Her torn gown hung uselessly on either side of her. Her body, thin and bare, was exposed before me. The baby's presence forced me to be aware of the relationship between us. That is, of two people. Not manipulator and manipulated.

The baby floated off her belly. Up into the air. Up through the ceiling. Gone.

Time began.

Kyrethe screamed, tried to cover her breasts with her thin arms.

I rolled off her, falling backward onto the bed. I continued away from her, trying to escape the space I had inhabited. My retreat carried me off the bed and I tumbled onto the floor. I realized I was crying. I stood, and as if I had woken up in strange surroundings, had no idea where I was.

Kyrethe cried, her sobs wracking through my head; memories of my own tears. I had felt remorse after my most horrible crimes—the murder of my father, the mutilation of the two of you—but this damaged me in new ways. Pain ripped at my throat from my crying. I curled my fists, beat myself in the face. The center gave loose, the rationalizations all gone. What I did I did. If I had expected more from my mother, then I could not simply slough off my dangerous behavior on her. I must expect more from myself, as well.

But these notions came only as strange buzzing sounds in my mind. Only one true thought came to me: Flee.

And that I did, rushing from the room, tripping twice on my way to the door. Down the stairs. Morning sunlight poured in through the windows. The wash of blood everywhere! Everywhere! When I reached the entrance hall I rushed out of the tower, desperate for the relief of the morning air.

The glare of the sea's molten rock reflected into the clouds, as did the low light of the morning sun. The clouds churned, and as they bled across the sky, it seemed my head had somehow split open, my emotional innards spilling out into the universe. Within and without my thoughts, desolation.

Kyrethe's sobs clawed their way out of her throat. Floated out of the windows. "NO! NO! NO!" she screamed. In her tone, the confusion of the betrayed. She could not understand what had happened. Had she not taken care of me? How could I have done such a thing?

She did not know, and neither did I.

I ran on, desperate to leave her agony behind. Over coarse stones. Up small hills and across tiny, dry rivulets. What had taken me days to travel I now raced across in minutes. Soon I was at the island's edge. Thick and slow, the sea's molten lava rose and fell against the black rock. Kyrethe's tears of betrayal hacked their way into my ears.

I huddled down, kneeling on the rocks. Covered my ears with my arms. Now what was I to do? In similar circumstances in the past I ran away. Carved out a new life for myself. Assured myself that an aberration had taken place. That it was the interaction of that person and myself that had caused the problem.

But now a sea of lava cut me off from the rest of the world. I could not run. If I had thought of that before I touched Kyrethe I never would have done what I did. As I stared out at the sea, out at the sun, now bloated and bright red over the horizon, I began to laugh. No humor, but a laugh. I could not believe the situation I was in. Trapped on an island, the only other person the victim of my attempt at rape. Had not that damned baby promised my freedom?

I stood, screamed for the child to present himself. I looked around wildly. He did not appear. My tirade continued, and as I shouted I stomped around the rocks. I demanded to know why he had imprisoned me on the island. I had assumed him to be Lochost, the Passion of change. Freedom. But now I demanded to know if he was Vestrial, the Passion of enslavement, in disguise. Still no answer.

Like a child embittered at learning how difficult life can sometimes be, I stomped and stormed endlessly. My shrill words managed to drown out Kyrethe's cries, which might have been the entire purpose of my tirade. At some point, when I could shout no more, I settled on the rocks. Sat glumly. Kyrethe's cries had stopped, and a sweet silence unfurled over my small, desperate corner of the world.

Somewhere, a boy was in pieces. Here, a woman was whole, but imprisoned by her father's curse. And I—I was no more than a monster. There had been a creature in my head once, and I thought I had killed it. But it had left something terrible in my life. A lesson on how to live. I was a better pupil than I would have liked.

10

I woke without remembering I'd fallen asleep. I felt drained and worn. My age had finally caught up with me. Trapped on the island, everything could catch up with me. I'd spent my sleep arguing with my family, getting you and Torran to understand that pain is the defining point of life. Trying to get Releana to understand she could try to hide the two of you from pain, but it would find you nonetheless.

I had made sure of that, of course. Had provided the pain myself. And it wasn't just the pain of the knife. It was the betrayal. That memory had repeated itself in my thoughts again and again.

And so, when I woke, I tried to shake the thoughts from my head. If I had been home, I would have gone off to steal something from Kratas. Motion and acquisition kept my mind from indulging in the painful habit of self-reflection. But there was nowhere to go. Nothing to steal. Nothing to do but visit the tower—and I certainly would not do that. And with nothing else to occupy my attention, your screams came back to me.

I had not dreamed the screams. Had, in fact, not thought of them for a long time. But now they came to me as if we were all in the Theran airship once more.

I drew the blade. Your small faces. So happy to see me at first. I had claimed to be your father, had given you the attention from a man that you both so craved. When I arrived, it could only mean everything was all right. But I was not your father, and I reached for each of you and mutilated your faces . . . To win against the Overgovernor. I would have done anything to win. In a world with no trust and only pain, what actions were too costly for victory?

So your screams filled the air. As they filled my thoughts now. I could not get your screams out of my head.

I paced. They did not go away.

I walked the circumference of the island. They did not go away.

The sound of your mother crying became a part of the cacophony in my thoughts. Tears flowed as I made her do things that had nothing to do with love, but which I demanded of her to prove love. I walked faster and faster, stumbling over the rocks.

My father's begging me for love was added next. He wanted me to know he had tried. Tried so hard. And I rejected him for his weakness. No. I killed him for his weakness. I had thought then, Either I kill him or we both die. Just as I had thought, Either I cut apart the faces of my sons, or we all die. The thoughts did not come to mind that clearly. Analytically. But they were present. I definitely thought them after. Justifying my actions. Forgetting one option. Not killing. Not betraying the love of my sons. Paying the price for retaining my humanity.

I ran on around the island, the voices and sobs swarming my thoughts like flies around rotted meat. In fact, I waved my arms around my head, as if I could somehow wave off the memories.

Then came the sounds of my mother's screams—your grandmother. She was driven mad by listening to my voice when I was a boy. She was placed in the center of the kaer's atrium. We—everyone there—stoned her to death. They thought she was possessed by a Horror.

I was possessed by the Horror. I did it! I did it to her! And her flesh tore off in bits and pieces as the rocks struck her. She died begging for mercy and babbling insistently.

So I listened to her screams and only after a long while realized that her screams had replaced all the others. I realized I had stopped running. I had been crying. With the sleeve of my shirt I dried my face. I stared out at the sea. Evening was falling now. Above, the clouds were tinged with gold. Below, the sea was endless and scarlet and black.

I settled down on the rock. There was nowhere to go. Nothing to do.

My mother's screams still haunted my thoughts. Within a few minutes all the other voices came back—the tears, shrieks for mercy, shouts . . . But all came softer now. I gave them my attention. They settled in my heart.

For a long time I listened to the sounds, torn between the despair and a strange kind of happiness. Not happy I'd caused the pain, but happy I could acknowledge myself as the source. I had done these things, and strangely, there was comfort in admitting it. A strange lightness radiated from my heart outward, and the screams floated on this lightness, leaving me.

Then the sound of Kyrethe's cries floated down from the tower. This newly caused pain, so immediate, shattered the lightness of my spirit. My fists clenched. How could I have done such a thing? Always, before, some strange excuse existed. Gave me pretense for my terrible actions. This time, what could justify my attempt at rape? Not the need for safety. Not even bitterness or anger. Just habit. The habit of pain.

I stood, began pacing. Despair welled in my soul. It seemed that the older I became, the more terror I was capable of creating in the world. Kyrethe's cries seemed to fill the air, approaching me from all directions. Like a giant snake, loathing encircled my flesh, tightening around me. I sat down again, buried my face in my hands. Who did I think I was? I was an old man. Lonely, bitter. I could not change. I had no chance of hope. That was for people from better childhoods than mine.

I was aware of a presence beside me. I thought that Kyrethe might have somehow found me. But when I looked up I saw myself. Open sores ran down my double's flesh, and blood flowed freely. Surprise is too light a word for my feelings, and I remained seated, mouth agape.

"Do you mind if I join you?" my double asked. Wordlessly I motioned to a rock beside me. He smiled, sat down. "Getting tired of all of this, aren't you?"

"Excuse me?"

"Going over this in your head, again and again. How many years now . . . ?"

"All of them. Most of them."

"I'd be exhausted."

"Who are you?"

He smiled. Old wounds opened on his cheeks and blood dripped down his flesh. "An old, old friend. Your bitterness."

"Raggok?" I asked, for it seemed I could be speaking to none other than the Passion of bitterness. He nodded. "Are you the shadow that has been haunting me?"

He looked at me carefully. "Well, haunting is the wrong word. You call us up and there we are. This shadow, if it is a Passion, is not me, and I couldn't tell you who it is."

"Oh."

"But in any case, don't you think it's time for all of this to end?"

"End?"

"Yes. It's been such a long, ridiculously pathetic life. And here you are, still cycling through your misery. How many times have you had these ideas? You know, you all—you name-givers—each build a story for yourself. The story may not be remembered by others. Most aren't. But it is a story. And when the story is done, it's time to die."

"It is?" His words caused a tinge of excitement in me. The possibility that my life was finally over, not from cowardice or failure, but simply from dry fact, was very intriguing. How I longed for rest.

"Yes, you do, you long for rest. It's done, your story, and you aren't even aware of it. You keep thinking something new is going to happen. But it won't. It will keep grinding like this until someone finally kills you or you die of old age. Why don't you do yourself a favor? End it now."

The abruptness of the offer stunned me. I gestured

back to the tower. "But Kyrethe . . ." I began, as if I might somehow help her.

"Will be much better off without you. Come, now. You've already broken her heart—the first person she's encountered in four decades tries to rape her. You might as well have been her father." He laughed. A horrible, petty, bitter laugh, full of cheap knowledge. "And that's the point, isn't it? You might as well have been her father. He might as well have been you. You might as well be your mother, for all you did for Kyrethe. You might as well be your father. Your parents might as well be you, now, for your behavior toward your children. Your sons might as well be you. You are no longer yourself, J'role. You don't think of yourself as you anymore, and you're not. You're not really alive. You're a collection of behaviors passed on to you, repeated by habit. You're stuck. You're going to keep grinding the same ideas and notions over and over again. You have nothing really left to offer yourself. Even the world. What kind of a gift could you truly ever give to Kyrethe but what you gave?"

"That wasn't a gift," I said sharply. His good-natured discussion of my attack was beginning to grate at my mind.

"Of course it was. You gave her something. It's one of the only gifts you've got in your limited inventory of presents. But it was a present. You've given her something, and she took it, and she'll remember it for the rest of her days. Which probably aren't much longer. That's how her life will probably close. Her story will end:

'And then she was nearly raped by a man she thought might, in her hope of hopes, offer her the love she so desperately longed for. A few years later she died.'

"And I don't think we even want to think about the fates in store for Neden, or your boys."

"How can you be so flippant about all this?"

"It's just the way it is, isn't it?"

"The way what is?"

"Life. Your life, at least. Lonely, absurdly painful. You attract despair like a Horror to a widow's mind. Aren't you tired of it?"

"You're awfully calm about all this."

"I'm your Passion of bitterness, J'role. The tirades are over. You know it's true. Who has time to stomp and shout anymore? It's a fact. You're tired of living. You're tired of having hope and having it stamped out."

Raggok was right, and it surprised me to realize how happy I was to hear him saying the words. My life really was over. Whatever I did now would only be a repetition of what I'd already done. If my life was a story, it was becoming astoundingly dull.

The baby appeared beside me.

"J'role, don't listen to this part of yourself. You can always hope. Free yourself from . . ."

"Shut up!" I snapped at the child. I smiled. "You're an annoying little infant, and I'm tired of your strange hope and your mysterious directions. Neden is probably dead by now . . ."

"You need time . . ."

"I'm sixty! What time do I have left?"

"It isn't easy. These things . . ."

I stood, as did my double. He extended one hand, and I took it. As our flesh touched, the hands melded together. We flowed into one being, my bitterness and I. "Ready?" I asked myself. "Oh, yes." The two of us walked to the edge of the island, right up to where the rocks met the lava. "This is going to hurt," I said to myself. "As if we can't stand a little pain," I replied. Memories of the Elf Queen's thorns and a thousand other atrocities shot through my thoughts. The levity of the moment left me. I really had wanted to be happy. I had wanted to leave behind a life that others could hear about and be inspired by. But it was all for nothing. Nothing could ever work out.

The baby appeared before me, floating in the air, trying to prevent me from stepping into the lava. "Listen. I can't tell you about what's going to happen, because I'm your Passion of hope, and you don't know what death is like. But I'll tell you this. If suicide was a good idea, word would have gotten out, and more people would be killing themselves. There's a reason why people try to stay alive . . ."

With my voice full of pity for all my lost opportunities, I said, "I have no more reasons," and leaned forward.

"NO!" the baby shouted, his face contorted in horrible pain.

I fell through the child, and as I slipped through him I remembered the potential for hope. The desire for one more chance. The belief that things could get better.

But then it was too late. My flesh splattered into the molten lava. A steam of blood rose up around me as my flesh melted. I screamed, and without thinking scrambled as if I might be able to save myself from my self-dictated fate. The fall from the airship had been one kind of doom—long and indeterminate. This death was not that.

In a moment I was dead.

PART THREE

Death and Life

1

"Come on, come on! We've got to get you set up!"

Bodies pressed against me from all directions, squeezing down on, pushing up at me. Elbows pressed against my sides. "Excuse me," someone said. "Sorry," said someone else. "Will you watch it!" said a third. Humans, dwarfs, t'skrang, and all the other name-giver races crammed against me, and I could see nothing beyond the endless throng. It seemed impossible that I should be able to move, but I passed through the crammed multitude as if moving through water. Limbs slid out of my way just as I approached, filling in behind me as I moved on.

"Come on. Come on." Someone tugged at my hand, and I looked down to see the words *Come on Come on* wrapped around my flesh, wavering, like a long white snake swimming underwater. The words shifted and changed, and as they re-formed themselves into new words, I heard, "We're almost there."

I glanced around, and astoundingly, everyone was writing. Let me repeat this, for I myself did a double-take as I realized what was happening around me.

Everyone was writing.

In one hand each person held a writing tablet, in another each held a stylus. Their tablets were pressed up against the backs of the people next to them, or propped up on their knees, or in the crooks of their arms, and so on. The other hand busily carved out pictographs. As I passed an elf I asked, "What are you writing?" He stared at me sadly for a moment; then, as if in shame, he bent his head down and continued to work.

Not everyone was sad. Some people seemed absolutely gleeful as they wrote. They carved quickly, sometimes laughing. Others stopped and looked at their writing, thinking it over. Of these, there were, again, both smiles and frowns. No one seemed to tire, though. But a few did seem bored.

As the writers finished one tablet, it rushed away, floating through the collection of bodies just as I did. Instantly, another tablet would appear, and the person would begin writing again. All the tablets traveled in the same direction that I was traveling, as if we were all heading for a central point, around which all these people were floating.

"What is everyone . . ." I began to ask, but the words on my hand re-formed themselves and said, "Here we are!"

The words led me to a small space between a few dwarfs who were busily scribbling away. With a bit of pushing on the part of the words I was tucked firmly inside. A tablet appeared in one hand and a stylus in another. I looked around for some sort of guidance, but the words had vanished and the people around me were completely engrossed in their writing.

But it did not matter. My hand began moving by itself. Without any will on my part, it moved to the top of the tablet and wrote: MY STORY

A calm flowed over me then. If I was to spend my time in the realm of the dead, or wherever I was, scribing my tale, that seemed a pleasant enough experience. I had always loved telling stories. Having an eternity to work on it would be a pleasure.

My hand, though, continued writing, without my willing it to. It wrote:

I WAS RAISED TO MISTRUST OTHER PEOPLE AND THINK MYSELF WORTHLESS. AS I GREW OLDER, MY LACK OF TRUST MADE ME KEEP THOSE I LOVED AWAY FROM ME. TO MAKE SURE I NEVER GOT TOO CLOSE TO ANYONE, I DID HORRIBLE THINGS TO THE PEOPLE I LOVED. THUS I PROVED MYSELF WORTHLESS. BITTERNESS BECAME MY FINAL COMPANION. I DIED. THE END.

The word stunned me. First, it seemed rather short. I was sixty, after all, and I had planned to write something much longer. Second, all the details were missing. Yes, I was raised by my parents to mistrust other people. Yes, my mother betrayed me to a monster, and that did little for my self-esteem. But all the *details* were missing. Why was I so miserable? What did I do to people? In all the details was the pain. And pain was all I had to offer to a narrative.

But this confusion and frustration was nothing compared to what happened next. The tablet rushed out of my arms, heading off to whatever destination all the tablets headed for, and another tablet appeared. Again, without willful effort on my part, my hand began to write. I wrote: MY STORY

Then:

I WAS RAISED TO MISTRUST OTHER PEOPLE AND THINK MYSELF WORTHLESS. AS I GREW OLDER, MY LACK OF TRUST MADE ME KEEP THOSE I LOVED AWAY FROM ME. TO MAKE SURE I NEVER GOT TOO CLOSE TO ANYONE, I DID HORRIBLE THINGS TO THE PEOPLE I LOVED. THUS I PROVED MYSELF WORTHLESS. BITTERNESS BECAME MY FINAL COMPANION. I DIED. THE END.

Then I wrote it again. And again. And again.

I must have done it some fifty times before I turned to one of the dwarfs beside me. As I continued to write, I asked, "When do we stop doing this?" He turned to me, a frighteningly glum expression on his round-cheeked face, then looked back down at his work. I turned to a happy dwarf and asked the question again. The dwarf smiled and said, "Stop? What else could you do? Your life is done."

I wrote MY STORY, followed by:

I WAS RAISED TO MISTRUST OTHER PEOPLE AND THINK MYSELF WORTHLESS. AS I GREW OLDER, MY LACK OF TRUST MADE ME KEEP THOSE I LOVED AWAY FROM ME. TO MAKE SURE I NEVER GOT TOO CLOSE TO ANYONE, I DID HORRIBLE THINGS TO THE PEOPLE I LOVED. THUS I PROVED MYSELF WORTHLESS. BITTERNESS BECAME MY FINAL COMPANION. I DIED. THE END.

"Yes," I said, "but there was more."

"Certainly, certainly," said the dwarf with a smile as he finished his life story again. "But I don't think Death is that concerned with the details."

"But this doesn't mean anything," I said, starting again.

"It's gibberish?" he asked with surprise.

"No. I mean, my life. The way it's written. It's meaningless."

The dwarf's arm stopped moving for just a moment, as if he'd suddenly regained some control because of the importance of his thought. "I don't think lives have meaning. Other than the meaning we give them. That's why we have words. So we can define things. Define ourselves. Define what matters to us."

"But here, what I'm writing, there's no . . . I never got around to defining my meaning."

He looked at me, very serious, and said, "I'm sorry to hear that." He stared at me a little longer, his hand still working away as we continued to look at each other, gazes locked. Then he put his attention back on his story. He smiled at what he wrote.

I was too flabbergasted to do anything for some time. Even to think of being upset or angry. My hand just wrote and wrote and wrote. I wrote the short, pathetic narrative hundreds of times. Finally I turned once more to the pleased dwarf. "There seems to be some sort of mistake. I didn't mean for my life to be like this. I've learned my lesson, or whatever, and I'd like to go try again. Death is imprisoned. Correct? It *is* possible to get out of here."

"I think you need someone in the world of the living to do something. Someone to do some sort of tremendous feat to encourage a miracle." He smiled, delighted with an idea. "Do you have anyone who will miss you? They might try to raise you from the dead."

I needed to think about it for only an instant. "No."

His smile melted. "I really don't know what to say then."

Frustrated, I asked, "So, what's your story." My tone was childish. It frustrated me that he was so happy writing his tale over and over again.

He smiled at me bashfully. "No. I really don't think I should. I don't even know if we're allowed to."

I wrote: BITTERNESS BECAME MY FINAL COMPANION. "Come on," I snapped. "What are they going to do? Kill you?"

He smiled at that and said, "All right." He looked down, and as he wrote he recited his story.

"My story. I was orphaned and left to die." Already I felt uncomfortable. I knew he was going to take a horrible fate and make it good. "I had no faith that anything good could come from interacting with people. I trusted no one. I thought I would kill myself. As I thought about it, I realized that if made pretend I was dead, I could live out the rest of my life without risk of failure. I was already dead, so what would it cost me to trust people? I trusted people and spent the rest of my days enjoying the company of others." He laughed and said, "The End."

"I tried that," I exclaimed. "The death thing."

"Isn't it utterly ridiculous?" he exclaimed, expecting me to join in his mirth.

But I said, "It didn't work! Or, it did, but somehow I let it slip . . . I went back . . ."

"I am sorry," he said, eyes sad once again. "I really am." He looked back down, smiling at the preposterousness of his narrative. How could he really end up happy by lying to himself about being dead? Yet it seemed to have worked.

I continued to work as well. Hours passed. Days. I wrote and wrote and wrote. No stars or sun turned in the sky. Time became meaningless. All that mattered was that I had to write my narrative again and again and again. I kept waiting for some change to come in the words. It seemed that at some point I would be allowed to learn a little lesson. Come to terms with some element of my past. But no. Nothing changed. I was trapped writing the same thing over and over. At some point, after I'd written it thousands and thousands of times, a terror crept into my comprehension. I'd be doing this forever. No variation. No relief. No change. No happiness. I'd lived my life. It was done. This was it.

I wrote: MY STORY

I WAS RAISED TO MISTRUST OTHER PEOPLE AND THINK MYSELF WORTHLESS. AS I GREW OLDER, MY LACK OF TRUST MADE ME KEEP THOSE I LOVED AWAY FROM ME. TO MAKE SURE I NEVER GOT TOO CLOSE TO ANYONE, I DID HORRIBLE THINGS TO THE PEOPLE I LOVED. THUS I PROVED MYSELF WORTHLESS. BITTERNESS BECAME MY FINAL COMPANION. I DIED. THE END.

I had to get out. I didn't know how I would do it. But by the hundred millionth time, I knew I could no longer sustain this agony. Ultimately, my life was too boring to read over and over. Something had to be done.

2

My only clue as to the geography of the land of Death was the tablets that flew from our hands and traveled in the same direction. Even if they did not travel to an important place, it would, I reasoned, still be a place. If I could at least reach a place, I would have some point of bearing.

I spent a long time calling for help, demanding that someone take me to Death so I could speak with him. No one arrived, but a few of the scribblers smiled at me with smug wisdom, as if they'd seen my behavior oh, so many times before.

I tried to hang on to my tablet as it flew off, but my life story slipped through my fingers again and again.

Finally I struck on the idea of grabbing someone else's tablet as it went by. The problem, the first one, lay in the fact that my hands automatically kept writing my story. They were no longer mine to control. However, in the moment between the tablet leaving my hand on completion and the appearance of a new blank tablet, I had a small moment of rest. In that moment I tried to extend my arm. I found I could do it. What was difficult was waiting for a tablet to fly by near me at the same time my hand was free. Each time I wrote the words THE END, I looked around for a tablet near me. They passed by from all directions, each one distracting me from all the others. I never made a choice of which one to grab for, and so all of them rushed by.

After waiting for what seemed forever, scrawling my simple, miserable narrative over and over again, I decided to focus on one area—to look in one direction and ignore the other options. As I wrote the last period, my hand was freed from its task of holding the tablet and I saw another rushing toward me. My fingers caught at the tablet, hanging on to the edge for just a moment, and then the tablet flew on. This encouraged me, however, for at least my plan was possible. The pull the tablet exerted was probably strong enough to drag me on.

"What are you doing?" asked the happy dwarf.

"I've got to get out of here," I answered, looked for another tablet flying nearby.

"Ah."

"There's no way to get out of here," said the miserable dwarf.

"I've got to try."

The happy dwarf said, "Yes. He's got to try. What's the risk of trying?"

"What's the point?"

"I take it your story didn't come out too well," I said.

"Useless," answered the miserable dwarf as he scratched it out once more.

"Actually," said the happy dwarf, "they all come out the same in the end. We all die. It's in the living of it that the tension lies."

"You were a stupid idiot!" barked the miserable dwarf.

"Did you two know each other?" I asked.

"No. But look at him. How can you review your life and be happy."

"But my life is so absurd," said the happy dwarf. "I've got to laugh."

"Absurd?" I asked.

"Certainly. I've read it to you. I spent my whole life needing to make myself perfect. I mean, that's not in the story, but I know it's there. My parents were always so proud of me when I did something. I was a stone-cutter, and they loved my skills. Loved them and loved them. Heaped praise on me for how I could cut up a gem. But no gem was ever good enough for me—because the more perfectly I cut it, the more praise I would get. As I grew into an adult, more people praised my abilities. I strove for perfection in all things. I became the guildmaster in Bartertown. I bullied everyone around me to be perfect as well. I dismissed everything that fell below my standards—and let me assure you, everything did." He began laughing, as if looking at someone else's memories from a great distance, and seeing all too clearly the foolishness of the poor man. "Everyone respected me, but no one came near me. I never fell in love . . ."

"Me neither," said the miserable dwarf.

"I think I did," I said. "But I'm not sure."

"*That's* what I meant," the miserable dwarf said. He seemed completely confused as to exactly what his life had been about. If I had suggested we had all been born tadpoles, he probably would have considered it a possibility.

"Well, I thought I did, but I think now I didn't," said the happy dwarf. He continued writing as he spoke. A few of the other bodies crammed around us began to listen, but most kept to their task, faces glum. "I would give advice, and people would listen. I would cut gems, and everyone would come to look at them. I was spoken about. But I don't think many people spoke to me. They were afraid I would cut up their words as deftly as I cut diamonds."

"That doesn't sound very happy or absurd," I said.

"Well, that's the thing of it," said the dwarf, with a barking laugh. "I was *miserable.* I didn't think my cutting was very good. I'd come home from work and my wife would compliment me . . ."

"I thought you said you didn't fall in love," said the miserable dwarf.

"I *didn't* love her," the happy dwarf said without missing a beat, then carried on. "She'd compliment me, so proud of me, and I'd think her an idiot—because I knew how useless and incompetent my work was. Nothing I did ever was good enough for me. I'd order her around the house, trying to snap her into something worthy of my approval. She thought I was so wonderful, and I so wanted her to realize what a terrible person I was. Only then would I be able to respect her." For a moment a flash of loss passed across his features, and he smiled as if in amazement. "And she was a wonderful woman! She had so much love!"

"You said you didn't love her," said the miserable dwarf.

"I didn't. She loved me. So this was my life. One day an expensive order came in from Throal. And I picked up a hammer and got ready to smash every one of the gems that had been entrusted into my care. I wasn't even aware of the fact until I was about to do it. I wielded the instrument with the same casual habit I used with my cutting tools. I raised it over the first diamond, beautiful and clear blue, and just before I brought it down, knew what was at stake. My wife came in and said, 'Dear?' I looked up, saw her staring at me, her expression of love and concern. The hammer felt ridiculously heavy in my hand. Feeling out of place in my own life, I put the tool down. It occurred to me I had no idea why I cut diamonds."

"I'll bet you didn't even like cutting diamonds," the miserable dwarf said.

"No, actually. That was the interesting thing about it all. I ended up continuing to carve diamonds and gems until the day I died, when a giant eagle had a heart attack and fell to the earth, crushing me to death. I loved the work. People would bring me rare stones with so much potential for such beauty, and my job was to bring that beauty out."

The miserable dwarf was becoming irritable now. "Then what was the business with the hammer?"

"I hadn't ever *enjoyed* it. Well, at least not from the first times I'd done it. I'd traded in my love of the activity for the approval of everyone else. I hadn't paid attention to my own passion for the work in years. I turned the task into one I did only for money and the approval of others."

"What did you do?" I asked. His story was different than mine. But I heard similarities in both our tales. I thought I might learn something from him.

"First, I cancelled the contract with Bartertown. In fact, I got rid of all the work I'd scheduled for the next few months. I had a bit of money saved away, and knew I'd be all right for a while."

"I'm sure your wife appreciated that," the miserable dwarf grumbled.

"She was very supportive, actually. She wanted me to be happy. She had always wanted me to be happy. My misery had made her miserable."

"Why did she stay with you?" This *was* pertinent, for I could only believe that Releana had always expected some sort of transformation to take place within me. Why else had she given me so many chances?

"She loved me. And for that I have no explanation. Whether it be my wife's love for me, or anyone's love for someone else."

I had never believed something so simple could be the reason. My mind had reeled out countless excuses for Releana's affection. She had no taste. She was weak. She was an idiot. She felt a need to save me. She had nothing better to do with her time. The possibility that, despite all my flaws, she might simply care for me, came as a tremendous shock. "What did you do?" I asked.

"Well, as a craftsman in the jewel and gem trade, I had, over the years, accumulated quite a few stones of my own. Small pieces. Not the stuff of marketable value that might appeal to princes and kings and wealthy merchants. But attractive nonetheless. And they were mine. I took them out of storage, where they'd been waiting, some of them, for years, and set them out on a black cloth in my workshop. Each of them, a dozen in all, sparkled different colors in the sunlight that rushed in through the window. I spent a day just looking at them, thinking about how to cut each one. And then I got to work. It took me months, for I wanted to try some cuts not so obvious. Because they were mine, I could take the risks I needed to take. Most people, you know, want to buy what they've bought before. They think they're getting something new, but usually they're not. As a cutter it was rare that anyone expected me to try something different. But now I wasn't working for anyone else. I was working for me.

"So I spent months on my delicate stones. A strange peacefulness came over my household. Without a need to busy my wife with countless words, as my own thoughts had so busied my head with countless criticisms of myself, we actually had the silence we needed to be able to speak to each other. I discovered that she loved to take long walks through the streets of Bartertown at twilight. I had thought she rushed out of the house to avoid me. But I soon learned she did not rush. That was my own imagination at work. I also learned, once I asked, that she would love for me to accompany her on occasion. Not all the time, for as she said, 'These are *my* walks.' But sometimes. So we wandered the city. Without the need to judge everything poking at my mind all the time, I was able to listen to the voice of the people around me, and to see all the sights, the small ones, I'd missed so often. A child helping another child up from the ground. A man whistling a song as he carried lumber. A woman peeling the skin off an orange, eyeing it hungrily in anticipation.

"Things lost the meaning I'd previously assigned them. Success was found in the details of daily life fitting together calmly, not the ability to bully those around me and prove them incompetent. On these walks my wife held my hand. Perhaps for the first time I really felt its touch. It was a wonder to me. For all our time together I'd seen her body as a collection of items to be judged. I had kept most of my thoughts to myself, but I think she always knew. But now—how do I say this?—her flesh was no longer flesh, something isolated from her. It was an embodiment of her life story and who she was in the present. I was drawn to her not only because her body was appealing, but because it was one way for our stories to meet, merge, connect."

Almost everyone in the dwarf's immediate area was listening now, even as their hands continued to write out time after time their narratives. Some smiled wistfully at the dwarf's words, others looked down glumly. Still others had tears in their eyes. All of them, I'm certain, were reflecting on their own lives, before their deaths, when they had had the chance at living, the chance now gone. I know I was.

"What did you do when the money ran out?" said the miserable dwarf with a bit of a sneer. He clearly wanted to find some loose thread of despair hanging from the happy dwarf's narrative tapestry.

"I went back to work, of course. One does what one must to eat. But the work was different now. It was during this time I imagined killing myself. I really thought it through, because I felt the dragging depression of my past picking at the edges of my newly found joy. I thought: If I kill myself, my wife will be sad, and my neighbors will have something to talk about for a while. But with time, my death, which would be the defining moment of my life, would be forgotten, along with my life. Others, even my wife, would have to get on with theirs. That would be all. But with that in mind, I could live as if I had died. Freed from the need to succeed, I could enjoy this second, accidentally found life. I could work at cutting precious stones not because I *had* to, but because I chose to. So I surrendered my life to the Passions, and decided to live with the absurd notion that I could be happy, not because I had a reason to be happy, but because I had no reason *not* to be happy."

Only the sound of the scratching of stylus against tablet continued after the happy dwarf had finished. The lot of us, our bodies pressed up against one another, remained silent for a long time. Until finally someone coughed, and one by one the others turned their attention back to their own stories. Stories that, for better or worse, they would apparently write out again and again for the rest of eternity. I could only think that the realm of the dead was filled with more regret than any place I'd ever heard of.

"I can see why you smile when you write your story," I said.

"It's utterly ridiculous," he agreed with a foolish grin.

The miserable dwarf snorted in agreement.

"And enjoyable for that," I said. "But now I must try to get back to the realm of the living."

"Disappointed with your tale?"

I'm sure I rolled my eyes as I thought of *that* matter. "Oh, yes. But there's also a little boy who's been cut up into little pieces—"

"Dead?"

"No. Living. The last time I saw him."

"Incredible."

"We all have elements of the absurd in our lives."

"We just have to make sure we don't notice only the tragic."

I thought about that. "Yes. And a woman who I hurt—" My voice trailed off.

"Your wife."

"Her, too, actually. But a woman, recently. I—attacked her—"

He winced at this, and even the miserable dwarf looked up from his miserable story and stared at me. "Raped?" asked the happy dwarf, now not so happy.

I could look at neither of them. "Yes. I stopped myself, but the intent . . ."

The happy dwarf, now not so happy, asked, "Are you certain you want to go back? It seems as if things didn't work out for you in the realm of the living."

With my eyes now fixed on him as if I needed his permission to go on, I said, "All I have carried with me from my life is regret. I need more than that if I'm going to be trapped writing my tale over and over."

"You'll never get out of here," said the miserable dwarf.

"He might," said the happy dwarf, his spirits rising again.

"I must."

"All you can do is try, you know. Success is never guaranteed. But at this point . . ." He shrugged his shoulders.

A tablet rushed toward me as my hand finished writing THE END. I reached out and grabbed it with both hands.

"Good luck," the happy dwarf shouted after me as the tablet dragged me along through the infinite mass of bodies. Another tablet appeared in my arm—a tablet for me to write my story on, and I placed it on top of the tablet I clung to. My hand with the stylus began to write my short, desperate narrative again and again.

I swooshed through the throng, knocking people out of the way. Alone, the tablet would have passed easily between people. But dragging me along made getting between the dead difficult. Several times my grip became tenuous as my arm slammed into people. But I held on—hoping the tablet would lead me back to my life.

3

As I rushed on I read the story the tablet contained. I read it in small chunks, for I could only see it in the glimpses afforded me in the times between my finished tablet flying off and my new one arriving. The story read: MY STORY

I SAW LIFE AS A SERIES OF DOORS. WHEN I WAS YOUNG THEY STOOD BEFORE ME: OPPORTUNITIES. WHEN I BECAME OLDER, THEY CLOSED BEHIND ME, ONE AFTER ANOTHER. LOST OPPORTUNITIES. MY LIFE GOT SMALLER AND SMALLER. I SPENT ALL MY TIME LOOKING BACK AT ALL THE CLOSED DOORS. THE FINAL DOOR CLOSED. I DIED. THE END.

When I finished the story I took grim comfort in the notion that this narrative's author seemed in some respects to have been more miserable than me.

My journey seemed interminable. I tried to think of how long I had been traveling. Or even how much time had passed since my death. But I could not think in terms of time. I could remember specific incidents since my arrival, but I could not comprehend the space between them.

So I traveled on, passing hundreds of thousands of

people, all busily writing away. The possibility that the tablets in fact led nowhere came to me. Maybe they circled this strange place or eventually ended up in the hands of another writer, the words mysteriously vanishing.

This idea had only just occurred to me when suddenly I spotted my mother.

I saw only a bit of her face—the right eye and forehead buried in a tangle of troll limbs and t'skrang tails. The bit of her looked as if she was in her mid-thirties, the same as she had looked on the day my people had stoned her to death in the kaer. In shock I let go of the tablet and came to an abrupt stop.

At once I began making my way toward her, grabbing at arms and legs, pulling myself along through the mass of people. A few people glared at me, but most ignored me, simply grunting a bit as I climbed over or under them. An eternity of interminably performing the same task would breed a certain lack of interest in anything, I suppose.

When I reached her, she was busily writing away, her forehead furrowed in deep concentration. Her skin did not show the cuts and livid bruises from the stoning. But in a way she looked older than I'd remembered. She did not look up as I grabbed her arm. "Mother?" I said.

She looked up then, eyed me with suspicion. Cold eyes. "What do you want?"

The two of us were both writing our life stories, inches apart from each other, packed up tightly against all the dead of the Universe. For the first time since my arrival I felt a strange panic at all the bodies around me, trapped in too small a place with too many people.

"I'm J'role. Your son, J'role."

She examined me. "My son is a little boy." She turned back to her work.

I looked down at my hands. They were wrinkled and worn. I was *older* than her.

"I was a little boy when you died. I lived for fifty years more. I am J'role."

She looked up at me again. In her throat, the slightest twitch as she swallowed. I thought she might reveal something. Finally. Some sort of truth. Or something. An exchange. But she said, "And what do you want from me?"

"I . . . I don't want anything from you. I want . . ." What did I want from her? There was something, but I couldn't put it into words. "I wanted to see you. To talk to you."

She looked back down at her writing. "Talk then."

"Don't you . . . ? Aren't you the least bit . . . ? I don't know . . . Curious, at least. What happened to me? Something?"

Her chin began to tremble. "I really don't want you here. Near me."

"I'm sorry."

" 'I'm sorry,' " she mimicked. " 'I'm sorry, I'm sorry, I'm sorry.' You and your father. You couldn't stop apologizing. You were so much like him."

Now, as when she had said the same thing to me years earlier, a pain stung through me. "I liked being like father."

"I'm not surprised."

"What was wrong with him?"

"If you couldn't see it then, you'll never know now."

"Why couldn't you love us?" The words surprised me.

She looked up, sharp-eyed, ready for a fight. She said, "I did love you."

I believed her. I said, "Why didn't you show it?"

Her mouth opened, then closed, like a beached fish desperate for water. "I did."

Again, without thinking, I spoke. "No. No you didn't."

"I don't know."

"You put that creature in my head." My voice took a rising tone, a wind picking up speed through the leaves of trees just before the crash of a thunderstorm. "I was eight years old and you were my *mother* and you put that thing in my head."

"I thought you would be all right?"

"All right! All right?"

"I had to protect your father and me. It said it would kill me. And you were so young. No one would suspect . . . It said it wouldn't hurt you . . ."

"I couldn't speak! Why didn't you tell anyone? Why didn't you get help?"

"It would have been bad for us." She paused, then her voice rose to match mine. "You were just a boy. What did you understand about life in the kaer? We were all trapped. Frightened. Frightened of the Horrors. Frightened of each other. Any weakness, any sign of corruption could get you killed."

"You died anyway," I snapped, strangely satisfied, childish.

"I died when you were born." I could say nothing. A long pause settled between us. She said, "I did love you."

"You just wanted me dead."

"I wanted you different."

"Different?"

"You talked too much. Like your father. The two of you, with that laugh. So—busy! You couldn't stop moving. Run here! Run there! You wouldn't stop. I just wanted you to sit still once in a while. Just to stop. Why couldn't you have been who I wanted you to be once in a while?"

Her words confused me. My memories of my childhood were filled with images of being still. I thought I had only learned my love of motion after my mother's death. After everything had gone wrong. As an escape from the misery of my life.

"Do you want to know what happened to me, mother?"

She remained silent, simply writing. Then nodded.

"Things didn't go very well."

"Things don't."

"For some people they do. Not for me. Not for you. You have grandchildren."

She looked up.

"Two boys. Samael and Torran. I haven't seen them for a long time, but one is a swordmaster adept, the other a troubadour adept."

"A troubadour," she repeated with regret.

"He likes what he does. I hear he's very good at it."

"What kind of life is that? Making up stories for people? Great artists can do that. Who does he think he is?"

"He enjoys it."

"Your father got nothing from it."

"Father liked it. It made him happy."

With teeth clenched, her tone imploring me to finally explain a deep mystery, she asked, "Why?"

"I don't know why. He just did."

She looked away, completely dissatisfied with my answer. More silence between us. Then she asked, "Do you want anything else?"

"I've always wanted your love."

"I gave you that. You had that."

"I wanted to be loved for being me."

"That I couldn't do. There was so much wrong with you. If you'd ever listened to me . . . With time . . ."

" 'There was so much' . . . !You put a monster in my head! And now you judge me for it?"

"The monster came for you. How do you know you didn't deserve a monster in your head?"

The scratchiness of bile began to rise in my throat.

"You don't know, do you?" she said accusingly. "I think you deserved that monster. It came for you, and I gave you exactly what you deserved."

"I was a little boy."

"Other boys knew how to behave."

"You called it misbehaving because you were my mother. Other mothers could accept how their boys behaved. I was only being a little boy."

"I don't think so. When I spoke with other mothers I was so ashamed to have to say my son spent all his time daydreaming."

"If it caused you so much shame, why did you talk to them about me?"

This gave her pause, and then she said, "I wanted people to know what I went through with you. How hard it was to raise you. To raise you with that day-dreaming father of yours. You don't know, do you? You don't know, do you? You don't know what I went through raising you."

Her cold words sent my thoughts reeling. Dead or not, I wanted nothing to do with her anymore. A terrible anger rose up in my thoughts. "What is your story?" I shrieked. I wanted it to be something truly terrible. She pulled away, hiding it from me. "Goodbye, Mother. I won't trouble you anymore."

She finished her story and it slipped out of her hand. I reached out and grabbed it and was on my way again.

My mother had written: MY STORY

MY PARENTS TAUGHT ME THAT FAILURE OF ANY KIND MEANT FAILURE AS A PERSON. THOUGH I COULD NEVER ATTAIN PERFECTION, I SPENT MY LIFE TRYING TO MAKE SURE THE PEOPLE I LOVED WOULD NEVER FAIL AS I ALWAYS DID. EVEN IN THIS I FAILED. AT THE TIME OF THEIR GREATEST NEED, I FAILED THEM. I FAILED TO MAKE THEM STRONG AND PERFECT, AND SO THEY COULD NOT HELP ME. I DIED. THE END.

The thought of my mother writing her self-centered tale over and over again filled me with a strange mix of morbid glee and true sadness. Things about her I had always suspected, but never knew for sure, made my hatred of her come full-blown from deep in my heart. I was glad she was trapped here, everyone else safe from her. Yet a part of me mourned the loss of a mother. Not the woman who wrote the story, but the mother I wished I'd been born to. Someone who . . . I could not find the words. I did not know what I would want from a mother. But I knew that I would have wanted someone else. How my life would have been different with another woman!

The tablet dragged me on and on, and I began to fear that truly I would continue my useless motion forever. Then, after a passage of time I could not quantify, I saw a silver light ahead. It came only in bits and pieces, for the bodies crammed together blocked the view of what was ahead. But as I drew closer, the silver light grew brighter and brighter. Wider and wider. Within seconds, or so it seemed to me, a wall of brilliant silver light loomed before me, stretching out in all directions as far as I could see. It was to this point that all the tablets traveled.

The throngs of people did not press against this wall, but floated several yards away from it. With only seconds to go before I reached it, I realized that the massive wall curved slightly, so that it most likely formed a giant sphere. All the bodies of the dead floated around this sphere, piled up against each other for all eternity.

Several people looked at me as I rushed by. A few called out, warning me to stop. The tablets, so many I could not count, rushed toward the silver sphere and disappeared inside, dissolving into the sphere's walls. I did not know if they were destroyed upon impact or had somehow passed through the sphere's walls, perhaps entering a land contained within the sphere. I had no idea of what I should do—whether to let go of my mother's tablet or whether to let it drag me forward. But then I remembered my fate if I did not challenge myself to move on: I would spend the rest of time writing out my pathetic tale. That I could not bear. I tightened my grip on the tablet and rushed into the silver wall.

4

The tablet vanished from my hands. With more momentum than I would have liked, I bumped along a long stretch of dead, dry grass, coming to a stop only when I'd become completely dizzy and disoriented. The stylus had left my hand, and no new tablet appeared for me to write my story again. If anything, I had freed myself of my terrible, endless fate.

Sensation and pain had abruptly returned, and I moved slowly, my old body tired and weary. The light from the sky caught my attention first. Above churned molten rock—swirls of black and red moving in great circles. The land I rested on was on a small island, maybe three or four miles across. The lava sky came down to the edges of the island, cutting off all escape. The legend of Death's imprisonment came to me immediately, and I knew Death was nearby.

The landscape was enough to confirm this notion. The ground was hilly and covered with short, dead grass. Trees, all gathered in scraggly copses, stood with bare, withered branches. Not a bird sang or a monkey moved about. The red lava sky, swirling improbably above, cast a terrible, stark light upon the land. Everything seemed made of shadow.

I waited, expecting some sort of attack. A monster of some kind. Agents of Death.

Nothing.

Waiting a while longer, I wallowed in the space of the island. Though small and surrounded on all sides by lava, it was far less cramped than the realm of the dead I'd visited earlier. The desire to never return to that place—at least not until I had made a story I wanted to write again and again—moved my legs forward. Without a specific plan, I started walking.

The dead grass crunched underfoot. The uncomfortable noise echoed dully in sharp contrast to the silence of the tiny land. With each step a solid thrum of anxiety traveled up my spine. Even Kyrethe's tears would be comfortable company in such a lonely place. Knowing that the weight of Death's Sea not only pressed down toward me, but cut me off from the rest of the world—the rest of all living things—added to a growing apprehension.

The hill I climbed was taller than those in the immediate area. From its top I saw that the rest of the land was no different from what I had already seen. Except for one feature. Toward the center of the dead island, on top of a massive, flat hill, stood a lovely building. White stones made up its base. From the base rose thick pillars, which formed the building's four walls. On top of the pillars rested an angled roof, which sloped down along the length of the building's longer sides.

The roof cast a deep shadow across the interior of the building, so that between the pillars I could see nothing. Though the structure was beautiful, it filled me with dread. The red glare of the lava above reflected off the smooth, white stones. Like the firelight of Mordom's henchmen back in my kaer, and the Death Sea's reflection on Kyrethe's white sheets, the sight brought to mind blood. This train of thought led me to think of the Elf Queen's thorns, my father's death, my mother's death, the mutilation of . . .

Blood and gore filled my narrative. I was weary of it. It wasn't just that my life was filled with violence. It was that my eyes saw spilled blood whenever possible. My imagination ran rich with the stuff. When anything suggested blood, I picked up the suggestion and let it wander around my mind.

Like the Horror in my head decades earlier. Things moving about in me. Old habits. Old sights. Old responses. I didn't want them, but they remained.

The building was the only item of interest in sight, and if I was to do anything to change the circumstances of my life, I would have to approach it.

Before long I realized I had misjudged not only the size of the island, but the size of the building. Both were much larger than I had originally assumed; most likely because I could not at first comprehend the size of the lava ceiling above me. As I walked on and on, the building loomed bigger and bigger. It towered above me. The pillars as wide as castles, high enough to reach the clouds. I had once thought that if I were to ever meet a dragon, the creature's size alone would freeze me in my tracks. Though the building did not live, its size had the same fearsome effect. At the base of the hill I simply stopped, my heart filled with dread. Some things are just too big to go near.

But again, what choice did I have? I started up the

hill, which was steeper than I had at first thought. After great exertion I reached the base of the building, which was made of white stones and several hundred feet high. From its top rose the pillars, which lifted toward the sky. As I leaned back, now directly under the pillars, the sight made me dizzy. Quickly I looked down at the ground, but it took me a few moments to regain my sense of balance.

Farther down I saw giant stone steps leading laboriously up to the top of the white stone base. After resting a bit against its wall, I walked to the stairs and began to climb. Each step was as tall as me, and had I not been a thief and used to climbing walls to reach valuables waiting within well-protected towers, I might not have made it. The climb up the stairs took what seemed hours, and I had to rest several times.

I could not see what waited on top of the base until I cleared the final step. When I had finally pulled myself up, my breath caught in my throat and I froze. Before me, dark and strange in the shadows of the roof, rested countless tablets. The kind on which I'd written my story. Dozens of them gathered in tall stacks in and around massive walls that rose haphazardly up to the ceiling. It took me a moment to realize that the walls themselves were also tablets. Piled so high and thick that they vanished into deep darkness above me.

The sensation of being dwarfed, both by the pillars and now the stacks of tablets, only increased as I pulled myself up onto the top of the base and stepped under the dark shadow of the massive roof. As I moved further in, the slight sound of my footsteps and breath echoed off the bare stone walls. The walls of tablets opened up into countless doorways, and I realized I was standing before a drunken and massive maze. The desolate, red-sky landscape behind me seemed a comforting memory now.

As silently as I could, I walked forward, choosing one of the openings in the walls at random. Along the ground were scattered countless tablets, all inscribed with the brief summation of too many lives to comprehend. Soon the walls cut me off from whatever illumination had slipped between the pillars, and I walked in absolute darkness. With one hand against the left wall, I tried to keep track of the way out as I walked on. But I quickly realized that many of the walls were small islands of tablets, stacked up one against another and disconnected from the rest of the stacks. It was, in fact, not a maze, but simply a disorganized collection of tablets. I encountered large, empty spaces with small stacks grouped between larger stacks. I found stairs leading up to platforms, also made of tablets, that ended in dead ends. Retracing my steps became a common necessity.

Soon I had no idea where I had come from, where I was going. The deep blackness poured into my vision, allowing me no rest from apprehension. I kept thinking some creature would leap out and rend me. But if there were monsters, they possessed a perverse patience. Nothing at all could be heard. I moved slower and slower, waiting for an attack. Surely, in such a strange and puzzling place, there would be monsters and guardians of some sort.

Then I thought to myself—remembering all the things I had done in my life—what need is there of monsters when J'role walks the maze?

Laughter, soft and distant, barely present in the air,

distracted me from my thoughts. A woman's laugh. It came, it seemed, from many directions. As I moved around trying to find the true source, it stopped. I waited, standing in the darkness, my breathing as quiet as I could make it. For a long time nothing more drifted down the corridors. I thought I heard a sigh, but it was too soft to help me seek out the source. The waiting continued, and then I finally heard someone let out a gasp of "Oh!" followed by the sound of weeping. Moving quickly, I found an opening between two stacks where the sound seemed the most firm. Releasing my concern for subtlety, I moved as quickly as I could through the corridors, trying to find the source of the noise before the tears stopped.

I heard the last few sniffles echoing down the corridor before the silence once more descended. I was close. I moved on in the direction I had been traveling. Thoughts of strange stories came to me, and I wondered if the sounds were the lure of a monster that would lead me deeper and deeper into the dark stacks, and then leave me there to die.

But as I turned a corner I saw the thin trace of red firelight flickering against a wall much further down a long stretch of stacks. Anxious and frustrated, I did not hesitate, but moved quickly down the long stretch of stone tablets. As I drew closer to the source of the light, I could see how high the tablets rose above me. Two walls of tablets stood on either side of me, dissolving into darkness hundreds of feet up and seeming to lean into each other as they rose. I could not be certain, but it looked as though they reached higher than the ceiling I'd seen from the outside would allow. Somehow, the interior had grown taller and taller as I'd traveled deeper into the building. Contained here, I felt certain, were all the infinite tablets written over and over again by all the infinite dead. Overstuffed passions and failed dreams, glimmers of hope and joy. My deep terrors and evil deeds seemed as if they were being squeezed from me, and I wondered how I could have so squandered my brief stay in the realm of the living.

Ahead, the firelight glowed brighter and brighter. Another bend in the corridor revealed another larger area. This one, however, contained a great many fires burning in urns crafted from bones. My eyes, accustomed now to deep darkness, could see nothing against the brilliant flames. But from that deep blackness between the flames I heard a woman's voice. With surprise, she said, "J'role?"

5

I stepped into the room, my eyes adjusting to the bright firelight. The urns, six of them, formed a large circle in a room made up of stacks and stacks of tablets piled up endlessly. In the center of the room sat a large table made of gray stone. Stone tablets were scattered over the table. Behind the table was a chair, also made of stone. A lovely woman, in her mid-thirties, rose from this chair and smiled at me. Her hair was short and black, her posture confident. Something about her eyes reminded me of Releana. Again she said, "J'role?" She smiled, a quizzical and pleased smile, as if she could not have foreseen my arrival, but now was so happy that I had, in fact, arrived.

For my part, a strange emotion came over me. From the way she stood when I arrived and the way she said my name, I felt from her a great affection. And with this affection she gave me, she drew forth from me an equal affection. It seemed, somehow, that she was a daughter—a daughter I knew I'd never had. But she warmed to me with what I imagined flowed between parents and children who love and respect each other.

"I'm . . . Yes, J'role," I answered. Before I could phrase my question—who was she and how did she

know my name?—she was out from behind the desk and walking briskly toward me. Her eyes were red from crying. She spread her arms wide and came to embrace me. Pressed her face against my cheek. At first I did not know how to react, but she held me for so long that I felt compelled to do something. So I encircled her with my arms and returned the embrace. We remained so for some time, and I felt the weight of my life slipping off me.

Eventually she stepped back, took my hands in hers. "You've been through so much, haven't you? I'm so, so sorry." She turned, and at the wave of her hand two chairs appeared, each carved of fine, shiny red wood. Leading me to them, she said, in an almost chiding voice, "Now. What are you doing here?"

She motioned for me to sit, but I said, "You're Death?" She stopped, smiled. Nodded, eyes bright with humor at my confusion. I said, "I was expecting someone more—"

"Evil? Menacing? Let me assure you, at times I am."

I knew that the Passions, when they appear to people, take on different forms—forms that make sense, though sometimes obliquely—to the viewer. I asked Death if her appearance was like that.

"Somewhat. It's very complicated." She sat down. She did not offer me the other chair, but seemed content to let me stand or sit as I desired. "Now, I assume that you . . ."

Abruptly I knelt beside her, took her hand in mine. I could not stop myself. "You remind me of someone."

The touch of good humor melted from her face,

leaving her sad. "I will look like someone you lost in life. I am Death."

"I never met anyone who looked like you before. Your eyes . . . They remind me of my wife's eyes. There's something about you . . ."

She looked down at her arms as if they were a new piece of jewelry or a gown tried on for the first time. "I look like a young woman to you? About the age of your boys? I may well be the daughter you might have had."

"I could have had a daughter?"

She shrugged, squeezing my hand. "Perhaps. Maybe with Releana, if things had worked out . . ." Her voice trailed off. She obviously did not want to discuss what might have been.

The notion of having a daughter filled me with both sadness and excitement. Sadness for the loss, excitement, for this woman seemed so confident and sure of herself. After a moment's thought, this confused me, and I said, "I can't imagine my boys being as sure of themselves as you are. I don't think I could have been the father to raise you."

She held her words for a moment, then decided to speak. "You're probably right. I am a person you lost in life. Someone that could have been part of your life, but also that could not have been. I am the lost opportunity of your life."

A sadness of a kind I had never experienced before coursed through me. I had always regretted my past. The possibility of lost futures had never entered my mind. As I looked up into her lovely face, I thought how wonderful it would have been to leave such a person in the world. To be remembered by people speaking of her—so strong and confident. Not singing songs of the cuts I made on the faces of my boys. I lowered my head, and tears began to fall.

"Shhh, shhh," she said, soothing me. She put her hands on my shoulders and drew me close, patting me. "It's all right. It's all right."

"It's not all right," I said. "Everything. Everything went wrong."

"But you're dead now. Nothing else can go wrong." She said the words as if they were more of a comfort to her than to me.

I pulled back. Still on my knees, I said, "That's why I came here. I must return to the realm of the living. There are things that I must—I don't know. Finish. Take care of."

She smiled, knowingly, suddenly full of age and playful wisdom. "Everyone has things to finish and take care of. Life, by its nature, is incomplete. That's what I offer. Completion."

I didn't quite know what she meant, but decided not to press the matter. "Yes," I said, my tone as tactful as I could muster. "Yes, well, I want that incompleteness again."

She sat back. Eyed me carefully. Stood. "I don't think you do." She walked behind the desk, raised her hand. Within moments a stack of tablets appeared on the table. Among them were tablets I'd written out. But when she read them out loud, she did not read the words I had written. She scanned them quickly, picking out key phrases. "Betrayed by mother. Father drank excessively. Mentor tortured you during initiation as thief adept . . ."

"What you're reading isn't what it says on the tablet."

"It's what I can see in your words. When you wrote your brief story, you layered it with thoughts and memories."

"Why do you make us write it again and again?"

She looked at me with slight exasperation. "Each time you write it, you invest something else into it. By focusing on it again and again, you remember more and more."

I realized I didn't care about the tablets, and pressed on with my need to live again.

"No," she said. "You're dead, you're mine now, and you'll write out your story until the end of time. Or until I've figured you people out."

"What people?" I asked.

"All of you. You people. You living people."

"What do you want to know?" In a moment of foolishness, I thought if she simply put the question straight to me, I could answer it and be on my way.

She placed her fingertips on the desk, and stared at me for a moment or two. Then she said, "Why do some people press through adversity while others succumb to it?"

"What?"

She repeated the question.

"I have no idea." I became incredulous. "What has that got to do with all those people trapped writing their stories over and over again?"

"I don't understand people. I want to understand."

So enchanted had I been with her mortal guise that I'd forgotten that she was, in fact, Death. Her reference to "people" snapped me back. "Is that why you kill us? To understand?"

She looked down at the table. "I've been through this with you mortals before. You never understand. Neither of us should make pretend you will. But I have a special fondness for you, J'role. You have been through so much horror in your life, and still you went on. I'll be as clear as I can. Unless there is closure in life, unless there is death, there is no meaning, nothing for me to learn from. It is not simply that mortality gives all of you perspective—a sense that your days matter. It is that only upon someone's death can a life story be told. Until that point, there is always the possibility that the arc of the narrative will change drastically. What had before been mere insignificant details can suddenly take on major importance. What was once the major thrust of one's life can suddenly change into meaninglessness. Only in death can the proper study of a life be made."

I took several steps back from the table. "We die only because you want to understand us?"

"Yes," she sighed. "The Universe made you all, and now I want to understand you. The Passions don't appreciate it, but there it is. They would want you all to live forever."

"What would be wrong with that?"

She looked at me, confused. Smiled. "Wrong? I didn't say it would be wrong. It's just not what I want."

"You cause all the grief among the living for your own *curiosity*? You kill people, leave orphans, widows—"

She stood straight. "I don't think *you* should chastise me for causing grief, J'role."

"No. I suppose not. So we die and then write out stories until you learn everything you need to learn from us—"

"I never stop learning. I could read each person's story over and over again. There's always something."

I slammed my hands down on the table. "I don't want to write the same story forever and ever. I must get back. You *must* let me out of this. I've been living in the past—in the pain of my childhood—*forever*! I need . . . I need to be an adult. To live in the world, not trapped in the pain of years past."

She sat down, visibly upset. "You should have thought of that before you tossed your life away into molten rock."

"That was a mistake!" I said, clutching at my forehead. I wheeled around, overwhelmed by the insanity of the words, the ideas. "I want to take it back."

"Death isn't like that. *I'm* not like that."

"Please," I said very softly. "People have gone back. I know it happens. A man I killed went back. Please. I want to do what you said. Change my narrative. I don't want to be trapped in the old story anymore."

"Those people, those who return, have people who care for them," she said matter-of-factly. "Who work hard to make miracles happen."

"I don't have anyone like that," I told her through clenched teeth. "No one will miss me."

Her face softened. "I know, J'role. But you have a place here. I care about you. I really do."

In that moment I knew she did. She really did. My story, my pain, meant something to her. And not just because I was an interesting subject for study. She cared about people simply because we all mattered to her. I had at first thought her search for understanding some sort of cold exercise, but I realized she really was filled with empathy and compassion. I felt my resolve weaken. If I went back to the realm of the living, I would risk failure again. If I stayed with Death, I would be safe. My memories would be of pain, but I would know them. There was comfort in that.

But Neden. "There's someone I must rescue."

"Others can do that. You life is over."

"*I* have to do it."

"You can't."

"And Kyrethe. She's alone—I . . ."

"I know. She will die there. Or not. It is no longer your concern."

Her words were true, and the truth struck me powerfully. They weren't my concern. I did not have to do anything. To care. Yet I did. I wanted to get back to them. To help.

She studied my face. "You aren't willing to accept that, are you?"

"No. I can't. I mean—I can. I just don't want to. I'm *choosing* not to."

She smiled at that. "Interesting. Why did you kill yourself then?"

"I told you. A mistake?"

"A dramatic mistake."

"I'm a dramatic person."

She laughed. "I don't give up the dead lightly. I so want you all near me. But sometimes, if someone can help me understand, I'll give them a second chance at life."

"Yes," I begged.

"Then tell me. Why do some people persevere through adversity, and others become swallowed up by it? Why did you surrender your will to the Therans, and your wife bend her entire being to the act of escaping? Why did you survive for sixty years, despite all the horrible things done to you and all the guilt you suffered for the horrible things you did to others, only for you to one day decide to remove yourself from a life in a strange impulse?"

The questions were so big they made me step back. In my mind there was only a black void. I could not, for the life of me, think of even how to approach the question.

"I don't . . . ," I began, then realized the truth would not serve me well now. "I need time."

"Time you have plenty of," said Death. And with that she vanished.

6

She took the table, the chairs, the massive urns with the fires. She took everything but the darkness. The abrupt departure startled me terribly, and for a while I simply stood, waiting for some new surprise. But when nothing happened, I settled to the floor and tried to figure out Death's mystery.

I never did.

I thought of the two dwarfs—one happy, one miserable. The happy dwarf pulled himself out of his misery when he raised his hammer high. Why?

I thought of my mother, trying to make everyone perfect because she wasn't. She sacrificed me to her fears of the Horror, rather than confronting the beast itself. Why?

I thought of Releana, who may have sometimes lacked hope when we sought you and Torran, but her perseverance never failed. Why?

Kyrethe in the tower, alive after all these years, scratching out her story in stone. Waiting for her life to turn. Why?

What allows two people from almost the same background to be faced with similar circumstances—

painful, harsh circumstances—and one to overcome the circumstances, and the other to wallow in misery?

Theories popped into my head, one after another.

The Passions gave us unexpected impulses. But we called on the Passions. They could not give what we did not already have.

Some souls were just different than others. But that would not explain what was different about the souls, and that I could not figure out.

Some days were worse than others. But depressions sometimes lasted years. Why did some end and others linger on?

I hadn't a clue.

I waited a long time in the darkness, thinking and thinking until I could think no more. Why do some people persevere and others become overwhelmed? I still do not know.

Death finally returned, and I was glad, for I had become frustrated and wanted only to seal my fate.

"What can you tell me about mortals and my question?" she said.

"I have nothing to add. It is as much a mystery to me as to you."

"Strange how mortals always say that. I'm Death, not like you people at all. I understand that mortals will be difficult for me to comprehend." She smiled. "But that you are still a mystery to yourselves. Despite all of your trade and the cities you build and your magic—you still don't know who you are."

"Will you please let me go?"

"Why do you want to leave me?"

She said it with such sincere concern that I didn't

know how to answer at first. But neither could I stand the idea of writing my story again and again. I said so.

"But it is *your* story," countered Death. "Revel in it."

"Really, I can't. I've lived it. If I'm going to write something for the rest of my life, it's got to be something different."

"No, J'role. This is the life you made for yourself. This is the story you'll write."

I didn't think to argue that some of my life had been handed to me by my parents. I felt doomed. Then I remembered what I'd overheard about Mordom's plan. I asked, "Is it true that when enough blood is spilled in the lands around your sea, you will be released?"

"I have heard as much, but I do not truly know."

"But it might be true."

"Yes. It might be."

"And if you are one day released?"

"I will claim people more often. Resurrections will be impossible. I will gather more and more stories, and I will keep those stories here."

These words disquieted me, but I made my proposal anyway. "The man I mentioned before, who was raised from the dead, Mordom—" She smiled ruefully, nodded. "He has a plan to prevent a war from taking place in Barsaive. He plans to resolve a conflict between Thera and Throal peacefully, through guile and deception." Death was interested, and leaned toward me. "If I were to stop him, the conflict would continue, and it would most likely lead to violence."

She thought for a moment, then walked around her desk and sat down. "J'role, this isn't like you. Your violence comes unexpectedly. Helping me become free?

That requires both premeditation and the acceptance that you might soon be responsible for countless lives being cut short."

"Only if the conflict then leads to violence."

"Which, knowing mortals, it most likely will."

"It's a risk I'm willing to take." I surprised myself when I said this. Backed into a corner, I was willing to try to prevent Mordom's plan at the risk of releasing Death.

"No guilt?"

"It's not just for me. I don't want Mordom to complete his plan. I don't want him to hurt the boy. I don't want him to control Throal."

"But it is for you. You're asking me to let *you* go. My question to you is, why should I? Someone else may stop this Mordom. Or countless other things could go wrong. Why should I release you to handle this?"

"Because," I said slowly, the response growing firmer in my head as I formed the words, "if you let me go back, with such a firm goal, when I return, as I undoubtedly someday will, the story I write might well reveal something about the nature of your question. Certainly I've reached a very low state. If I fail, and cannot transcend myself, then we'll know about the power of failure. But if I succeed, surely something can be gleaned as to why some people move on with their lives."

A smile, pleased and coy, formed on her lovely face. "You're very good. I wish you well, and I hope your actions make the blood of Barsaive flow freely." She waved her hand. All of my tablets vanished from the table save one. She picked it up and handed it to me. "Destroy it, and you are free."

"Where will I be when I'm . . ."

"Resurrected?"

"Yes."

"Somewhere in time and space near the point in time and space of your death. It is imprecise. Mortals who raise the dead call that person to them. But when you destroy the tablet, you destroy the story. The ending no longer exists."

"Minutes from the time I died? Weeks?"

"Anything. Near."

"I could end up standing on your sea and die again instantly."

She smiled. I knew immediately that she had already considered that option. "But at least you'll have tried."

"That would make it a new story, wouldn't it?"

"Oh, yes."

I raised the tablet. Death looked at me, eyes sad. I did not want to disappoint her. I did not want to disappoint myself. What if I went back to my life, and things remained the same? What if they became worse? Fear crept along my strength, tickling it gently, distracting it. I had already made a mess of my life. Why did I think I could do it better now?

I met Death's eyes. She loved me. I could see it so clearly. For her, I was a fascinating person with a fascinating life. She loved people. She did not dismiss me in the face of all others who had lived and died. Suddenly I knew that whatever might come, my life, my narrative, did matter. I mattered. Death, I realized, looked at me with the eyes I wished my mother had possessed. She had given me something my mother never had. A sense of worth.

I dashed my life's story to the ground.

7

Up through molten rock. Fiery liquid flowed around me, burned with exquisite heat. It melted my flesh, burning off one layer at a time. Everything I'd loved about pain came to me, pleasing me. I'd grown comfortable with it over the years, and it reminded me I was alive. It was what I knew.

But soon the heat and pain grew too much for me to bear. No longer controllable—like wounds I inflicted on myself, or the bites I had asked for from Releana, knowing she would only go so far. The heat penetrated deeper than my flesh, into the center of my being. The source of my life, my soul, was scorched by the terrible, fiery blast. The molten rock poured into me. I had never realized how pain of the flesh meant *nothing* against pain of the soul. The agony of my life coursed through me, not as a dull ache that met me each day as I awoke, or the nagging longing for something better, a happiness now lost but remembered from better days. I remembered this:

A boy, me, six years old. I sat inside my home, on the floor. Before me, a collection of wooden blocks my father had been given by his father, handed down through the generations in our kaer. The light was soft on my skin, light from glowing, warm white moss. My focus, on the blocks. I was building a city—what my father told me cities had looked like. Walls around them. Tall buildings. Streets. My small hands, still awkward with the large blocks, moved them carefully into place. Composing, somehow, without training, with an eye toward balance. Scale. I knew when things looked right. Changed them when they were off. The task of construction absorbed my thinking; time passed without notice. We knew we might leave the kaer soon. It might happen when I was still a child. I had dreams then of helping to rebuild the world. I would construct cities. Plan for the happiness of others. From the dreams of my mind and the minds of others, towers would be built. Reality would be formed from dreams. And through it all, the habit of pleasure. Building from a love of building.

I had not remembered the moment for years and years. In it, everything had been right. I was alive, being me, and that had been enough.

The loss of decades of my life to misery swept through me all at once. I screamed, molten rock gurgling through my throat. I wept—tears of blood rushed down my cheeks. Everything I'd gotten used to, the compromises, one after another, accepting life as one endless disappointment so that I no longer felt the full surge of misery, suddenly came clean and fresh into my awareness. It washed away all my assumptions, my habits of misery. I became all too aware of my pain, and it seemed impossible that I should live as I had.

I knew that I had to stop the pain. It was all over. I did not know how to do it, but the pain had to be healed. Getting by would no longer do. Death would not do. I needed to be healed. I wanted to live the promise of *life*.

I broke the surface of the molten rock. The bright light of day blinded me. And suddenly, I was alive.

I stood at the top of the stairs reading Kyrethe's story, the words she had carved into the wall:

Should I kill myself?

I was twenty when I came here. How old am I now?

Why do I still live?

How many years?

Everything was quiet. Though a moment ago it had been bright outside, now it was night. The red light of Death's Sea spilled in through the windows, shining bright in the glass vials on the shelves. I pressed my fingers to my chest. I could not believe I truly lived, that I had flesh on my bones. I smiled, a strange lightness overtaking me. Truly now I felt freedom for the first time in so many years.

The baby, Lochost, the Passion of freedom, appeared beside me, smiling. An inversion of the normal: a baby smiling proudly at an adult. "I didn't think I'd ever see you again." His voice was small and slight, like that of any child.

I reached out, taking him into my arms, his floating body coming easily into my embrace. He was warm and comfortable against me. I thought of you and Torran and realized I'd never held you with such abandon. Freedom does not come from escaping the entanglement of other people's lives.

I cried for a moment, just a moment, and his small hands pressed up against my neck. His fingers curled slightly. Relief came to me in throbbing waves. Then he said, "J'role. You must hurry." It took a moment for the words to register. As I held him away from me, he said, "If you wish to retain your freedom, stop yourself now."

"Stop myself?"

He nodded.

I looked around the room. Something about it seemed familiar. Not just the place. The time.

I understood.

I raced down the stairs, leaving the child floating in the air, ancient concern on his small, smooth face.

8

I sat on the edge of the bed. Kyrethe's bed. My back to me. My fingers on Kyrethe's gray hair. This was not a Passion, as Raggok had appeared before me as me when I committed suicide. This was really me. It staggered my powers of comprehension. "It's very complicated," Death had said, and so it was.

The scene was exactly as it had been—when? In my memory, some time ago, the night before I killed myself. But also *now*. It was happening now. At the base of the stairs I stood stunned, astounded by the sight. The red light of the lava caressed the coiled white sheets of the bed and canopy. Kyrethe slept peacefully, unaware of what I was doing. It was strange—stranger than I can ever express—seeing the events unfolding. The situation was mine. I'd already lived it. But now I was outside of it. I'd slipped out of myself.

"Stop!" I shouted at myself. Kyrethe, of course, did not stir, unaware of any sound in the room.

My double turned, shocked to find me standing at the base of the stairs. I—he—stood. Turned his head slightly. Examined me. Mouth open slightly.

And I examined him. His face shocked me. So dark, twisted. So much anger. A scowl etched in granite. Did

I really look like that? Could I really have never noticed?

"Who are you?" he asked.

"You," I replied.

He stepped toward me. "You're a Passion?" As he walked closer, a shadow began forming from the wall behind him, seeping out into the room. He was breathing quickly. I remembered breathing quickly the night I attacked Kyrethe.

"I'm you," I answered.

"No. You're not. You've an idiotic grin on your face."

I knew I was not smiling, but touched my mouth to be sure. No. I was not smiling. What did he see in me? I said, "I'm you, and you've got to stop this madness."

"I don't know who you are—which Passion—but I'm turning my back on you. I'm not doing anything wrong. Just touching her." He stepped back to the bed. Sat down at the edge. Carefully picked up her hand. Gently kissed it.

"Leave her alone," I said firmly.

"Leave me be," he answered. "I have no need of you here." The shadow had worked its way up to him. It was as deep and dark as the dead sky of a cloud-covered night. It was so palpable that I couldn't believe I had ever doubted its existence.

Taking a few cautious steps forward, I said, "I'm not a Passion. But you feel the thing beside you. You must. That's the Passion ruling you now."

He froze, aware of the thing beside him, but also unaware. I knew because he was me, and I'd lived my life getting more and more used to that thing near me.

"Go away," he said to me, and took Kyrethe's hand and raked her nails lightly over his face.

My revulsion with myself the night I attacked Kyrethe had overwhelmed me. Had led to suicide. But seeing it before me, played out, so disturbed me that my breathing stopped. That was me! For the first time there was no screen of pain between my actions and my thoughts. My hands began to tremble. Kyrethe was so helpless. She had no power. What had I thought I was doing? There was no sexual component to my actions at all. Nothing but power. Abusive, cowardly power. The perversity of my actions came clear to me—perhaps fully for the first time.

"Stop it!" I screamed.

He did not look at me. "Go away." He began running his tongue along her wrist.

I grabbed him, dragged him off the bed. We tumbled to the floor, the red-lit stone a blur of sharp pain against my right elbow, my back. He ended up on top, whirled around, slammed his right fist, backhanded, across my chin. My lip slammed up into my teeth and blood curled out over my flesh, slipped into my mouth.

The shadow swirled around my other self, coming to rest behind him. Took form. A tall man with a ram's head. Bloody sores covered the Passion's flesh. Raggok. The Passion placed his hands on my other self. Instantly, in my eyes, I saw the madness. I'd never seen it before, only experienced it. But I knew it immediately. The same madness that had let me kill my father. Let me mutilate my sons. Let me run from Releana's soft touch.

"Don't . . ." I began, but I—he—was possessed by the Passion of bitterness. I saw so clearly how he hated me. He raised his fists high, brought them down toward my chest.

I tried to roll out of the way, but Raggok waved his hand. Suddenly, memories of my mother's touch, her fingertips on my chest as she placed the Horror in my head, came back to me. I froze. Unable to move. The fists slammed down. A sharp crack across my ribs. Pain like a razor's edge sliced through me. I exhaled, a sound like wind through trees, and found I could not breathe.

My other self raised his fists again. Between the painful memories of my mother's betrayal and my cracked ribs, I found I could hardly move. *But how I wanted to.* For the first time in my life I faced death and did not see it as simply part of the day. Death, I realized, had been waiting for me all along, because I had been waiting for her to take me all along. I risked death in the hope I would lose the risk, and finally be freed of life without being viewed as a coward. But now, now I wanted to live. I had something I'd never thought I could have again—hope. And losing it so quickly drove me on to struggle.

The child appeared above my head, facing me upside down, smiling. He leaned down, kissed my forehead. His touch freed me of the crippling memories. A breeze coursed through my damaged chest, and I found that I had enough energy to roll out of the way. My other self slammed his fists down into my right shoulder. Painful, but not lethal.

I swung my hand up, blocking another blow. We were both old men, somewhat weary with life, but driven, as always, by fresh violence. I slipped away from him, scrambled up. Turned. "We don't have to do this," I said. The thought of attacking myself was much like looking over the side of an airship when the ground is far, far below.

But my other self did not need to believe me; probably could not. He did not know what I knew. On his face, that rage. He carried his hatred in his flesh, and let his flesh bring his hatred to the world. He ran at me.

The blows went back and forth. I swung, he ducked. He swung, I parried. We staggered. We sprawled.

It is strange to fight yourself. I knew all my own tricks. I ran the same game endlessly against myself, thought all the while I was making progress. But all the while, the habits in my head were known—if you will—by my head. Just when I thought I'd outsmarted myself, had finally found a new plan of attack to get me out of the rut, I'd—that is, he—would counter and bring me back into the old habits.

The two Passions hovered at the edge of the conflict. Painful memories lanced my thoughts, and Lochost freed me each time. The longer the struggle continued, the less the thoughts interfered. There was little to do against the damage I could inflict on myself.

It was clear after a while, however, that I—he—meant to kill me if he got the chance. And why wouldn't he? Wouldn't he soon be committing suicide?

After he gave me a terrible swift kick, sending me reeling toward the bed, I glanced at Kyrethe. My impact on the bed startled her, but she only shifted, rolling back to sleep. Looking at her, I remembered the happy dwarf's words about how he saw his wife's body. She was no longer an object of lust, a thing to be *done to*. Her flesh embodied her story. When he touched her, he did so because he knew her story, because he loved her story, wanted to read her story. Add to her story. I knew Kyrethe's terrible story. I could see her now not as something to conquer, but as a person to communicate with—perhaps through the flesh, but in so many other ways as well.

But if I did not survive the fight, she would be at the mercy of my other self. He approached, carefully, and I got off the bed, leading him away from her.

Blood poured down from my split lip. I could feel where my skin had turned sharp red along my face and chest from his blows. Thinking had become difficult, and I moved with cautious steps. So did he. We were two battered old men.

He lunged toward me, sending his fist up toward my chest. I suspected as much, ducked out of the way. Grabbed his arm. Twisted it sharply, turning it around his back. He screamed out in terrible pain. But I did not know how else to end the struggle. It seemed I had little choice but to kill myself once more.

He collapsed to his knees. Tried to turn around. I brought my knee up into his face. He sprawled backward, a smear of blood dripping from his broken nose. Knowing I needed only a moment to collect myself with a tricky strategy to escape, I dropped down on him, driving my knee into his stomach. He gasped. I grabbed his head, slammed it down. A sharp crack of skull against stone. His hands fumbled for my neck, found it. The grip, strangely strong. I slammed his head again, and he continued to strangle me.

As my efforts continued, his grip weakened. But I was already beginning to black out. I wondered briefly if this was my end, to commit suicide all over again, finally removing myself and all possibilities of my life forever.

Then, out the corner of my eye, I noticed that Raggok and Lochost had become completely still. It was as if they were frozen in time and space, the same way other mortals are frozen when Passions appear as a specific individual. But this time, the Passions had frozen. My encounter with myself had transcended the Passions. Whatever was to occur as we reached the moments of our respective deaths was ours to discover, and ours alone.

I no longer had the strength to slam his head against the floor, so I turned my attention to his throat. Because I was on top of him, I had the advantage. I only needed to lean down on him, force the constriction of his throat. A gurgling noise came from his throat.

He looked terrified. The madness was gone, and I saw a lonely old man, the flesh wrinkled, the life going from him. He knew he was about to die, and realized what that meant. The hope and opportunities gone. Everything I had confronted in the realm of the dead he was becoming aware of now.

A joy took possession of me. I pressed my hands tighter on his throat. I wanted him to DIE! Suddenly I knew what a terrible monster he was, this thing that had been my life before the new me. A strange confidence slid into my thinking; a peculiar knowledge of what was right and what was wrong. Unshakable. I was right, he was wrong. His hands slipped from my throat. His eyelids fluttered. The new certainty thrilled me. I had lost all doubts about killing him.

A darkness seeped into the edges of my vision. I ignored it.

As he died, my new, doubt-free self became stronger. Nothing could ever make me waver. Nothing could ever make me think about another person. Years had been spent worrying about the pain I'd caused others. What about my own pain?

The darkness wrapped all the way around me. Tightened.

The face beneath me turned slightly blue. I laughed. A terrible laugh that raked the last shred of compassion in my ears. But I did hear it. I looked down at the old man. The lines in the face, their clarity, startled me.

Killing myself again.

I released my grip. His mouth open, the tongue visible. Just a shallow breath. Touching his skin, my worn, wrinkled fingers touched his worn, wrinkled flesh. I did not want to kill myself anymore. I remembered Death's last look.

Worth.

If I was worth something, was not my old self worth something? Hadn't he tried for sixty years to attain something more? He failed, but kept trying. Hurt people, but kept trying. Others, I knew, would judge him harshly. Wanted him dead. But he was me. If I couldn't draw him close, who would I ultimately be?

I leaned down. Touched my cheek against his. His pain became mine. Our flesh flowed together. Finally letting all the hatred out of my body, I lay down beside him, put my arms around him. Held him close. I held a story in my flesh as well, and embraced it. Past and present became one, ready to risk the future. The pain of my life mixed with hopes of happiness, producing the possibility of compassion. The evil of my past joined with my desire to make amends, allowing me to become—me.

9

I opened my eyes. My other self was gone. I was just me. The shadow was gone. The child was gone. Or rather, not visible. Both bitterness and hope resided comfortably in me now. The fight had exhausted me, and I could not get up. The floor was cold, but horizontal, and that was enough. Closing my eyes, I slept.

Kyrethe woke me up when she tripped over me.

She called out in surprise, falling forward. Kyrethe called out again, asking if I was the man from downstairs. Instinctive discomfort seized my emotions, for I felt terrible and shamed by what I had done to her. How could I possibly explain myself?

Then I remembered: I hadn't done it. Or at least, she did not know I had done it. To her, it had not happened. I smiled, my face, I'm sure, cracking under the strain of smiling so broadly for the first time in so many years. Suddenly the Universe wasn't turned against me, nor I against the Universe. I stood, moved quickly to where she sat crouched, waiting for a possible attack. I let my fingers touch hers, pushing hard enough for her to notice me despite her lack of touch. She pulled away quickly, then tentatively extended her hand again. She took my hand in hers and squeezed it tight. Then I took her other hand and placed it on my face so she could be certain it was me.

With the same awkwardness as the day before (years might have passed in the realm of the dead, for all I knew, but for Kyrethe only a night had gone by), she pressed her fingertips against me. Her need to search out every curve and line of my flesh tickled and amused me, and I laughed. When her fingertips found my smile and traced the shape, she smiled too.

Behind her, light from a clear blue sky rushed in through the windows, illuminating the sheets with pure clarity. The sky itself fascinated me, the little bit I could see through the rectangular window. I did not think I'd seen the sky so blue before. Then I realized I'd never really noticed it. A strange airiness entered my chest, and I felt grateful to the Universe for taking the time to construct colors for us to enjoy.

Kyrethe and I stood. Hand in hand. Her grip on me so tight it hurt. I let her hold on tightly, because it was the only way she could keep track of me.

The sky caught my attention again. I thought back to the day when I created the city. I thought, "What am I going to build today?"

When I looked at the beautiful woman whose hands I held in mine, I knew that today I wanted to build a friendship. I led her to the bed, sat her down on the edge. "I need my water," she said with her strained and awkward voice. In response I took her finger and jabbed it firmly into my chest. Then I placed her hand in mine, as if I were giving her the cup, and raised her hand to her lips. Then once more I pointed her hand to me.

She smiled. "Thank you."

I went downstairs to get the water.

There, at the fountain, I saw the statue of her father. Standing imperious, the source of the precious substance that sustained his daughter's life. Arrogantly, I hated him. Then I remembered my own crimes, and silenced myself.

When I returned with the cup, I saw that Kyrethe's face wore an expression of fear mixed with impatience. She could not allow herself to truly believe I would come back, perhaps. Or waited for the attack that she knew, properly, was possible. Picking up her hand to place the cup in it once again startled her, making her tremble. But again, after a moment, she relaxed. She took a long sip, and then said, "You're feeling better now?"

Her words, strained and awkward, did not make me embarrassed, as they had the day before. Now I heard in them hope and strength. Perseverance. I raised her hand to my head, nodded. She laughed.

"Have you had any?" she asked, extending the cup to me. I took it, drank. The lovely liquid tasted more brilliant against my tongue than it had the day before.

Wonderful things were possible in life, despite everything to prove the contrary.

I smiled. I raised her hand to my smile, and she smiled again.

What was I going to build? A friendship.

Days passed. I wanted to go after Neden, but there was no way off the island. I called for Lochost to help me, but the Passions do not arrive upon request. They are present simply when their Passion is present. Instead of fretting over what I could not do, I did what I could. I treated Kyrethe well.

Each morning and night I brought her water. For days she jumped whenever I touched her. After a week, she took my arrival with stoic stillness. But another week passed before my touch was something she could take in stride. That she could enjoy.

When it finally happened, I decided to give her a gift. The only thing I could think of—and I had waited many days before I thought it would be appropriate to give it to her—was to massage her hands. At midday I took her fingers in mine and rubbed them between my own fingers. She was startled, wary, at first. Pulled away.

I was disappointed. Angry even. But I thought it through, reminded myself that she had her own very good reasons for distrusting a stranger who wanted intimacy with her. She held the hand I had tried to massage in her other hand, cradled it. Then she looked up, a little bit toward me, concerned. I raised her hand to my face. Smiled. She sighed, smiled.

Days later, unexpectedly, she extended her hands toward me after drinking from the morning cup. I took them, and she waited. Coyly, she smiled. I understood. I massaged her fingers. Though the feeling in her flesh was gone, the muscles still knew the truth of motion. It was a simple action. I tended to each finger separately, then moved on to the back of the hand. The heel. Then placed the whole hand within my hands. Then I did the same for the other hand and the other fingers. Halfway through she was sighing. Her happiness took her out of herself, out of her awareness of me.

This went on for another week, until she offered, after I had massaged her hand, to massage mine. Her touch was rough, for she could not feel me except by pressing hard. But she did it with generosity. And I, as you know, have always had a penchant for rougher affection. Her massage did not lead me down the bleaker elements of this, though. No thoughts of blood came to mind. It simply felt good.

After another week we added arms to our mutual exchange, and sometime after that we would take turns lying on the bed, rubbing and soothing our old muscles. That after so many years of life and solitude, for both of us, that we should have this opportunity simply to relax in each other's company—

I'd been on the run for so long. Stealing. Pursued by the agents of angry merchants. The soldiers of King Varulus after me for my crimes against my sons. To lie on that bed, face down, Kyrethe straddling me with her thin body, her hands pushing down on my shoulders, with nowhere to go and nothing to run from. I was trapped with patience, and patience became my friend.

How long had gone by, I do not know. The days had blurred into casual pleasure. Clouds floating leisurely through a perfect blue sky. One day I straddled her hips, massaging her shoulders. The most extraordinary thing happened. I wanted to touch her. Not to hurt her, or draw blood, or have her tear my flesh. But simply to—share. Her story, the narrative bound up in her flesh. To read the tale with my fingers.

I touched my fingers to her face lightly, forgetting, for just a moment, her condition. There was no response. No smile in turn. No sigh. Not even a shock of surprise. She could not feel. And with that lack of response, the impulse died in me. If she could not feel my touch, it felt tainted. Touching was not something one person could do. Both people touched. Without the sharing of the touch, one person was master over the other. I had lived my share of enslavement, as well as dominating those who had no power.

I did not know what to do, whether to go on massaging her. I wanted more. Wanted to give myself. Finally I remembered her words in the story, those telling how her mother used to hold her. If I could not touch her with love gently, I would hold her with love firmly. I got off her, slid next to her. She got up, alert, ready for trouble. Not from me. She reached her hand out for mine. But she did not know why I had stopped the massage.

Placing my back against the headboard, I pulled her close. This startled her, and then she was afraid of me. But when I did not pull her, she slowly, hesitantly, lowered her head against my chest. I waited until she was comfortable with it. Her hand pressed against my chest, as if ready to push herself away from me, ready for trouble.

I put my hand on hers, just heavily enough to let her know I had done it. Nothing dramatic. Flair was for the stories. Here, with our damaged lives, a slower pace was required. Finally she let her weight press against mine. After a moment of tension, she sighed. Comfortable. With the words of her narrative in my mind, I wrapped my arms around her flesh. I tightened just enough for her to know my arms were around her. Her father may have imprisoned her touch, but around that prison, I offered a siege of affection. She sighed again, snuggled against me.

Strange. I felt strange. Good, but strange. Different. No motion. No frantic need to escape affection or prove it. Simply present with someone. Offering something simple, and receiving something simple. Yet so—so—There are no words for it, I suppose, which is why we share part of our stories with touch.

10

We rested like that for a very long time. Fell asleep. When we woke, we were still in each other's arms. I went to get the liquid from the fountain. We drank. Then she pulled me close, and we held each other again. Outside, through the window, the stars shone clearly over the red, glowing sea. I remembered all my star maps, my attempts to correlate events in my life with the patterns of the stars. At no time had I ever conceived of circumstances so strange and so gentle in my life.

After a while I found myself becoming fidgety. But Kyrethe seemed content to hold me tight. Thoughts of my mother returned, panicked me. Made me tighten my grip. Kyrethe simply cuddled closer. I relaxed again. A ridiculously obvious revelation flashed across my thoughts—Kyrethe was not my mother. Would never be.

I relaxed.

Days passed. Massages and cuddling. Kyrethe wanted to dance. Dances from her childhood, close and intimate. I was completely unprepared. Since Garlthik had initiated me in the ways of the thief adept so many years before, motion was a very private thing. Secretive and silent. Her dance—danced to a tune she hummed so badly it made me laugh with pleasure at her earnestness—made us dance together. Closely. Slowly. With care and respect for the other person. It took me time. I kept moving away from her, embarrassed. She was patient. She taught me to wait. Hand in the hand. Hand around the waist; each touch, mattered.

Dancing. Massages. Hugs. I did not kiss her, for I still did not want to take from her lips what her lips could not receive.

She startled me awake one night with abrupt motion. I tried to calm her down, but she jerked her arms away from me, sitting back. In the starlight I saw her touch her face. A smile appeared, which quickly dissolved as tears filled her eyes. She touched them, the tears, and pressed her hands together. She smiled again. Placed her fingertips against her lips. Rubbed the moisture against them. I only had time to realize what was happening when she put her hands out blindly toward me, found my face, and pressed it as she had so many times before. Exploring. But this time the touch was light. She could feel.

Her breathing became surprised and labored as her body wracked with sobs. She laughed as tears streamed down her face. "I can touch!" she exclaimed. "I can touch!" Laughter and tears came to me as well, and in all of my life, as a witness to many strange events, I had never seen anything so miraculous. We embraced, our tears mingling on our cheeks, and more tears came to me as I realized how wonderful it was that she could feel my tears.

Our faces became slick from our tears, and we laughed and pulled away from each other. Over and over again she told me she could feel. She touched my face again, then the fabric of my ragged clothes. "Torn!" she shouted with glee. She grabbed the fabric of the sheets, clutched it in her hand. Drove her face into the material. She stumbled out of bed, still blind, but too excited to care about careful movement. She froze on the smooth stone floor, smiling, letting the soles of her feet enjoy the sensation of stepping out of bed; a sensation so long lost to her. She then scraped her feet against the floor, sliding, twirling. Then she dropped to the floor, pressed her face to the stone.

A breeze came in through the window, warm and dry. Instantly alert, she raised herself from the floor. She started for the window. I was out of the bed in a flash, hand on her elbow, making sure she didn't plunge to her death in her haste. "Air! I can feel the air. A wind!" We reached the window. The breeze caught up her hair, made it blow around her head. She smiled so happily—not a day over six, suddenly aware of the beauty of the world. She raised her arms wide, laughing. She turned to me. "Take me outside! Take me outside!"

And so I did. With care I walked her over the rough stones. "It hurts!" she said happily, for our feet were bare, and the stones did scrape a bit. "I love it! And the air! There is air everywhere!"

We reached the top of a small hill and she spread her arms wide. Laughing, laughing, laughing, turning every once in a while, lost in her perceptions. Never in my life had I seen anyone so beautiful. I had thought beauty was something that sat on the flesh. It is not. Beauty is the ability to perceive more beauty.

A new impulse of excitement clutched her wildly, and she blindly sent her arms out to find me. Our hands met, and she pulled me close to her. Softly, like a child with a careful secret, she said, "I can feel." The laughter had subsided now, and the weight of the miracle filled her voice. I touched her lips with my fingers. She pressed her fingers against my lips. Tentatively, we touched each other's faces, exploring cheeks, forehead. The curve of the ear. Our hands slid around the back of each other's head. We drew closer.

We kissed.

The air around us, warmed by the sea, swirled in light breezes. Sweat began to form, smooth our skin, sliding. Kyrethe's breathing increased in pace. She kissed my neck. I pulled her closer. Her hands fumbled for my clothes and with unexpected energy she ripped my shirt open.

The time of patience had come to an end.

I scooped her up in my arms. All the while I carried her she kissed my chest. Pressed her tongue against my flesh and tasted my sweat. Dragged her fingertips down my back. I felt the Passion of Astendar around us, encouraging our frantic abandon into lust. Without noticing the steps of the journey, we arrived at the bed. Our clothes on the floor. I kissed her shoulder. She ran her hands over my head. Both of us sighing—gasping—with pleasure. All of her was a delight to touch. To discover. She seemed to enjoy exploring me as well. Each of us finding each spot that made the other laugh with the joy of touching. Being touched.

Frantic in energy, but slow in time, we delighted each other for hours. When finally I entered her, the coupling spread out to all our flesh, now shared, our stories intertwining, not as an incident, but as a shared narrative.

Time passed, thrusting. Nips and licks; laughter, sighs and gasps. She began giggling uncontrollably. Her laughter, her belly shaking wildly against mine, was infectious. We laughed and laughed, our laughter transforming into shrieks of ecstasy, bodies quivering wildly, arms and legs wrapped tightly against each other for love and safety. Our bodies froze, tense, Astendar with us, discreetly, somewhere, I know, the moment extended by the Passion's presence, the world outside no longer a concern. We had, damaged though we both were, met, connected. Shared.

Long gasps rushed from us as we exhaled, time starting again. We did not unravel our limbs, but stayed tangled, flesh against flesh. Content. Sweaty and wet. We kissed. Again and again. A long time, until sleep came over—well, me at least. And perhaps for the first time since I was a boy, I slept well.

11

She woke me with her touch. Trying to get me in shape. "Let's do it again," she said, when she realized I was finally awake. She smiled coyly, biting her lip. I had my doubts about such a feat so soon after the previous night's activities. But we took our time, slower now. Even more care. And after several hours we were once more in each other's arms.

She said, "You hold me the way my mother did."

A warm gladness spread through my chest, for I knew how much her mother meant to her. Then an idea slammed through my skull. Pulling her closer to me, I said the words that her mother had said to her many, many years earlier:

"You are my love. You matter to me because you are you. Everything about you is what I love, the good and the bad, because without both you would not be what I love."

She did not respond in any way. But I realized that I had said the words as if by rote. But now, after my encounter with Death, I also realized their power. I said them again, this time thinking how meaningful it would be to me if someone said them to me. I spoke the words again. She lifted her head, as you might listen for the buzzing of an insect you cannot see.

I got up, sitting across from her on the bed. "What is it?" she asked. I took her hand in mine. Looked into her face. "You are my love. You matter to me because you are you. Everything about you is what I love, the good and the bad, because without both you would not be what I love."

She looked around, certain this time that something had happened.

"My name is J'role. You, Kyrethe, are my love. You matter to me because you are you. Everything about you is what I love, the good and the bad, because without both you would not be what I love."

Hesitantly she said, "J'role?"

I repeated the words again and again. So many times my voice became sore and creaked. But each time Kyrethe could hear a bit more. Until finally a smile of shock possessed her face, and she stood up on the bed and jumped up and down shouting, "I can hear! I can hear!" Almost immediately she dropped to her knees and took my face in her hands. "You are J'role? J'role. J'role. J'role. J'role. J'role. J'role. J'role. J'role. J'role. J'role. J'role. J'role. J'role. J'role." She tried my name out countless ways, learning how to hear how she spoke all over again. At one point she looked overcome with sudden disappointment. "I can't talk. I sound terrible."

"You sound like you," I replied. "And that is more than enough for me." She smiled, and I did too. It seemed the more I gave her, the more comfortable I was with myself. I felt like me more and more.

"Tell me—" she demanded, childlike again, impatient. "Everything."

"About what?"

"You, the world. Let me hear words again."

And so I told her my story, as she had told me her story with her writing on the tower wall. For hours and hours we spoke about ourselves, and what our lives had been like, the stories bound in our flesh now released through words. Into the night. Through the night. Into the morning. Toward noon. We collapsed with yawns and laughter into each other's arms, surrendering to sleep.

Later that night I awoke, and wondered how I could bring her sight back. The secret to ending the curse seemed to be helping Kyrethe relive what it had been like to be loved by her mother. But how could I show her her mother? I could never know what the woman looked like. I had no magic to create the illusion even if I had known. I felt as if I had failed her. For a long time I stared out at the stars.

The next day she once again woke me. No sex this time. More talking. And talk we did, hours and hours more. At one point she said, "It is our pain, you know, that is the source of our love."

"That sounds very sad," I replied, and meant it.

"Not at all. In fact, more's the joy for it. For from our shared sadness came this unexpected happiness. Who would have thought?"

And her words made me so happy.

I told her about her brother, and Neden, and my desire to save the boy. This made her very silent. I did not know what she was thinking, but I held her close, and let her have her thoughts. Then, finally I said, "Kyrethe. I think I am the one who broke your father's curse." I explained to her how I had held her, and how I had repeated her mother's words. And she smiled and touched my lips with her fingers. Then I said, "But I don't know how to return your sight. I can't show you your mother. I don't know what she looks like."

She said, "I do not need to see my mother. For she is you."

The cloudiness in her eyes faded. A new spark of awareness appeared in her face, and she focused her gaze on me. She gasped, looking at me full with sight. A broad smile appeared on her face.

But immediately I felt uncomfortable, and I realized how I had enjoyed being hidden in her darkness. "And how do I fare in your sight?" I asked with mopey tones.

She took my face once more in her hands. "Are you still so foolish," she said with soft tones, "that you do not know that the kindness and love you give comes back to you in equal form?"

She held me close, and now *I* cried, for I had not known. Had, in fact, braced every muscle of my body against betrayal and pain all of my life, for I had never expected love. The image of the star castle came to me, my fortress against pain. It was not merely a shelter, I realized, but an assumed way of life. I hadn't considered the way my mother had treated me to be anything but normal. I had nothing to judge it against; I had been a little boy. Life was simply pain. Rather than working from the premise that my mother had done something horrible to me, I had assumed that I had done something wrong. That I deserved what she had done to me. All my life had been spent forging pain for others on the order that my mother had forged pain for me. Not just to cause pain. But because I had to justify my mother's actions, had to make her actions true—the way the Universe really worked. To admit that love could exist would have meant my mother was wrong. Such a conclusion is not easily reached.

So now I pulled Kyrethe close, and let all my shock at my mother's actions finally pour out. Six decades near death, and I was finally ready to let go and face the world honestly, not in an attempt to protect my mother.

Kyrethe and I were, I realized, changed. Free.

A cool, gratifying wind rushed into the room, whipping the sheets around us with tremendous force. Just past Kyrethe's large hands, massive baby's hands with stubby fingers reached down for us. Picked us up, one in each hand, and suddenly we were airborne. A miracle of the Passions.

Death's Sea passed below us so quickly that it looked like a mere blur of red. I glanced at Kyrethe, held in the palm of Lochost's hand. Her body was fearful, clutching tightly at the Passion's thumb. But on her face she wore a wild smile of excitement. She could not believe she was flying—freed not only of her sensory prison, but of the prison of the island. She laughed out loud.

I turned up to look at Lochost. The child's face did not remind me of me any longer. Instead, his features shifted between those of all people of all races—so quickly I had to turn my head to avoid dizziness. I heard him laughing, though, the laughter of far too much pleasure in the possibility of life. I knew that if I tried to contain all of the Passion's hope I would burst.

Suddenly we stood on the shore of Death's Sea. Lochost gone. The land around us was barren—rocky and dry and cracked. But we were far from the island and safe. The two of us looked to each other, then out toward the sea. What words could we use?

I extended my hand to Kyrethe. She took it. Silently we turned and walked away from Death's Sea. There was a boy to be rescued; a broken boy to be found and healed.

PART FOUR

The Corrupted Heart

1

Lochost had deposited us somewhere on the northern shore of Death's Sea. We could see that the Scarlet Sea was further north and to the west of us, so we had only to walk west to reach the Badlands. I had overheard the two Theran sailors say that was where they were taking Neden, and so it was there we would go.

We did not speak much at this time. Without the magical fountain of the island, we would need food. We needed to make good time to get out of the dry wastes surrounding the sea and that would require speed of our old legs. So we walked on briskly until early evening, when we came to a jungle. Sparse at first, it thickened quickly. Soon we found all the fruit we needed to replenish ourselves. A large stream gave us water. We settled under a tree, preparing to rest up for the rest of the journey.

I had built a fire, and we sat together, staring into it. The fire created a hut of light carved out of the darkness around us. Against the fire's bright glare, we could see nothing beyond the flames. I felt cozy and safe.

When Kyrethe spoke now, it was with more caution.

She wanted to master her pronunciation. Her efforts were succeeding terrifically. "I'm going to kill him."

I laughed, thinking her comment a grim joke. She stared at me as if I were insane. "Your brother? Mordom?"

"Yes. You know what he did to me."

"He accepted your father's murder of your mother."

"I guess I didn't write everything down. It was so difficult chipping away the stone. He did more. My father died before I left for the island. At the funeral they made me touch his face. Lifeless. But I recognized the shape. I started scratching at it, and people dragged me away. It was Mordom who had the island built. He probably hired a questor of Upandal. A powerful one. There are many of them in Thera."

"Why would he do that to you?"

"I'm sure he didn't know what to do with me. My father's actions had created suspicion, but nothing concrete. However, the family reputation had been tarnished. That's why Mordom went along with my father's wishes. Otherwise his own chances of advancement through the Theran bureaucracy would have been ruined."

"When I met him years ago, he didn't seem to be a Theran official. He still doesn't."

"He might not be. Our system of political rewards and punishments is harsh on all failures. The desperate plan you've described to me shows that he must be trying to prove that he is worthy of a place in the bureaucracy once more."

"He had to exile you for the rest of your life?"

"Guilt through association, failure through association, is very prevalent among my government. If my father's crimes ever came to light . . ."

"Why didn't he kill you then?"

She paused. Quietly, she said, "I guess he couldn't bring himself to do that."

"But you can?"

"You're not trying to defend him, are you?"

I put my hands on my chest. "I practically told Death I'd personally send him back to her. I just . . . I've told you, my family situation . . . I suggest that if you can avoid bringing more pain into your life, you avoid it. I'm not telling you what to do. Just suggesting you look out for it."

She glared at me, eyes narrow. Examining me all over again. She placed her hand on mine. "All right. Good advice. I still want him dead."

"Excellent," I said, stretching out on the ground. "I'll be there to back you up."

She remained sitting, and for a moment I felt bad. A part of me wished she would lie down next to me. It would be good to have her warmth again. But things had changed. The isolation of the island had provided an ideal for romance. There was, ultimately, nothing else to do. But complications of the world made things—complicated. Her talk of revenge against her brother certainly had put neither of us in a cuddling mood. Which, when I thought of it, was a good thing.

Smiling, I rolled over and fell asleep.

A tiger woke me. Its scent invaded my nostrils, and my eyes flashed open. The beast's green eyes stared into mine. Only a foot away. "Back!" Kyrethe shouted, and I almost jumped back on her command. But she was speaking to the tiger, and it retreated a few steps. I looked up and saw her walking toward me, amused. "I'm sorry," she said, and sat down beside me. I must have still been wearing my fear, for she said, "Oh, I'm sorry," and touched my nose. Her casual, almost childish nature in the matter confused me. The tiger sat placidly a few feet away, licking its teeth. When the thing yawned I realized my entire head could fit into its mouth in a single bite.

"You know this tiger?"

"Not well. We only met last night. But I think we'll get along over time."

I looked up at her. "You're a beastmaster adept?"

She laughed. "Very good."

As I sat up I said, "Sorry. I spent most of my life either hiding in the wilderness—meaning I saw nobody—or working with people in cities. I haven't met many people with your talents." I realized too that my image of her was of a completely helpless woman. The more she spoke and took action, the more I realized that she *had been* a helpless woman. She was no longer such.

"I thought we could use some help, eventually. She and I can get to know each other better as we travel. She'll be able to help us track Mordom."

"From what I know of your profession—I don't know how to phrase this. Being alone, without any chance of encountering an animal . . ."

Her eyes became cold, as they had been the night before when she spoke of killing Mordom. "It was very difficult. A part of who I was had become cut off from life." She stood up abruptly. "We'd better get moving."

For a short while we discussed our options. Two general courses of action presented themselves. First, we could try to contact the government of Throal. They would have the forces to overwhelm Mordom's independent venture. But Throal was far away, and I suspected time was of the essence. Mordom, on the airship, had suggested that the plan he had for Neden would take weeks and weeks to complete. Well, weeks and weeks had gone by, and if there was any time left, there was precious little of it. I still did not know what Mordom had in mind for Neden, but I could anticipate that anything that involved cutting the boy up and working on him for a few months would be nightmarish in scope.

There was also the matter of my illegal activities and the Kingdom of Throal's attempts to arrest me over the years. For crimes ranging from the mutilation of my sons all the way down to petty theft, I was *wanted*. Sauntering into the kingdom to announce what Mordom was up to would only expose me to people who wanted me dead.

The other option was to press on alone. We were already near the Badlands, where I knew Mordom was heading. If he needed weeks of work it would be the perfect place for him to set up shop without being disturbed. For reasons of time I wanted to head straight for Mordom, and contact Throal after Neden's recovery. This was the option I put forward.

Kyrethe hadn't given it a moment's thought, really. She had no concern for Neden or the place of Throal in the mess Mordom had started. She only wanted to find her brother. She wanted a closure of blood.

"You're welcome to come with me, of course. You

know these lands far better than I. I can use your help."

"Well, I think going to Mordom is the best course of action as well."

"The only course of action."

"Be that as it may, let's get going."

We were on our way. The tiger, a female who she named Jade for the color of her eyes, walked beside Kyrethe. Kyrethe petted her as we walked, and the huge beast would run up ahead, and then back toward us, obviously delighted by Kyrethe's company. I was slightly jealous, but happy that Kyrethe was so happy. I walked a few feet back, if only because Jade still made me very nervous.

Days and days of walking.

We reached a small village. Kyrethe waited with Jade in the jungle. Kyrethe explained that the tiger might have become too easily agitated. I could tell, though, that she also wanted to avoid being in the midst of a lot of curious people. Beastmasters are by nature a solitary lot, and her time alone on the island had probably exaggerated that. I told a few stories, earned us some food and supplies. When we set out again the next day, I had a sword at my hip, she a dagger. We also had dried fruit for the Badlands.

After a few more days, the land, though still covered with grass, began to writhe slightly underfoot. Ahead I saw the brown, dead region that was the Badlands. A remnant of the Scourge. for whatever reason, the Badlands had never healed.

I had never entered it before. The few times I'd approached it, it reminded me too much of how the Earth had looked during my youth. That had been not long after the people had begun to emerge from centuries of living in the kaers. some things don't heal as well as we'd like them to. The soil. The soul.

A day later we entered a landscape devoid of life. Or so it seemed. The obvious life was gone. But with care you could spot big insects with heavily armored shells scurrying along, then burying themselves in the brown dirt. Birds would suddenly appear from behind a hill, rushing into the sky, then dive to the ground once more, becoming hidden from view. A few bent and twisted trees and some ugly shrubs were the vegetation. But nothing seemed permanent, as if it belonged.

And, in fact, nothing was. Even as we made our way along a dry gully, I saw the sides of the gully shift position. *The very direction in which we traveled changed because the land itself moved.* This was the terror of the Badlands. Not only was it huge—about four hundred by seven hundred miles—but you could not depend on the landmarks. Slowly but surely the land moved. Jade walked more warily now. Her steps were no longer certain, and it seemed that she did not trust her claws and weight to protect her in such a place.

We had decided that once we'd entered the Badlands, Kyrethe would borrow Jade's sense of smell. That ability seemed more than strange to me. But beastmaster adepts could do it, and it would certainly help us. Jade was loyal to Kyrethe now, and had learned a few rudimentary commands. I learned however, that because beasts have no language, they cannot be spoken to, even if bonded with a beastmaster.

Jade and Kyrethe faced each other, and Kyrethe simply touched the tiger's nose.

When she stood she seemed startled. "This place is terrible," she said. I could only nod. It was obvious that she had perceived the truth of the place in a way I could not. Jade seemed disoriented as well, and looked to Kyrethe for guidance. Kyrethe lifted her nose in the air, sniffed—a comic effect, actually—and said, "Nothing. If there are people here, I don't smell them yet."

"It could take us days—weeks—to find him."

"Let's keep moving then." And she was off. Whether I was there or not, she would keep moving. As we trudged on through the sliding stones and shifting gullies, my jealousy returned. Strangely, I was jealous not of someone else, but of her. She was complete with herself. This feeling lingered until I remembered her history. She had stood up to her father and her brother. Had suffered terrible torture and punishment in order to declare what she believed was true. Of course she was complete. The fact that she had survived her exile clearly demonstrated that she was complete. If she hadn't been complete, she would not have survived, and I would never have met her. If she wasn't complete, I would not have laughed the way I laughed with her, made love with her the way I did. That we were no longer trapped on an isolated island with nothing better to do had not changed her. It did not even mean I was completely out of her heart. But the circumstances were different. What her concerns were—before me, now her brother—had changed. I could either accept that or drive myself back into bitter loneliness.

I knew the bitter loneliness all too well. Acceptance seemed an approach still full of novel possibilities, and I decided to try it.

We did, in fact, spend days searching. Twice we were attacked by Horrors waiting for prey. The fights were fast—we won both. But the creatures—things with tentacles and silver teeth—left me wounded and aching.

The dry earth seemed somehow to soak up moisture from my body. The land shifted with the sun, which made it beat on us mercilessly, without hope of finding a patch of shade. The place was warmer than any other I'd seen in Barsaive. An awful emotional irritant began to work its way into my spirit. I thought at first it was the oppressive environment. But no. I think, though I cannot be certain, that the land itself held poison for the soul.

We were into our second week of exploration, conserving our rations, discussing whether to turn back and replenish our food, when we finally stumbled over a clue to Neden's whereabouts.

2

Kyrethe raised her hand. Both Jade and I stopped. "Something near. Mountain dwellers. Dwarfs." She spoke softly, pointing west. Now I raised one hand, gesturing her to wait. With limping leg I started off toward where she'd pointed. Soon I topped a gully, crawling up on my stomach. The ground under my fingers felt warm. Smelled of things recently dead.

Several hundred yards away walked a group of dwarfs, about a dozen, with a few humans and elves. Had King Varulus learned of the plan—were these his agents come to rescue Neden? They wore armor, the dwarfs, but I did not see the red and gold standard of Throal. Perhaps they were lost, having wandered into my narrative by accident.

The effort I had just made in rationalizing why the dwarfs might be from Throal but did not look like it surprised me. A year earlier the quest to save a little boy from the hands of an evil magician would have sent me racing to the task. Redemption at last! If only I could prove myself with one bold stroke. Saving a child. What more proof would I need to show myself worthy of becoming, once more, a member of my people? Deserving love. Having a place.

But now, since my death, the need to prove anything was rapidly losing importance. If Throalic warriors were about, then they could handle the situation. I had other matters to attend to. Maybe seeing my boys. My wife. Or starting a new life with Kyrethe. Who knew? But taking action for the sole purpose of reclaiming my past—how could such a thing even be possible?

Back down into the gully I slid, the rumination still churning in my thoughts as I returned to Kyrethe. Of course, Kyrethe would go after Mordom, no matter what. Again I thought of how direct and simple things had been at the tower. What I had once seen as a prison now seemed the place where in all my life I'd been most free. The world itself demanded attention in so many ways. The threads of other lives, whether I wanted them to or not, wove themselves into the pattern of my life. There seemed no escaping it.

No, there was a way. To retreat once again to my home in the jungle. To turn my back on all people once more. To seek the solitude I had so carefully forged for myself. To once more find companionship with no one and nothing but the stars above.

I smiled at the thought. That was impossible now. The Universe had teased me out of my loneliness with Kyrethe's presence, and there was no going back. More to the point, I simply liked being alive too much to return to my former loneliness. I wanted to interact with other people, for no other reason than to do it.

And so, as I walked up to Kyrethe, I realized why I wanted to pursue Neden. Not to put myself in the good graces of my fellow name-givers, which was an action born of vanity. But because I wanted to be involved. Running toward and away from each other, helping each other, laughing and crying with each other. That's what we did.

No, the metaphor is off. It wasn't that we were all threads forming a huge tapestry of life. We are all the stars of the sky reflected on earth. But instead of the static pattern I'd so desperately tried to build for myself, we are in constant motion. There is nothing to be known, nothing to be counted on. Our interactions with each other create a mess. One either embraces the mess, or one hides from the truth behind an elaborate framework of lies. How many years had I spent studying the stars? And how much more had I learned about myself and my fate by throwing myself into the mess?

I told Kyrethe what I had seen. We agreed we would follow the group, seeing if they were involved with Mordom. Maybe they would lead us to him. If not, if they were headed out of the Badlands, we would form a new plan then. Still using Kyrethe's borrowed sense of smell, we followed the group from a distance. We lost the trail every so often as the wind shifted, but through the next two days we succeeded in staying with them.

On the second day, they stopped and made a large camp, replete with tents showing the banner of Throal. With confirmation that they were from Throal, I thought we would be safe in approaching them. But Kyrethe said, "Didn't you tell me that this king of Throal had sent his son away because his own home was not safe?" When I nodded, she said, "Then what makes you think that anyone from Throal is your ally?"

I had not thought about it that way, though I should have. It occurred to me that Kyrethe, who was a

Theran, still had her people's propensity to see the political ramifications of any situation the way most of us breathe. Though she'd been far from such intrigues since the age of twenty, her instincts were so sharply honed that she could still pick up trouble from third-hand sources. I told her I needed to find out either way. She agreed that we required more information.

That night, with their bright orange campfire as our guide, Kyrethe, Jade, and I moved up quietly, getting close enough for me to hear the murmur of voices. A single word shouted in laughter. Dwarf guards stationed at the edge of the perimeter kept a vigilant, somber eye. And around a large fire a trio of dwarfs sat quietly speaking to one another.

"I'm going to take Jade's sense of hearing and move up closer," Kyrethe said.

"I've got the skills to get closer," I said. "It would make more sense for me to do it."

"You'll have to get even closer than I have to."

She had a point, and I agreed to wait behind. She meditated for a few moments, then placed her hands on Jade's large head. Ever so gently she ran her fingers through the tiger's fur, then touched her ears. The tiger panted lightly, pleased.

When Kyrethe turned to go, I touched her hand. We'd had little contact of kindness over the past few days. The nature of the Badlands had made us quiet and irritable. "Kyrethe," I said, "I just wanted to tell you that, of all the women I have ever met, you are the most ridiculously driven." I had meant to say something appropriately meaningful and sentimental. But I think, by speaking the truth, I fared much better. She smiled at my words, suppressed a laugh. She extended a hand and took one of mine. Her skin, worn and old, felt wonderful. A woman worth knowing. She said, "And you the most confused. But let me tell you something. All the men in my life have known exactly what they wanted to do, exactly how they wanted to live. They knew what was right, and they did it. A passionately Theran trait. And let me also tell you, I used to think that was wonderful. During my years of isolation I had time to think about that, though. A touch of uncertainty in my father or Mordom would have made my life a great deal easier. Thank you for showing me the other side of life." She tugged on my hand, pulling me close. We kissed. Passionately. Eventually Jade rolled onto her back and pressed her head against mine, trying to remove me from her mistress' attention. Softly Kyrethe laughed, and then she was focused again. With the careful movement of a predator, she started off for the camp, crawling on her stomach. Jade rested beside me, watching her, panting with impatience.

I could still see her for the first few hundred feet. Then her gray robe blended into the land, and she vanished from my sight.

The camp, however, was perfectly visible. About fifteen minutes after Kyrethe left my side I saw one of the dwarf guards looking with curiosity in the general direction where Kyrethe would be. Had he heard something? He started walking out of the firelight to investigate. I began moving forward. Whether these people were loyal to Throal or not, Kyrethe would be in terrible danger if discovered. She carried with her the Theran air, and that could spell her immediate death.

With the pain in my leg still burning a bit, I began

to move forward. I could silence the guard without making a sound. All I had to do was get out there fast enough.

Then a commotion in the camp caught my attention. Another entourage approached from the other side of the camp. At its head—Mordom. I could just make out his thin face, the sealed eyes. The eye-palm upraised, allowing him to see. Jade sat up, licked her lips. The dwarf guard stepped back into the firelight, preparing himself for the arrival of Mordom's group. I relaxed.

I saw Mordom and the others greet one another. Small, collapsible stools were set up around the fire. A large group of dwarfs, humans, elves—and of course, Mordom—gathered. The discussion was soft and I could hear nothing they said.

But all I wanted was Kyrethe's return. Mordom had obviously come from where he kept Neden. From what I knew of a beastmaster adept's talents, Kyrethe would be able to track Mordom's path back to Neden. With Mordom out of the way we would only have to deal with whatever guards he had left around the boy. It would actually be possible to rescue him!

More than a half an hour later my patience was beginning to fray. I scanned the darkness for Kyrethe's return. What was taking her so long? The distraction had passed, the guards were watchful once more. She could not press her luck too much longer.

Then, against a slope ridiculously close to the camp, I saw her. She was still moving forward, seeking out patches of darkness to get as close as possible. But she was closer than she had to be for eavesdropping. Then I saw something glitter in her hand, reflecting the starlight above. Those in the camp could not see it, for she had hidden herself in a shallow gully as she continued to move closer. I knew, though, exactly what it was, and a terror passed through me. I knew that within moments I could lose both Neden and Kyrethe. She had her dagger out, and there was no doubt she meant to kill her brother *now*.

3

"Stay," I said to Jade. Kyrethe had taught the tiger that command, and I hoped she would obey even though it was only I who spoke the instruction. Then I was out in the shadows, moving swiftly through the shallow gullies and ducking behind the low rises that separated me from the camp. I moved much faster than I would have liked. Had to keep myself nearly standing in my haste. But time was the key.

Within moments I saw Kyrethe just ahead of me, moving up. So slowly—and then she began getting up on her hands and knees. She was too close for further subtlety. There was nothing for her to do now but rush forward. I hastened my pace, my leg tight with short jabs of pain with each step, until I was on her. She had left her crouch and was about to sprint. I launched myself onto her back, covering her mouth. The two of us hit the ground. I landed on my back, and, with her back against my stomach, tried to keep her still. I wrapped my legs around her, keeping one hand on her mouth and my other arm around her stomach.

She fought fiercely, aggravating the pain in my leg. But death waited if I were to give in and let her go. We were only yards from the camp's perimeter.

"Shhh. It's me. J'role. Stop."

She paused. Then, with greater fury and energy than before, struggled wildly once again to free herself.

"Stop it. Please. Listen. Mordom will die. You can kill your brother, I'll help." She gave a muffled gurgle. "All right. You can kill him yourself. But please. Please. I beg of you. We can get to Neden now. He'll be lightly protected. We can follow Mordom's tracks back to where he has the boy. Please. Please. Help me rescue the boy. The death can wait. Death is always looming. Saving this boy—this is something we have to do now."

She stopped struggling. I waited, wondering if it were a trick. Then I realized I would never know. After a few more moments I let her go. Without a word she rolled off me, face down, breathing. Her anger was palpable. But she did not run off toward Mordom.

"We'll get him," I whispered.

"Quiet," she said. She was listening to the discussion now. They were all so close. I raised my head above the gully's top and saw Mordom clearly in the firelight.

"He's dead?" he asked.

"That's the word from Kratas," said a dwarf who wore the symbol of Throal on his shoulder. Traitors must be deep within the ranks of Throal, for the man was a general in the Throalic army. "Vistrosh assured me his agents dispatched King Varulus three weeks ago."

"Kratas?" wondered Mordom. "Isn't that the city Garlthik One-Eye rules?"

"It doesn't matter," said the general. "Vistrosh and Garlthik are bitter rivals for control of the city. He's competent. If he says the king is dead, the king is dead."

Mordom was not satisfied. "If Garlthik is even near the source of the information . . ." Mordom's voice trailed off, searching for the right words. "He has this . . . loathsome talent for getting into the middle of things that aren't his business. For having access to knowledge that he should in no way possess. For turning the worst of luck to his advantage."

"Mordom," the general said firmly. "Garlthik tried to infiltrate our efforts. We dispatched his agents."

"Even worse news."

"Enough. I have told you the deed is done. How is your work progressing . . . ?"

"The 'deed' better be. If this is to work . . ."

The general held up a hand. His face, already red in the firelight, grew redder. "We betrayed the prince's escort. We arranged for the king's hiding place to be betrayed. Now. The prince's mind. How goes your work?"

"Well. I'm almost done. The poison is already at work."

"Can we take him now?"

Mordom shook his head. "He is mindless. A coma. A few more days will have him behaving with reactions typical for a boy his age."

"Can I see him now?"

"I don't think that's a good idea. He's—as I told you, there would be risks. He's near death right now . . ."

"But he is going to live?"

"Oh, yes. Mountainshadow's guidance has been—

incredible, really. We'll have him ready for you soon. But you must be patient."

"Varulus opened up our kingdom to all of Barsaive, polluting our land. He took on the responsibility of fighting Thera and trying to bring justice to all the land. Our resources are nearly bled dry. We don't have much more time."

"And soon you will have an heir ready to do whatever you say. When you march back to Throal, the boy safely in your care after a daring rescue, you will be able to put all things right."

"And Thera and Throal can become the allies they were in the past."

"Oh, yes," Mordom said, smiling. "Assuredly that."

I tugged on Kyrethe's robe. She sighed, nodded. Carefully we headed back to Jade.

"We've got to find him now. Now is our chance."

"J'role. Did you hear what my brother said? Your boy is near death. What are we going to do when we find him?"

"Something. Anything. But you also heard your brother say that he'll soon be some sort of puppet for the traitors."

She stopped, looked at me, studying me. "This matters to you, doesn't it?"

I was startled into realizing it did. I nodded. "Why do you wonder at that?"

"From everything you've told me about yourself—it just doesn't make sense in a way." Then she stared off into the distance. Then smiled. "In another way, it does. When this is all over, when your boy is rescued and my brother dead, I think I'd like to stay here in your land. There's something interesting about this place. Something I don't see in Thera."

It had never occurred to me she would return to her home. I did not say that. Sixty years had given me some tact. But I was happy to learn she was settling toward whatever it was that I was settling toward.

We continued on. By making our way in a wide arc around the camp we found Mordom's trail. The soil had shifted because of the nature of the Badlands. But the number of people who had walked with Mordom, along with Kyrethe's tracking talent, allowed her to pick up the trail. Soon, with only a few false leads, we were on our way back to Mordom's lair.

Taking a break at one point, Kyrethe asked, "Who is this Mountainshadow Mordom mentioned?"

When Mordom had mentioned the name, it had struck a memory of some sort, but I had not been able to place it. I was still not able to remember when Kyrethe asked me about him.

After we'd moved on for another twenty minutes I saw a guard on a large hill ahead of us. He sat low to the ground, without a fire. I pulled our group behind a rise and said I'd go scout and take care of the guards. Kyrethe said she'd take Jade along the trail and take care of anyone who might be backing the scouts up. I wanted to discourage her at first. To keep her safe. And then I realized that being safe was not who Kyrethe was. It might frighten me, because I cared for her, I realized. But that was who she was. We split up.

It took me a bit of work to get up onto the hill, for the guard's position was a good one. Then, when I arrived, I saw that there were two guards, not one. A dwarf and a troll. The two of them sat staring out over the ragged land. The starlight turned the dead earth silver.

Surprise would last me only for the first attack, so the troll would be my first victim. I waited for the right moment. Patience, when dealing with death, is a virtue that cannot be underestimated. Finally the dwarf got up to stretch. As he stood, he turned to look out over the land. At that moment I rushed forward, sword out. They heard only a slight scrape of footsteps against dirt, then my sword was buried deep in the troll's neck. He gave out a sharp, crooked gasp.

The dwarf was good. No panic. He had his axe in hand even as I whirled toward him. I tried to jerk my sword out of the troll to parry his blow, but it had gotten stuck in the troll's thick muscles. "Alarm!" the dwarf cried as his axe cut through the air. I jumped out of the way, leaving myself some room to maneuver.

We moved about the hilltop wildly, me dodging, him laughing as he swung his weapon. Twice I maneuvered myself back to my sword, and both times he drove me away from it. On the third attempt I wrested it free and brought it up for a decisive parry. He charged me then, for my sword would quickly outwork his axe in combat. I brought my sword up in a feint, forcing him to the right, then whirled and struck him across the arm. He cried out and fell to the ground. Another swing smashed in the side of his head, and he fell still.

But not all was silent. From below I heard heavy breathing and the cry of more guards. I ran to the edge of the hill and saw two humans and another troll rushing up the hill at me. *Now* panic filled me. No surprise. Badly outnumbered. Slightly winded.

I had momentarily forgotten about my support, however. Jade's roar cut through the night air, so loud and so brazen, it was as if she owned the night. Certainly in that moment the three guards and myself were willing to give it to her.

They turned, suddenly aware of a greater danger than an old man with a sword. She rushed up with incredible speed, her grace all the more impressive for her size. In the guard's moment of distraction I hopped down the hill and sliced one of the human guards through the back. Jade leaped into the air and plowed into the troll's chest. He gave out a horrible scream as Jade's claws ripped through his muscles and her fangs ripped deep into his right shoulder. The last guard, turning this way and that in search of more surprise threats, left himself open for my blow. I caught him on the arm. My attack sobered him and he came at me.

Beyond him, at the base of the hill, I saw another human guard appear, running out from a cave entrance. Kyrethe, who had been hiding within a shallow gully, popped out and made a credible, though amateurish, attack at the man's back. He screamed out and crumpled quickly. In the starlight, her dagger glistened shiny scarlet.

Beside me, the troll and Jade went after each other. The tiger's attack had determined the course of the fight, however. Soon the troll could not even scream.

The final guard and I went at it for a few attacks and parries. But I had the advantage of higher elevation, which I kept and used to keep pressing him further and further down the hill. Finally he tripped and cut himself on his own blade. It was little effort on my part to finish him off.

We gathered, Kyrethe, Jade, and I, at the base of the

hill. There a large cave opening waited. The starlight illuminated no more than the first few feet, and then darkness choked the cave. I could see, however, that the cave sloped sharply downward.

"A dragon," I said.

"What?"

"I remember now. Hearing about him in village east of here. There's supposed to be a dragon living in the Badlands. His name is Mountainshadow."

4

We stopped. Didn't look at each other. Just into the mouth of the cave. And then, starting at the same instant, we laughed. "Doom awaits us all," I said.

"But so regularly?" joked Kyrethe.

Our laughter stopped abruptly. A moment of sober reflection. "Thank you for helping me," I said.

"Well, despite the fact that I want him dead more than anything—helping an innocent boy does make me *feel* better."

We held hands a moment, and then, with Jade walking alongside, entered the cave. The guards who had come out of the cave had brought torches. Kyrethe picked one up from the ground and carried it as I moved ahead searching for traps and alarms. I could find nothing—Mordom had probably counted on the Badlands themselves to keep people out of his way—but remained vigilant nonetheless. The cave sloped down deeper and deeper until it finally opened out into a large cavern. Torches burned in metal stands that illuminated a small section of the cavern. Around us the walls were rough and covered with ancient stone. Off to one side were a dozen cots. To another, several boxes filled with scrolls. To another, a lab area with tables covered with beakers and books.

"Where's the dragon?" Kyrethe whispered.

"Don't know," I replied. I'd never seen a dragon before, but had heard of their vast size. Still, the cavern was so large it might well hold several dragons. "Maybe it's out killing or something."

Kyrethe's voice suddenly was drained of life. "J'role."

I turned and saw her pointing at a stone slab. Neden rested on it, eyes closed. His flesh had been put back together. Not even a scar remained. But a strange latticework of glass tubes had been constructed around him. One end of each tube was connected to beakers that held strange potions that emitted ghastly lights of different colors. Each tube rested on a series of stands around Neden's slab. Some of them had fires burning beneath them, others boiled of their own nature. The tubes from the beakers pierced the boy's flesh, and bloody welts boiled up about the tubes.

I moved quickly beside him. His breathing was shallow. His flesh a pale blue. I wondered if it was safe to remove the tubes. Were some of them keeping him alive?

Probably thinking along the same lines, Kyrethe asked, "Do you think we should really try this?"

"I don't think we have a choice. If they finish, the damage may be permanent." With that I extended my hand, almost touching one of the glass tubes. It occurred to me that if I removed the tube, the liquid within would spill out all over the floor. I looked around and saw some clay used to stopper the tubes, and picked some up.

"What is all this?" Kyrethe asked.

"Your brother has a talent for dealing with Horrors. An affinity. I believe some of these materials are poisons, extracts—something—from Horrors he's studied. Others are probably keeping Neden alive while portions of his soul and mind are being corrupted."

She was silent a moment, and then said, "I can't believe he's my brother."

I turned my head, stared at her. For one flash of an instant all her age and hard-edged determination vanished and she became terribly naive. I don't mean this in a bad way. I know too many people who accept the world's terrors with a shrug. Her ability to know dark truths and still be stunned by them I found wonderful.

"I'll go wait by the entrance, to listen for more guards."

"All right," I said, and put my attention back on the glass beakers and tubes. I extended my hand, ready to take a tube and pull it out. I had decided to pull them out one after another, in quick succession, for I had no idea which should be removed first. If some of them were keeping Neden alive, I obviously could not stop those from flowing into his body for too long while the poisons continued to flow into his mind.

I touched a tube. My vision flashed white. A solid hum raced up my arm, knocking me up off my feet, sending me crashing against the floor.

"J'role!"

Kyrethe was next to me when I opened my eyes. Dizzying so thick I could not find words to speak filled my head. She asked me what happened, and after a few moments my thoughts cleared and I told her. "We're going to need help," she said.

Getting up, I said, "We don't have help." The shock had made me ornery, and I was more determined than ever to free Neden and get out.

"That's strong Theran magic. It doesn't come lightly, and isn't broken lightly."

"Me neither."

She smiled. "All right. But what are you going to do?"

"I've been stealing all my life. I've learned a few things along the way. This isn't the first time I've had to get past magical protection."

The trick was, it was powerful magic I'd need to draw on. I had not meditated for a long while, and my focus on my talents had become weak. My intimacy with Kyrethe, my concern for Neden had pulled me away from the focus of my thief magic. "I'm going to need time to meditate," I said.

"We don't have time."

"We don't have a choice. We can't just smash the glass off him. We'll rip every vein in his body to shreds."

She nodded. "I'm going to go outside. Mordom will probably stay with the dwarfs tonight—but we don't know."

"Yes," I said. But I was already slipping away from her, becoming drawn into the loneliness and strength of my profession. She walked away, and I thought about loneliness. Focused on my need to rely on myself, commit myself to no one. That's how a thief adept draws his magical strength. Usually it takes about half an hour. I'd done it so many times all my life. But even as I started I knew this time was different. I couldn't find the loneliness. Even though I knew freeing Neden depended on my success, I didn't want to focus on being alone anymore. I'd had enough of it in my lifetime. In my first encounter with Neden I'd played all kinds of games to trick myself into helping him—thinking he might be a source of ransom. But now, as I looked at the young boy on the stone slab, I only wanted to embrace him. I wanted to help and admit I wanted to help him.

Five minutes passed. Ten. Fifteen.

I couldn't do it. I still had my talents as a thief. But I could not find the focus to do the amazing—which is what was required.

I set myself to the task of doing it once more. Ten minutes passed. All I could think of was trying to build a new life with Kyrethe.

There seemed to be no point in trying anymore. Something had slipped. Who I had been was no more. Even if I needed to be that person.

I walked up to the tubes. I might not be able to avoid the pain, but perhaps I'd be able to stand firm in the face of it. To accept it. Not enjoy it as proof of a bleak Universe. Nor withdraw into myself in an attempt to hide from it. Just confront it. Part of life, however unpleasant.

Bracing myself, I extended my hand.

"J'role!" Kyrethe shouted, nearly making me jump.

"What!"

My anger caught her off guard. She froze for a moment, then remembered her panic and raced over to me. "There are airships coming. Two of them."

Excitement coursed through me. "Maybe the Throal forces have come for the traitors."

"Or maybe Mordom has turned on the traitors and ambushed them."

"Your mind takes wildly cynical turns."

"I could be right."

"You could at that."

From the tunnel entrance came Mordom's voice. "HURRY!" he shouted, and the single word echoed down the cavern.

I said, "We didn't hide the bodies."

"No. But I did, when you were meditating."

"We'd better hide ourselves."

We tucked ourselves into a dim portion of the cavern, far from the torches. Kyrethe called Jade over and we all waited.

Mordom appeared, along with several of his guards. Blood ran down the right side of his face. He seemed terribly jostled, his overbearing manner diffused through fear. "Get those scrolls there," he shouted at one of the guards. He ran toward Neden, performed a series of hand gestures, and began removing tubes from the boy's body. He did it with great care, pulling the tubes out in a deliberate sequence. I was suddenly grateful I had not tried it.

"We can get him now," Kyrethe said, her voice barely able to contain the lust for violence.

I put a hand on her shoulder. "Just a moment more. Please."

Mordom finished and shouted for two of the guards to help him. Only three had accompanied him into the cave. He might have left some out by the cave's entrance, but it seemed safe to assume that his numbers were not greatly reduced. The dwarf general rushed down the entrance tunnel now. "We need that dragon of yours now, magician!"

Without looking up, Mordom said, "He's neither mine nor yours, General. I don't think he'd be much interested in helping us in this matter. He's very peculiar. The airship is hidden outside. We just have to get the prince onto it, and get away."

The general's agitation would not be assuaged. He ran up to Mordom and tugged on his robe. "They might catch up to us!"

Mordom turned sharply, slapping the dwarf with his eyeless hand. "Are you such a coward? Are you afraid of being exposed before your people for your crimes? You're not worthy of either your people's respect or their derision. You are a sycophant who hides behind the strength of others."

The dwarf began drawing his sword. Mordom, as if pulling out a handkerchief, casually touched the general's forehead. Before the dwarf had even finished drawing his blade, he screamed. His flesh began peeling away, exposing muscle and fat. The loose skin started to twist wildly around the dwarf's body, coiling around itself. The dwarf dropped to his knees, clutching his bleeding face. Mordom turned back to Neden. The guards' attention was captivated by the terrible fate of the dwarf. Mordom shouted at them to help with Neden.

"That's enough," Kyrethe said. "Jade," she commanded sternly. "Attack!"

5

As the group before us turned, the tiger sprang forward, leaping onto Mordom even as he attempted to ready a spell. The guards drew their weapons as Kyrethe also rushed forward. I, as surprised as the guards, followed her into the battle.

Swords. Cuts. Parries. Thrusts. Screams and claws. With the aid of Jade, we managed to quickly dispatch the guards. However, my wounds from the Horrors and the battle on the hill were starting to weaken me, and soon I was down as well. Mordom was bleeding heavily from the chest, and staggered against Neden's slab. His breathing was terribly labored, and as he exhaled, blood gurgled up.

He stared at us, I on the floor, Kyrethe standing a few yards away, Jade at her side. Her right arm bled, but she seemed calm enough confronting her brother. I don't think he understood why we didn't finish him off. Then, as he looked at his sister, recognition dawned in his eyes. He mouthed her name, but no sound issued.

"Yes," she answered.

He looked down at me, remembered I'd fallen off his airship near his sister's island. "How did you . . . ?"

"He did what you never thought of doing, Mordom. He loved me."

His voice sounded like leaves cracked underfoot. "I'm so sorry."

This softened her. I saw her shoulders relax. I tensed, waiting for Mordom to react. But the attack never came. He simply rested his weight more heavily against the slab. Perhaps it was the weight of memories long forced from his thoughts. From outside the cave came the sound of battle. Shouted orders.

I brought myself to my feet. "The boy, Mordom. Will the boy be all right?"

He turned to Neden. Looked down at him. Laughed a strange little laugh. "No. That is, he'll be fine for the purposes that I—but for what you mean—" He turned back to his sister. "Kyrethe. I . . . I'm so glad you managed to . . . I didn't think it was possible to break Father's curse."

She simply stared at him. "I want to kill you."

He slumped even further. "Yes." Raised his eyeless hand to his face. "That would make sense."

She looked at me. "But I don't think I will. Blood on the hands is difficult to remove."

The clatter of feet approached. I turned toward the entrance and saw a horde of dwarfs arrive. At the head was—King Varulus! His beard was whiter than the last time I'd seen him some forty years earlier and his face more deeply lined. Yet he moved with the ferocity of a father out to protect his son. His soldiers quickly surrounded us. Some checked the bodies of the dead. We were all suspect, and they held their weapons toward all us.

He rushed up to his son. Cried the boy's name. Tried

to awaken him. As if dreaming, Mordom said, "You can't . . . He isn't asleep . . . He's nothing now. There's nothing to wake." His gaze never left his sister.

Varulus whirled on Mordom. "Wake him. Put my son back together."

"Some things are impossible to do. I can give him the illusion of life. But he will never truly have it."

"I don't believe you. I don't know what your ambitions are, but you will get nothing from me. Undo your handiwork or die now."

"My ambition," said Mordom, and then he sighed heavily. "My ambition—" He faltered again. It was incredible that the man who now stood before me, his presence shrinking by the moment, torn to shreds by the horrors of his own past, was the man who had haunted my nightmares all of my life. When next he spoke, it was obvious that his thoughts had wandered completely from the immediate situation. "My ambition is to finish my father's work. To live my father's . . . To make sure things work correctly this time. No failures."

Varulus ignored him, turned to Kyrethe.

"I am Kyrethe. A recent prisoner on an island in Death's Sea."

"There are no islands in that sea."

"Things you cannot see still exist."

He turned to me, annoyed with her sharp answer. "And you? Can you help my son?"

"I am J'role." All the guards present took a half-step back. Varulus, who knew from Releana that the mad clown he sought was the same boy he'd met in the hanging garden years ago, peered into my face. His bushy eyebrows raised up in surprise. "So you are. I really thought you'd died years ago, your legend the work of many hands."

"I got around. I stole a great deal."

He stepped toward me. "You did this to my son?"

My voice was now flat. There seemed little hope of explaining the truth, and my bland acceptance of a terrible Universe was slipping back into my thoughts. "No. I wanted to help him." I thought back to hearing Neden's cries in the jungle when Mordom was pursuing him. "I very much wanted to help him."

Varulus looked at me suspiciously, but seemed content with my words for the moment. He turned back to Mordom. "There is nothing you can do for him. Truly?"

"No. Not to reverse it."

"And you are Mordom."

"Oh, yes."

"You have committed crimes in the land of Barsaive for sixty years now. You kidnapped my son, poisoned him with this plot to rule Throal through him . . ."

Mordom snapped out of his stupor. "How did you know? All my preparations . . ."

Varulus smiled. "I was told to ask if you thought I was dead."

"Garlthik," Mordom sighed.

"He told me you would guess. He'll be happy to hear you haven't forgotten him. I don't like dealing with his kind, but he cut me an offer I couldn't refuse when he heard I was after *you*." Varulus signaled to several soldiers. Suddenly they surrounded Mordom, forcing him to the ground. Varulus raised his sword and placed its tip at Mordom's neck. I stepped forward, an instinct, I suppose, trained by pain. Kyrethe placed her hand on my arm. Stopped me. "I want you to know," continued Varulus, "that I know you've died several times. That you have a network that labors diligently to bring you back. I'm tracking those people down. This might be your final death."

Varulus' words struck a memory in me. "King Varulus, I too have died and come back." My words surprised the dwarfs. I said, "There is something I wanted to ask Mordom about the realm of the dead."

"Do you realize how impertinent you are being?"

"Always."

Varulus weighted my request. "Ask."

"When you were there, Mordom, did you have to write your story again and again?"

Mordom turned to me as if I were mad. "In the realm of the dead one is deprived of all senses, but is constantly aware of all the beautiful sights and food and smells and people that surround you. I spoke to Death once—she entered my thoughts and told me she wanted to understand why we don't notice things until we're about to lose them."

As Death had said, "It's complicated."

"Then I send you to a punishment you so terribly deserve." Mordom raised his eye-hand, pointing it toward Kyrethe. He tried to form a word of goodbye or apology. But the king drove his sword forward. Kyrethe took my hand, squeezed it tight. Looked away. A gush of blood sprang up from Mordem's neck. With a sudden, short spasm, he died.

King Varulus sighed a heavy sigh, as if content with a job well done but saddened by its lack of significance. He let the sword slip from his fingers and turned toward Neden. With a careful touch, he stroked his boy's face. "There must be something. Something."

A soldier said, "Your Highness. We can get him to Throal. Our scholars can examine him there."

"Yes, yes," Varulus said distantly. But in his heart he did not think anyone could bring his son back from the soulless state Mordom had imposed on him.

From the dark recesses of the cave came a low, solid voice. "Your efforts will be in vain."

We all turned toward the source of the voice. A slow slithering echoed through the cavern. The dwarfs raised their swords.

The voice said, "But I can help. If someone is willing to take a risk."

From the deep darkness at the back of the enormous cavern emerged a massive dragon. His head, edging into the light of the torches, floated sixty feet above the ground. His forepaws had talons the size of great swords. He came closer and we all stepped back.

"What is this?" asked King Varulus softly.

"Mountainshadow," I answered. "If anyone can help Neden, it's him."

6

Mountainshadow's head snaked toward us, floating in the thick firelight on the end of a long neck. His wings, moist and folded innumerable times, rested along his body. A long tail slid slowly back and forth. King Varulus, sword drawn, rushed forward. "You can help my son?"

"I know how, but I cannot do it." The dragon's voice was removed—not just by distance. He seemed somewhat amused by the circumstances. How long had he been waiting in the shadows? Mordom hadn't even bothered to tell him an attack was coming. Was he always back there, watching, contributing to the scene at his whim, but invisible for all practical purposes?

Like me, as a thief. Present, but not participating.

Varulus did not shake his sword wildly. He did not shout. With the same tones that he used to keep his people together for all the years of Throal's political turmoil, he said, "You will help my son." The words carried a threat, soft and subtle: "If not, you will die. If not now, later."

"I will help. I am intrigued," said the dragon. Hot breath rolled out from his nostrils. I swallowed as the moisture in my mouth dried up.

"Quickly then!" demanded Varulus.

"Not so fast." The dragon smiled, the massive folds of his lips peeling back to reveal rows of terrible teeth. "I know how, but another will have to do the work."

"Then tell me!"

The dragon contemplated this. "No. Not you. I have searched all your minds, and you are the child's father. Your interests are too obvious."

Now the king did lose his patience. "What are you . . . ? Of course my interests are obvious! Yes, I'm his father . . ."

I raised my hand toward the king. Something had fallen into place in my mind. Legends of dragons mixed with my conversation with Death. Although we so often treat our lives as completely useless, lacking all meaning and beauty, there are many other beings in the Universe charmed by us. Curious to the point of obsession. Jealous. "I think, your Highness, that Mountainshadow has his own agenda. First, for helping Mordom, and now for helping Neden."

"By what right . . . ?" sputtered Varulus.

"By the right of his power!" I said, stepping toward the dragon, putting my back toward him, aligning myself with him. "He is not a name-giver in our meaning of the word, King Varulus. He is outside of our lives. He does not understand how we feel, what we live." I did not know exactly why I had taken this position, but it seemed vital that we end the puffed-up displays if we were going to save Neden.

The dragon's head appeared beside mine, the long snout extending far past me. His massive eye, the left eye, turned toward me, pale and yellow, as large as my head. "You understand things most people do not."

"I know now that our lives are much smaller than the ideals we set for our ourselves. But within that delicate life, that small life, there is more than we usually notice."

"Is that so?"

"I think so. I wanted to do enough deeds, even if terrible deeds, to make my life worthy of something to be remembered. But now I see that plan offered me nothing while living. If I could live well my final years, that would be something. That would be miraculous."

"You will be the one."

"You act as if you had not chosen me already." I knew he had. If there was a pattern to be found in the swirling stars of human life, this was it. Death, the great dragons—the forces that thought in ways beyond our understanding—they offered us greatness when we least expected it. By surrendering our lives to the mundane, we would be open to their arrival. They would pick us because we would be interesting.

"Yes. Exactly," said the dragon. "Interesting. You are a thief, a murderer, mutilator of children, rapist—" I glanced involuntarily at Kyrethe, my cheeks burning with shame. She stiffened, but did not know the full implications of the dragon's words. The dragon paused, observing the reactions of all present. "There is something interesting about you being the one to try to save Neden. You have no ties to the boy, nothing political or familial that binds you to him."

"No," I said softly.

"Yet, if I told you that to save him you would risk your very soul. Not death, but the very life substance that would normally live beyond your death, you would agree to risk this."

"Yes."

"Exactly," the dragon said, as if he knew this moment had been coming all along. "Exactly."

"I demand you let me be the one to do this," shouted Varulus. His warriors came to his side. I thought it certain Neden would die while we argued the matter endlessly, or used our weapons on each other.

"I don't think you could defeat me," said the dragon wearily. "But if you did, what would it gain you? Your son will be dead within the hour. I want to see how this thief does. My curiosity will be sated."

"Why are you doing this?" Varulus asked.

The dragon paused, turned his head slightly. "I don't really know. Not in a way that would satisfy you. But this thief is about to risk everything he is to save the life of boy he does not really know. I need to know how it turns out. Don't you?"

Mountainshadow instructed me to stretch out on the ground beside him. Neden was carried to us, and set beside me. The dragon had me place my hand on Neden's head. Then he placed one of his large, sharp foreclaws over my head. As the terror of the claws pressed around me, he said, "J'role, breathe lightly. For now you discover who you are."

"I don't think I want to find out."

The dragon laughed, good-natured, the sound low and echoing. "That is why you people are so strange. Are you ready?"

"What am I supposed to do?"

"I can only facilitate. The actions are yours."

Varulus stepped forward. "If my son dies . . . !"

"But what am I . . . ?"

The cavern vanished.

7

I stood on the deserted landscape from my youth. The ground was cracked and brown and endless. No trees. No birds. Nothing. A soulless wind touched my flesh for a moment. Died. The sun bathed all I could see harsh and dry. As I turned, I strained to listen or hear Neden. Nothing. When I turned halfway around, I saw the *Breeton,* half-buried in the cracked earth, tilted to port.

The ship still rested at the bottom of the Serpent River, ruined during the crew's mutiny so many years ago. But it also stood a quarter of a mile from me. Without thinking the matter over, I began walking toward it.

When I arrived, it towered above me. The wood was dry and rough. The paint pale. Splinters waited for the unwary. I called for Neden. No response came back. I walked around the ship until I came to the cargo-hold door. The doors were unhinged, and I was able to crawl inside.

Shafts of sunlight cut through the splintered hull. In the harsh light, dust swirled slowly. The stars, dancing. A dread pressed against me, though I sensed no one nearby. It was the past, the threat of memories and old patterns haunting me, that caused the fear.

I moved on through the ship, through the lower holds. I expected Captain Patrochian to arrive even though she'd been dead these many years. But who knew?

Suddenly the ship tilted. Boards creaked. The rush of water down the corridor. I looked toward the sound. No water. Light. Thick and golden. A swarm of stars coming to drown me, bouncing off the walls, sweeping each other along in a furious rush. I turned to run up the sloped corridor.

I wanted to run, but I couldn't move; a rope held me in place. I turned again. My father was drowning in the stars, the other end of the rope tied around him. He had not the strength to move on. His body weary, his spirit cracked in too many places. If he did not get help, he would die. But he was dragging me back toward him. He was so weak, weak, weak. Loathing clogged my mouth like rotted meat. He was everything I could not afford to be. I tried to drag him up, but in his panic he floundered in the water, dragging me back down.

There was only one way I could survive. I slid down the corridor toward him, arms extended. I grabbed him around the neck—

HE WAS SO WEAK!

And then a thought. If he was so much weaker than I, why could I not save him? Where was my strength?

I wanted to remove him from my life, deny him in any part of me. I could try again. Find all the strength that I'd wanted all my life. The impulse to destroy him was strong, but I hesitated.

Or try something different this time.

The stars swirled up around us, bathing us in light, their motion a constant buzz in my eyes. My hands slipped from my father's neck and fell over his shoulders. I drew him close. He cried and I held him, giving him the comfort he had so badly needed before he could be strong again. The stars rose up around us.

Then he was gone. The stars gone too. A strange peace floated from within me. Something finally put to rest. I touched my face. Felt my own flesh, but the old flesh of my father as well. Then I remembered Neden. I was closer now. Closer to him.

The ship was level. Bobbing in the water. I stood, rushed toward some stairs leading to the upper deck. The ship floated on a river of stars. To either side, solid night, without a moon or star to lend illumination. The ship's paddle wheel rolled forward, driving us toward a city that glowed so brightly that I could not stare at it. I traveled on for hours, a cool wind now blowing.

My mother rose from the river of stars. Hundreds of feet tall. I remembered her story in the realm of the dead. Her need to make everyone perfect. I felt myself a child again. She could control me. Destroy me. Panic clutched my chest. I did not have the strength to face her again. With desperate breaths I ran from her, running to the rear of the ship. If need be, I would leap off the stern when I got to it.

She stepped toward the vessel. The motion of her legs through the river of stars sent the ship rocking wildly. The stars rose up into the air, then rained down on the deck in great splashes. I clutched the rails, trying to keep my balance. I felt the fabric of the riverboat dissolving. The stars around me began to dim. I was leaving the place Mountainshadow had sent me.

Relief touched my cheeks. There were some things I would not be able to face, even to rescue—

Neden.

I could not leave him. The terror I felt at my mother's touch—what terrors was he living through now, victimized by Mordom's poison? I turned toward my mother. Her hand came for me. The ship's form became solid once more. The stars bright. She plucked me from the ship. Her face stern and unloving. She was a monster, not worthy of life. The things she had done to me . . .

In her eyes, the faces of my boys, their faces cut and bleeding.

I had wanted to be a father who would not spoil his children. Who would not hold back pain. Who would make them know everything about the horrors of life. Who was I but my mother?

My mother began to shrink. Still holding me in one hand, she became smaller and smaller. Soon we were on the deck of the ship. She grew younger and younger. A baby. In my arms. I cradled her. How had she been held? I rocked her and rocked her. As we sailed on she fell asleep. She grew smaller and smaller, until she finally disappeared within my own belly.

I felt her inside of me, this person. Living. Needing care. So much care.

Neden.

The citadel of stars loomed on a hill above. The ship's bow slid into a sandy beach and I disembarked. Trudged up the hill. There stood Parlainth. All of its walls and buildings alive with stars. So thick with brilliant light. Its magic and strength made me think nothing could get to it. It would be safe for all time. Then I remembered it was not safe. It had fallen.

I walked through the gates of the city. People filled the streets. No one saw me. More strangely, they barely noticed each other. They did not even seem to notice the beauty of their own city. Each walked with fear locking up their spines. They eyed the sky for threats of attack. They glanced suspiciously at their neighbors, searching for hidden clues of corruption. Their faces were the masks of the dead. Already buried. Ready to live out eternity writing the same story over and over again.

Ahead of me, floating from a courtyard, came screams of pain. The closer I got, the more huddled the people around me became, hunched over, gripping their arms around themselves. They seemed to think they could avoid hearing the screams by tightening themselves.

At the center of the courtyard Neden floated. Everyone kept a wide path from him, and I moved toward him without hindrance. As I got closer I saw that his body was stuffed with stars. They held him in place, in mid-air, like pins staking out a prize specimen in a butterfly collection. The stars made him glow from within, and formed terrible black-edge holes on his flesh that healed and appeared again and again.

When he saw me he burst out crying, calling my name. "PLEASE! J'role, help me." I did not know where he found the strength even to speak, but his words echoed across the courtyard. The people around us paid no attention. The brilliantly white buildings made of stars sat mute, beautiful, but were no help for Neden's pain. When I reached him he lowered his voice, begging me, as if I might ignore him like the others. "Please. Please. It hurts so much. So much. Please." His face was torn and twisted with pain; the stars in his skull burned their way through his flesh over and over. Whatever wish I might have had to keep him safe from the terrible pain I had suffered as a child was useless now. He'd been through it all. Perhaps even more.

I didn't know what to do. I turned around, looking for help. A clue from one of the citizens of the city. But they kept their eyes skyward, or stared at me with suspicion and ran on. "J'role, please. Get me off the stars."

Yes. The stars. They weren't in him so much as he was on them. They held him in place. They would be the means of controlling him. I just had to pull him off the stars. I extended my hand toward his. As I got close to his skin, I felt the terrible heat. Not just heat. Pain. The pain radiated from the stars. The pain of the unexpected, of disappointment, betrayal. The pain of life. It burned so hot that even before I reached his hand, I pulled away in fear. My father, my mother. I'd been able to embrace them. But pain itself? All my life I'd tried to hide myself away from that.

"J'role? Please, it hurts. So, so much."

The corrupted elves of Blood Wood had tried to protect themselves from the pain of the Horrors, and in doing so, had turned their own bodies against themselves. The citizens of Parlainth had hidden themselves as protection from the Horrors. Even though they had exiled themselves totally from the world, the Horrors had found them and slaughtered them. I had tried to teach my sons to be stronger than pain. They learned they could withstand terrible pain, but at what cost the lesson? I had hidden myself away all my life, trying to remain safe. But what had I saved?

I extended my hand. The pain of the stars burned through my flesh. No images now. Just the terror of life. The threat of things gone wrong. Of broken hearts. Stupid deaths. Hateful words spoken and later regretted. Actions of impulse that led to tragedy. *I did not want to touch his hand.* The connection itself would imply tying myself to him. Getting into the habit of tying myself to people. That meant more complications, more pain. I wanted to be alone again. Safe.

I thought, As safe as the elves? The citizens of Parlainth? My mother?

I took his hand. The pain ripped through my palm, cut up through my chest. I began breathing rapidly. Shaking. Without thinking I grabbed his other hand with my free hand. I screamed in agony as the act of concern culminated. It seemed I would never free him. Staggering, I backed up, pulled him from the stars.

He too, screamed, and the two of us filled the city with cries of agony. Then he fell from the stars, and I fell back and he landed on my chest. I held him close, my muscles tight, for I could not move at all.

Around me, the stars of the city's buildings began to dissolve. As the walls cracked when the Horrors attacked. No safety in stillness, shadows, loneliness. The pain comes for you wherever you are. The question is, will you count yourself among others in pain when it happens?

The city dissolved before my eyes. The stars, thousands upon thousand of them, swirled faster and faster, rushing up into the sky, scattering themselves where they belonged. Fixed and distant high above our mortal interactions. Their fixed paths and certainty were not mine to live by. I held Neden close. So, so close. He wrapped his arms around me. And we had done it. Shared ourselves against the pain of life, because that is what we do best.

When I looked up, we were in the cavern. Neden in my arms. Crying. His father standing before us. "Shhh. Shhh," I said. "There's someone here who wants to see you." I turned him around and when he saw Varulus, he called out, "Father!" and leaped into his father's arms. The old dwarf held his son tight. So loving.

Kyrethe knelt down beside me. "You were screaming. Are you all right?"

I felt very dizzy. Hungry. Ill at ease. Alive, with all the pangs that displeasure and misery can bring. I said, "Yes. Oddly enough, I think I am."

8

When all the greetings had been taken care of, Neden explained to his father what had happened back at the jungle, how I had tried to help, and how I did help. His father eyed me with suspicion, but finally decided to let me go. Varulus tried to chastise Mountainshadow for his actions in support of Mordom. The dragon listened politely.

Varulus offered to take us north in their airships, and we gladly accepted. While the dwarfs prepared to depart, Mountainshadow said to me, "Thank you."

"For what?" I said with a laugh. "It is I who should thank you. You gave me the chance to—complete things."

"But you risked yourself, and gave me knowledge." He seemed sad, and I could not help but think loneliness was a common trait among dragons.

"What did I risk? You said I would be—"

"You were in Neden's mind, though you carried your own images into it. You were sealed within it. If you had not freed him, you would have remained trapped within his thoughts. Your flesh would have remained in a coma, and your personality would have dissolved, over time, into the boy's. When he died, you would have been dragged to the realm of the dead with him. Your identity depended on freeing the boy."

I sighed. A strange thought.

"J'role. As you were in Neden's mind, so I was in yours. I know of your life now. I would be curious—now that you have lived through the things you have lived through . . . Have you any interest in contacting your family?" The dragon's tone was lighter than it had been earlier. It seemed more human.

"I hadn't thought about it really." As I did think about it, the prospect seemed daunting. "I really don't know what I would say. My boys . . . They know nothing about me, really."

"Maybe you should tell them."

"I have faced many dangers, Mountainshadow. But approaching my family . . ."

"Stories should be told. The truth helps."

"Sometimes."

"Oh, from what I've seen, it's not always pleasant. But it helps."

"I don't think I could do it."

"What if I helped?"

"What?"

"What if I wrote the first letter to your sons. Introducing you to them."

"You would do that?"

"At the least, I'm curious to see how it turns out."

"Very well."

We flew with the dwarfs back to my home. On the way, I thought of Mountainshadow's words about truth. I decided during the flight to tell Kyrethe about my attack on her—an attack that I never finished, but had been a part of me nonetheless. I remembered how I had kept so much from Releana, and that had always made me afraid to be around her. Although I was not the man who would do that now, I did not want the fear of it lurking in my thoughts, making me wonder if Kyrethe saw the monster hidden in me. I decided she should know, and then make up her own mind.

"Why are you telling me this?" she asked, shocked.

"Because I love you. I want you to know who I was. What I was capable of. I don't want to think I tricked you."

She did not hide from me, but she was withdrawn for the rest of the trip. When the airship reached my home, she said she would go out into the world for some time. She said, "I've spent so much of my time alone. I need to get used to being in the world before I settle with you." I do not expect to see her again. But strangely, I am content. The love we had on the island was true. And this time I did not try to hide from the world.

In the meantime, I have my house to clean up. I think I will move to Throal. Varulus offered me a home there years and years ago. I was in such a rush to move on, I never considered the offer seriously until now. It might be nice to be trapped in a kingdom with so many people.

But now you are here. And right now, you are all the company I could ever want. You have been here for me, with no real reason to listen, with no other purpose than the attempt at communion. It is, I think, these exchanges that keep us alive as much as food and water. We are not like the beasts, you know. We know more than they, and because of this, must work harder to be kind.

Epilogue

J'role's old hand wavered a bit in the air, uncertain of where to place itself. His fear showed so clearly. Fear of what, Samael was not certain. The blade Samael held on his lap? Or Samael's rejection?

Days had passed. Samael had remained cold and aloof. He had wanted to make things difficult for his father. His father filled the silence with his tale. The old man was so animated when spinning his narrative! So full of life! If only he'd become a troubadour instead of a thief. And yet, that was obviously not the way of it.

For a moment a sharp stab of smugness shot through Samael, for now he sat in judgement. But there was nothing he wanted to judge. His father stared at the wall, spent. Whatever he had wanted to say, he had said.

Samael stood, placed the sword on the ground. He knelt beside his father and took his wrinkled hands. "I hated you for so long for not being there."

"Yes. That would make sense."

"I'm sorry you went through the life you did."

"And I'm sorry you suffered through my life."

Samael smiled a rueful smile.

They were silent for a while longer, and then Samael said, "I would like to have you in my life. There are things I could learn from you."

"And I from you. I'm beginning to think that my profession is one for younger, sad men. But I've always loved to tell a good story. You, as a troubadour adept, could teach me much."

Samael smiled. "I could teach you a few things . . ."

"No. Everything! I want to become an adept."

Samael opened his mouth to tell his father he was so old. Wasn't it time to stop? Then he remembered the fate awaiting J'role—writing his story again and again. What better skill to acquire?

So he did teach his father the ways of the storyteller's magic, and the two of them traveled to Throal. There they regaled the citizens with outlandish narratives that they created together. Their fame grew and grew, and it was an odd night when they did not tell tales at the court of Throal, with King Varulus and his son Neden listening attentively.

Over time J'role and Releana did meet again. Though they were uncomfortable at first, soon they became good friends, with the depth of caring that can only come from shared pain. And even Torran, with caution, approached his father.

But it was Kyrethe's return that made J'role happiest of all. One day she arrived in the Kingdom of Throal. The two of them were tentative at first, as they had been on the island. Their courtship lasted several years, with Kyrethe trying to determine whether J'role was the man she had thought he was. In time she came to trust him as he trusted himself. They were married, and never had anyone seen so rambunctious a couple, with or without consideration of their age.

J'role would sometimes think, And when I die, I will be able to write again and again how much I loved her. His whole life story, in fact, the pain and pleasure, became his to embrace.

When he did die, he visited Death once more, and she gave him a large desk to work at. There, amid all the stacks of countless other lives, he wrote his narrative again and again. And each time he finished it he wrote the words:

AND HE LEARNED TO WRITE HIS STORY.

 ROC (0451)

FANTASTICAL LANDS

☐ **SHROUD OF SHADOW by Gael Baudino.** Natil is the last Elf—lone survivor in the Age of the Inquisition where there is no longer a place for her. Now, with her powers soon diminishing, she must slowly make her way to the final place where she will depart forever the world of mortals—but three things will intervene Natil from taking that final step. (452941—$4.99)

☐ **THE CATSWORLD PORTAL by Shirley Rousseau Murphy.** Come to the land where an enchanting young woman will reclaim her rightful crown and liberate her people, where she will travel from the Hell Pit to the very heart of the sorceress queen's court, and where she will magically transform into the guise of a calico cat! "A captivating feline fantasy!"—*Booklist* (452755—$5.50)

☐ **RED BRIDE by Christopher Fowler.** When John Chapel is offered a career change, his mundane life is transformed. He's drawn to Ixora, the woman of his dreams, and into a shadow realm—a place marked by murder and by the dark, unseen figure of a slayer who might reach out to claim not only their lives but their souls. (452933—$4.99)

☐ **BROTHERS OF THE DRAGON by Robin W. Bailey.** Caught in a war between dragon-riders and bloodthirsty unicorns, two brothers trained in martial arts lead the forces of Light toward victory. (452518—$4.99)

☐ **UNDER THE THOUSAND STARS by John Deakins.** Return to Barrow, a unique town in Elsewhen where even a worker of dark magic must sometimes work for the Light. (452534—$4.99)

☐ **HEART READERS by Kristine Kathryn Rusch.** They are called heartreaders—magic-bonded pairs who can see into a person's very soul and read the nature of his or her heart—and through their strength, a kingdom might thrive or fall. (452828—$4.99)

Prices slightly higher in Canada.

Buy them at your local bookstore or use this convenient coupon for ordering.

PENGUIN USA
P.O. Box 999 – Dept. #17109
Bergenfield, New Jersey 07621

Please send me the books I have checked above.
I am enclosing $__________ (please add $2.00 to cover postage and handling). Send check or money order (no cash or C.O.D.'s) or charge by Mastercard or VISA (with a $15.00 minimum). Prices and numbers are subject to change without notice.

Card #__________ Exp. Date __________
Signature__________
Name__________
Address__________
City __________ State __________ Zip Code __________

For faster service when ordering by credit card call **1-800-253-6476**

Allow a minimum of 4-6 weeks for delivery. This offer is subject to change without notice.

RoC
SF
ADVANCE